Dear Reader,

This is one of my favorite installments in the Mary's Bookshop series. The challenge for Mary in this story revolves around finding clues about her mysterious new friend. We all leave clues behind that tell people something about us. My sewing room would tell you that purple is one of my favorite fabric colors, that I'm in the middle of making a sorority T-shirt memory quilt for my youngest daughter, and that I often have several different sewing projects in progress at one time.

My writing desk provides even more clues about my life. I have all of the usual office supplies: paper clips, notepads, pens and pencils, etc. But I have more personal items too. On the top of my desk is a thirtieth anniversary card from my husband, along with two writing awards. There is an enamel box with old coins left to me by my wonderful grandfather, and a calendar with dates circled for a trip to Lake Tahoe to celebrate my sister's birthday. I have my Bible on a shelf, along with my journal and a daily planner. And there are colorful Post-it notes attached all over my desk—some with inspirational quotes, others with research information for my next book, and one with the ingredients for a new recipe I want to try.

These are small clues, but woven all together they tell a story. What story do the clues in your life tell about you?

Mary's talent for weaving clues together made this book so much fun to write. I hope you enjoy the newest mystery in Ivy Bay and enjoy searching for clues along with Mary!

Blessings,
Kristin Eckhardt

Secrets of Mary's Bookshop

A New Chapter
Rewriting History
Reading the Clues
The Writing on the Wall
By Word of Mouth
A Book by Its Cover
Poetry in Motion
Missing Pages
Between the Lines
By the Book
Disappearing Acts
A Classic Case
Cover Story
A Thousand Words
The Lost Noel
Work in Progress
Words of Wisdom

SECRETS *of* MARY'S
BOOKSHOP

Lost for Words

Kristin Eckhardt

Guideposts

New York

Secrets of Mary's Bookshop is a trademark of Guideposts.

Published by Guideposts Books & Inspirational Media
110 William Street
New York, New York 10038
Guideposts.org

Acknowledgments

Every attempt has been made to credit the sources of copyrighted material used in this book. If any such acknowledgment has been inadvertently omitted or miscredited, receipt of such information would be appreciated.

"From the Guideposts Archives" originally appeared in *Daily Guideposts 2007*. Copyright © 2006 by Guideposts. All rights reserved.

Cover and interior design by Müllerhaus
Cover illustration by Ross Jones, represented by Deborah Wolfe, Ltd.
Typeset by Aptara, Inc.

Printed and bound in the United States of America
10 9 8 7 6 5 4 3 2 1

Lost for Words

ONE

Mary strolled along the sidewalk on Main Street, enjoying the shade of the trees that lined both sides of the street. She'd taken an early lunch, prompted by her growling stomach and Rebecca's offer to work through the noon hour so she could leave early this afternoon to attend an academic quiz bowl competition at Ashley's school.

Mary wished she could attend also, but someone needed to mind the bookshop. Now that September had arrived, the tourist crowds were easing, but the shop still enjoyed a steady flow of customers.

She loved fall in Cape Cod. The cranberry harvest was just around the corner, and soon, migrating birds from Canada would enjoy using the Cape as a resting spot on their way to Mexico. The days were still warm enough to enjoy the beaches and go on hiking excursions through the golden dunes and salt marshes, while the nights were just crisp enough to light up the fireplace.

The cooler weather also seemed to increase her appetite. Mary had been thinking about lunch all morning, but now she had a decision to make. Should she enjoy some chocolate-chip pancakes at the Black & White Diner? Have a slice of pepperoni pizza or a cheesy calzone at Pizzeria Rustica? Or maybe indulge in a decadent banana split at Bailey's Ice Cream Shop and call it lunch?

The possibilities were all so tempting, but as she passed by the front window of the Tea Shoppe, she saw the signboard listing Tuesday's specials, including one of her favorite comfort foods: crab quiche.

While the Tea Shoppe specialized in a wide selection of teas, it also had a small café nestled in the far corner, where customers could enjoy homemade quiches and delectable pastries as well as a small selection of deli sandwiches and salads.

With her choice for lunch made in that instant, Mary walked into the Tea Shoppe and headed for the crowded café. She waved to Frances Curran and Virginia Livingston, both members of her sister's book club, as her gaze searched for an empty table in the crowded room.

"Mary," a man's voice called out. "Over here."

She turned to see Pastor Frank Miles and his wife, Tricia, seated at a small mission-style table. He waved her toward them, a wide smile on his face.

"Hello," Mary greeted them. "This is a nice surprise."

"We're celebrating," Pastor Miles said, rising to his feet. "Here, take my seat. I'll borrow an empty chair from another table."

"Are you sure?" Mary asked, hesitating. "I don't want to intrude."

"Nonsense," Tricia said with a smile. "We'd love to have you join us."

"Well, thank you," Mary replied, taking the chair that Pastor Miles had occupied while he went in search of another.

He returned carrying a chair in his hands at the same time the owner, Sophie Mershon, appeared to take Mary's order.

Sophie was blonde and lithe, a former ballet dancer who now ran a successful business. "Good afternoon, Mary," she greeted her. "What would you like today?"

"The crab quiche, please," Mary responded, "and a glass of raspberry iced tea."

Sophie turned her gaze to Tricia. "And how about dessert for you two?"

"Absolutely!" Tricia said, grinning, and then pointed to the teacup-shaped chalkboard that hung above the counter to advertise the day's specials. "Hazelnut cheesecake, please."

"And two forks," the pastor added with a smile.

Sophie smiled as she jotted down their order on the small notepad in her hand. "Coming right up."

"So what are you celebrating today?" Mary asked.

"Well," Tricia began, "have you heard about the Cape Cod Wildlife Rescue Foundation fund-raiser?"

"I have," Mary replied. The annual fund-raiser was held in a different town on Cape Cod each year, and this year was Ivy Bay's turn. "In fact, I just read about it in the newspaper. They're holding a concert, aren't they?"

"That's right," Pastor Miles replied, "and they're featuring local talent. Tricia auditioned for a flute solo last week, and the fund-raiser committee called this morning to offer her a spot at the concert."

Mary clapped her hands together as she turned to Tricia. "That's wonderful!"

"I'm thrilled," Tricia said, a pink blush coloring her cheeks. "I've been playing the flute quite a bit lately, since Trevor likes it so much, but I never imagined playing in front of a crowd. Frank talked me into it."

"She's very good," Pastor Miles said, a twinkle in his eyes. "Our grandson has wonderful taste in music."

"And books," Mary added. Trevor was the sweet eight-year-old son of the Mileses' daughter Kayla. He had autism and spent a lot of time with his grandparents. Pastor Miles often brought him into the bookshop.

"Kayla's planning to bring him to the concert," Tricia said with a smile, "at least long enough to hear me play on stage. I have a lot of practicing to do between now and then."

A few moments later, Sophie arrived with the order and set the plates on the table. Mary's mouth watered as she picked up her fork, eager to dig into the tender quiche. Then her glance caught Tricia, who sat staring at the cheesecake that had been placed between her and her husband.

A tiny frown turned down the edges of Pastor Miles's mouth, his fork poised near the cheesecake. "What's wrong, dear?"

"Nothing," Tricia replied with a wistful sigh. "I'm just enjoying the moment. I don't indulge in cheesecake very often, you know." Then she picked up her fork, and they both dug in.

Mary chatted with the couple as they ate, enjoying the relaxed atmosphere in the Tea Shoppe and the fragrant scent of spiced teas in the air. When she finished the last sip of her raspberry tea, she glanced at her watch and nearly gasped out loud.

"Look at the time! Rebecca will be sending out a search party for me if I don't get back to the shop." She scooted her chair back and picked up the bill Sophie had set next to her plate, along with a small box containing her leftover quiche. "Thank you so much for letting me join you."

"It was our pleasure," Tricia said.

Pastor Miles nodded. "It certainly was. It's always fun to share good news with friends."

Mary bid them good-bye and went up to the counter to pay for her lunch. She added the cost of two dozen butter tarts filled with raisins and brown sugar to the total amount, intending to take them back for her customers to enjoy this afternoon.

When she arrived back at the store, she found Rebecca straightening books on one of the shelves.

"I'm sorry I took so long for lunch," Mary said, the sack of butter tarts in one hand and her quiche in the other. "I lost track of the time."

Rebecca smiled. "No problem. I don't have to leave for another thirty minutes or so."

Mary glanced around the shop, noting a young couple holding hands as they perused the novels by local authors and a young woman seated with a book near the unlit fireplace. "How's it going here?"

"Nice and steady," Rebecca said, nudging another book into alignment with the rest of the books on the shelf. "I was just about to make another pot of coffee."

"I'll take care of it," Mary offered, eager to set out the tarts. She turned and walked to the back room, and then placed her leftover quiche in the small refrigerator. She grabbed a decorative glass platter on her way out and carried it with her to the coffee station. The bell above the door tinkled as a young couple walked in with two small children in tow, quickly followed by Rachel Hadley, who was due to return to Boston University in a few days.

Like Mary, the Hadley family belonged to Grace Church. The congregation had held an ice-cream social last Sunday for all the young members heading off to college. Mary had made a chocolate-chip cookie-dough ice cream that had received rave reviews.

While Rebecca attended to the new arrivals, Mary started a new pot of coffee and then began placing the butter tarts on the platter. Although Sweet Susan's Bakery next door was always brimming with wonderful baked goods, Mary also loved the small pastries available at the Tea Shoppe. When the platter was full, she was delighted to see one left over in the sack. She popped it into her mouth, enjoying the buttery flakiness of the tart and the sweet, fruity filling. Then she wiped up the crumbs at the coffee station and made a mental note to buy some more napkins the next time she went to the market.

Rebecca sidled next to her and whispered, "Mary, I need to talk to you."

Concerned, Mary turned to her. "What is it?"

Rebecca glanced over her shoulder at the customers browsing through the bookshelves, then turned back to Mary. "Do you see that woman sitting near the fireplace?"

"Yes," Mary said, glancing in that direction. The young woman looked to be in her late twenties and had dark red hair and a willowy figure. "What about her?"

"I'm not sure," Rebecca whispered. "There's just something...strange about her. She arrived here soon after you left, grabbed a book off the shelf, and sat down in that chair."

Mary didn't understand Rebecca's concern. Customers settled in to read at the bookshop all the time. "Well, we like our customers to make themselves comfortable."

"I know," Rebecca whispered. "But she hasn't looked *comfortable* since she got here. Every time someone walks in the door, she looks up and watches them until they leave again. I don't think she's turned more than three pages of that book in the two hours she's been sitting there."

Mary didn't know what to think. She glanced again at the woman, not wanting to stare. The woman wore a pair of denim capri pants and a white top. She looked well groomed and rather benign, to Mary's way of thinking. But Rebecca wasn't prone to drama and seemed genuinely concerned.

"I'll keep an eye on her," Mary told Rebecca. "And you probably need to get going if you want to catch the beginning of the quiz bowl contest."

Rebecca glanced at her watch. "You're right. I promised Ashley I wouldn't be late."

Mary smiled. "I wish I could see her in action. I'm sure she'll do great."

"I hope so," Rebecca replied. "She's really been studying her little heart out. And I'm going to videotape some of it, so you can watch it later, if you'd like."

"Absolutely," Mary said.

Rebecca gathered her things and then waved good-bye as she headed out the door.

"Be with Ashley today, Lord," Mary prayed softly. "She's such a special little girl."

The young family approached the glass-fronted counter, the two young boys with their arms full of books. Mary helped them check out and then glanced at the woman by the fireplace again. She stared at the young family until they walked out the door before dropping her gaze to the book in front of her.

Then Mary saw Rachel approaching the front counter. "Hello there. Are you all packed for college?"

"Packed and ready to go," Rachel replied with a bright smile. "But I just had to stop in and get the sequel to the book I bought here yesterday afternoon. It was *so* good."

Mary had stayed home to help Betty with some yard work yesterday afternoon, leaving the shop in Rebecca's capable hands. "Do you mean to tell me that you've already finished it?"

Rachel's green eyes flashed with glee. "I couldn't put it down! I stayed up until two o'clock in the morning finishing that book."

Mary laughed. She loved to talk about books with her customers, especially one as enthusiastic as Rachel. "I'm so glad you liked it."

"It was awesome! Have you read it?"

"Not yet, but it's gotten good reviews."

"The story is crazy," Rachel replied. "This really nice guy named Jack is being stalked by someone, but he doesn't know who. Then some weird stuff starts turning up in his house and he hears footsteps in his attic at night, but he never catches anyone. Then it turns out that the stuff in his house is stolen property, and he's arrested as a thief...." Rachel continued recounting the plot until she was almost out of breath.

"Are you sure you want to read the sequel?" Mary teased. "You do need to sleep sometime."

Rachel laughed. "Who has time to sleep when there are so many good books to read?"

"That's my motto too," Mary said, not willing to confess how late she stayed up some nights, lost in a good book.

"I'm just glad you had the sequel in stock," Rachel said, placing the book on the counter. "I don't think I'd have the patience to wait for it."

Mary smiled as she picked up the book and rang it up on the antique cash register. "Did you know there's a third book in the series?"

Rachel's mouth gaped. "Seriously?"

"It's due out next week. I could send it to you at college, if you'd like."

"That would be perfect. Can I just pay for it now?"

Mary nodded. "Sure. I'll just add it to your total." Then she handed her a piece of notepaper. "Just write down your address for me and promise that you won't let your reading interfere with your schoolwork."

Rachel winced as she wrote down her address. "I'm not sure I can promise. These books are *really* good, but I'll do my best."

Mary rang up her order and then placed the book in a sack. "Help yourself to a butter tart or two on the way out. They're delicious."

"Thanks, Mrs. Fisher," Rachel said, taking the sack from Mary before heading toward the coffee station.

Mary picked up the paper with Rachel's college address on it, then made a note to herself to send the book there as soon as it arrived at the shop. She spent the next hour organizing the order forms on her desk and going through the mail that had arrived while she was at lunch. Every once in a while, she'd glance over at the fireplace where the young woman still sat with the book open in front of her.

Rebecca was right. Every time new customers entered the shop, the woman would look up and watch them, her gaze following them around the shop until they took their leave. Then her gaze would fall to the book in her lap, but she didn't seem to be reading it—only staring at the pages open in front of her.

Mary walked over to the coffee station and placed some butter tarts on a small paper plate. She carried it over to the young woman. "Would you like a butter tart? They're quite good."

The woman hesitated, her deep blue eyes scanning Mary's face. Then a smile quivered on her lips as she reached for a tart. Her nails were trimmed and polished with a lovely pearl-pink color. "Thank you."

"You're very welcome. I'm Mary Fisher."

"It's nice to meet you, Mary." The woman took a bite of her tart, catching a crumb as it fell from her lips and quickly bringing it to her mouth again.

The tart disappeared in a matter of seconds. The woman eyed the plate in Mary's hand but didn't ask for more.

Uneasiness fluttered through Mary as she set the plate on the small table next to the chair. "I'm afraid I'll need to close the shop soon. Is there anything you need?"

"No," the woman replied, her voice almost a whisper.

Mary knelt down beside her chair. "Is there anything I can help you find?"

"I don't know." The woman looked at Mary for a long moment and then sucked in a deep breath. "I don't remember anything."

TWO

•━◆◆━•

Mary stared at the young woman in front of her. "What?"

Tears glistened in the woman's blue eyes. "I don't know who I am. I don't remember anything about my life." She choked back a sob. "I'm...scared."

"Oh dear," Mary murmured, gently placing one hand on the woman's forearm. "Don't be scared. I'll help you."

The tears spilled onto the woman's cheeks as another soft sob racked her. She buried her face in her hands, her shoulders quaking as she silently wept.

Mary knelt next to her, gently patting her back and saying soothing words of reassurance. "It will be all right. You're safe here." As she spoke, she sent a silent plea to God. *Please, Lord, help this woman.*

At last, the woman lifted her head and wiped the tears off her face. "I'm sorry."

"There's nothing to be sorry about," Mary told her. Then she walked to the front counter to retrieve a box of tissues. She carried it back to the woman, who plucked one from the box and blew her nose.

Rebecca had been right—there was something odd about the woman, and now Mary knew why. She continued gently. "So what brought you into my shop?"

"This." The woman reached into the pockets of her denim capri pants and pulled out a crumpled note, then handed it to Mary.

Mary smoothed out the paper and read it out loud: *Katie, Arrive at Mary's Bookshop at 1:12.*

What an odd time for a meeting, Mary thought to herself. The brief note wasn't signed, and the word *Katie* was handwritten, but the rest of the note was typewritten in black letters.

Mary looked up at her. "So...are you Katie?"

The woman shrugged. "I have no idea. The last thing I remember was walking on the beach this morning. I didn't know who I was or how I got there. Then I found that note in my pocket, so I came here, hoping that someone who knew me would be waiting. But...no one came."

Mary nodded, understanding even more now. "Well, Katie is a very pretty name. May I call you that until we find out who you are?"

"Yes, that's fine," the woman replied. "I mean, it makes sense that Katie is my name since the note was in my pocket, right?"

"It does," Mary agreed. "Did you find anything else that might be a clue to your identity?"

Katie shook her head. "No, just the note."

Mary studied the young woman's pretty face, trying to place her. She was about her daughter Lizzie's height, and slender. Her dark red hair was shiny and straight, hanging almost to her shoulders. It was parted on the side, giving her side-swept bangs over her creamy forehead.

Katie's white top and denim-blue pants and red Top-Siders looked like good-quality clothing, although not high-end. She had a pair of small pearl earrings in her ears, but no rings on her fingers. That meant she probably wasn't married.

She was well groomed too, which told Mary that she probably hadn't spent the night on the beach but perhaps in a house or hotel. But where? And how had she lost her memory?

"I think we should have a doctor take a look at you," Mary said at last. "Just to make sure you're not sick or injured in any way."

"I feel okay," Katie replied. "My right hand is sore, and I just have a slight headache, but that may be because I haven't eaten anything except that wonderful tart."

"And you only ate one," Mary gently chided. "I have something a little more substantial for you."

Mary headed to the back room and retrieved her leftover quiche from the refrigerator. When she returned, she handed the quiche to Katie. "Hopefully, this will make you feel better. You eat as much as you want while I call the doctor's office to let him know we're coming in."

Katie took the paper plate and plastic fork from her, eagerly digging in. Mary moved toward the front counter to grab her cell phone from her purse. She placed a call to Dr. Teagarden's office and explained the situation to the receptionist. After checking with the doctor, the receptionist assured her that the office would stay open until they arrived.

By the time she finished the phone call, Katie was standing on the other side of the counter with the empty plate in her hands.

"Thank you," Katie said, setting the plate on the counter. "I feel better now."

"Good," Mary told her. "Now let's go see what the doctor has to say about you."

———

Fifteen minutes later, Mary and Katie arrived at Dr. Teagarden's medical office. The large waiting room was light and airy, with small palm plants lining the walls and a television propped high near the ceiling in the far corner, next to the enclosed children's area.

Mary approached the reception desk, with Katie right on her heels.

"Hello, Vera," Mary greeted the woman behind the desk. Vera Colbert was about sixty-five and had lived in Ivy Bay all her life. She'd helped raise five siblings after her mother's death but had never married herself.

"Hello, Mary. You sure got here fast."

"Well, we're anxious to see the doctor," Mary told her.

Vera smiled at Katie. "I'm sure you are. The nurse had already left for the day when you called, so I'll take you back to the examination room."

Mary hesitated. "Do you want me to wait out here, Katie?"

"No," Katie replied, her voice hushed. "If you don't mind, I'd rather you come with me."

"Of course," Mary said. Then they followed Vera down the hallway to one of the examination rooms.

Vera ushered them inside, then stood in the doorway. "Dr. Teagarden will be with you shortly."

"Thank you," Mary said, then watched as Vera closed the door.

The small room had a green padded examination table and a dressing screen on one side and a cupboard and stainless-steel sink on the other. There were two green folding chairs between the door and the examination table, so Mary and Katie each took a seat.

Katie's hands lay in her lap, her fingers knotted together. A bird whistled from the towering maple tree near the window, the sweet song breaking the awkward silence in the small room.

"You'll like Dr. Teagarden," Mary assured her. "He's very kind and very competent."

Katie gave a stiff nod. "I hope he can help me."

Before Mary could respond, a light knock sounded on the door. Then Dr. Teagarden opened it. He strode in wearing his white lab coat and a pair of black trousers. His bright smile and soft brown eyes made most people instantly at ease.

"Hello there," he greeted them, giving Mary a nod. Then he focused on Katie, holding out one hand. "I'm Dr. Teagarden."

She shook his hand, wincing a little. "I'm...Katie...I guess. I don't remember my name."

"That's scary, isn't it?" Dr. Teagarden said, his deep, gentle voice like a warm hug. "But you don't need to be scared here. We're going to figure this out."

Katie's shoulders relaxed. "I hope so."

He kept her right hand in his, now gently examining it. "Does your hand hurt, especially your palm?"

"Yes," she said. "It feels sore, like it's bruised or something, but I don't see any bruises."

"And I don't feel any broken bones." Dr. Teagarden let go of her hand. "It's probably a muscle strain or a pulled tendon. Nothing too serious." He grabbed the rolling stainless-steel stool from under the cupboard and sat down on it, placing himself directly in front of Katie. "Now, why don't you tell me what you do know about yourself?"

"I found myself on the beach this morning," Katie began, "but I didn't know how I got there or anything else about my life. There was no one around me and no car nearby—no clues about my identity." Then she dug into her pants pocket. "Except this." She pulled out the crumpled note and handed it to him.

Mary watched him adjust his wire-rimmed bifocals as he read the note.

"Interesting," Dr. Teagarden murmured. "So that's how you found Mary?"

A ghost of a smile haunted Katie's mouth. "I camped in her bookshop for hours today, waiting for someone— anyone—to find me. But no one came."

"That's when I discovered her predicament," Mary interjected, "and called your office."

"I'm glad you did," Dr. Teagarden said, rolling his stool back, then rising to his feet. He reached into the cupboard and pulled out a folded hospital gown. "Katie, I'd like to do a brief physical examination, just to rule out any injuries you might have. We'll step out for a minute, and you can get into the gown." He handed the gown to her. "Just take your outer clothes off, please."

"Okay." Katie stood up, hugging the gown to her chest while Dr. Teagarden motioned to Mary to follow him out into the hallway.

He closed the door behind them and then turned to Mary. "Is there anything you can tell me that Katie might have left out?" he asked softly. "Any trouble with her speech or language? Any behaviors that seemed unusual?"

Mary shook her head. "No, not at all. The only thing that seemed a little unusual was the amount of time she spent in my shop. Most of that time, she read—or pretended to read. She was waiting for the arrival of whoever wrote that note."

"Did she complain of any pain or dizziness?"

"No," Mary told him. "Just a slight headache, but she told me she hadn't eaten all day. All I had to offer her were some butter tarts and leftover quiche from the Tea Shoppe."

"At least the quiche provided her with some protein," the doctor said with a smile. "And those butter tarts are my favorite. Sophie always gives the office a call whenever she bakes some."

Mary smiled. "Now that's some good customer service." She glanced toward the door, her smile fading. "What do you think is wrong?"

He gave a slight shrug. "I'd only be guessing at this point. I'll have a better idea after I examine her."

They chatted a few more minutes. Then Dr. Teagarden knocked on the door. "Katie, may we come in?"

"Yes," Katie replied.

LOST FOR WORDS ～ 19

They entered the exam room and found Katie seated on the examination table, the white paper under her crinkling as she shifted slightly.

Mary took a seat in the chair while Dr. Teagarden approached Katie.

"What happened to your knees?" he asked her.

That's when Mary noticed a fresh scrape on each bare knee. The skin around each scrape was slightly bruised.

Katie looked down at her knees, her brow furrowed. "I don't know. I must have fallen, I guess."

"So you have no memory of falling?"

"No," Katie said.

"Go ahead and lie down, please," the doctor told her. "Let's make sure you're not hurt anywhere else."

Katie did as he asked, her head resting on the paper-covered pillow at the top of the examination table.

Mary watched as the doctor assessed her legs and arms for any fractures or other signs of injuries. He did the same with her torso.

"Everything looks good so far," the doctor told Katie. "Go ahead and sit up for me again." He waited until she'd resumed a seated position, then began to carefully assess her neck. "Any pain when I do this?" he asked, gently turning her head to one side and then the other.

"No, it's fine," Katie replied.

Then he moved his fingers through her hair, gently pressing down on her scalp every couple of inches.

"Ouch!" Katie cried when he touched the back of her head.

"That hurts?" he inquired.

"Yes," she said, sounding surprised. "A little."

"You've got a nice little bump back there," Dr. Teagarden told her. "Do you remember hitting your head?"

"No," Katie said. "Is that why I have a headache?"

"Very possibly," he told her. "If you had to rate your headache between one and ten, with ten being the worst headache you've ever had—" He stopped abruptly, and his face softened with sympathy. "I guess that's not a fair question since· you can't remember anything. Okay, with ten being the worst headache you can imagine having, what would you rate it?"

Katie hesitated a moment, then said, "A three, I guess. It actually feels a little better than before. I think the butter tart helped."

"They always do," he said with a small chuckle.

He gave her a neurological exam that she passed with flying colors, then gently cleaned the scrapes on her knees before treating them with antibiotic ointment.

"Well?" Katie asked as he applied an adhesive bandage to her right knee. "Do you know what's wrong with me?"

"I think I do," he told her, opening another bandage. He carefully applied it to her left knee and then stepped back. "In my opinion, you have retrograde amnesia." He sat down on his stool, still facing Katie. "There are many things that can cause amnesia, such as disease or sedatives or psychological trauma. But I believe your amnesia is caused by physical trauma—specifically the injury on your head. Given the injury to your knees, you most likely hit the back of your head, and the impact caused you to fall forward onto your knees. The dirt and sand I found in the wounds indicates that this fall occurred outside—possibly even on the beach you mentioned."

"Possibly?" Mary echoed. "So it could have happened somewhere else?"

Dr. Teagarden nodded. "Absolutely. She could have become disoriented after the head injury and wandered from the original site of the incident before becoming aware of her surroundings."

"But my head is all right?" Katie asked him.

"I feel confident that you'll be fine," he told her. "You don't appear to have suffered any other neurological problems, other than the memory loss, and the injury doesn't seem severe enough to cause me concern." He stood up. "But I'd like you to go to the hospital for a CAT scan and a blood test."

Katie's eyes widened with concern. "Why?"

"Don't worry; it's just a precaution," he assured her. "Anytime you have a head injury that's serious enough to cause something like amnesia, then we want to see what's happening on the inside."

"And the blood test?" Katie asked.

"It's a standard blood panel," he explained. "I just want to make certain that you haven't ingested any medications or possible toxins that could have caused or exacerbated the amnesia." He walked with them into the hallway. "And I realize you don't know your insurance policy number or even if you have insurance. Don't worry about that for now. I'll call ahead and make all the arrangements with the hospital lab."

"When will we find out the results?" Mary asked him.

"It usually takes about a week," he replied. "I'll give you a call as soon as I have them." Then he turned to

Katie. "But if you notice any changes in how you're feeling, especially if your headache worsens, I want you to call me immediately." He pulled a card out of the pocket of his lab coat. "My home number is on there too. You can call day or night."

"Wow," Katie said, taking the business card from him. "Even with my amnesia, I'm pretty sure that doctors don't usually give out their home numbers."

He chuckled. "One of the benefits of living in Ivy Bay, I guess. Although it's possible you do know that. Retrograde amnesia most often occurs after an accident, such as your head injury. The brain is unable to retrieve information that was acquired before that injury, although the patient usually retains their intellectual, linguistic, and social skills."

Mary breathed a silent prayer of thanks that Katie's head injury wasn't more serious, but she still had questions. "How long will the amnesia last?"

He breathed a small sigh. "There are few hard-and-fast rules in the world of medicine, but I'd be surprised if her memory hasn't returned in full in the next week or two."

"A week or two?" Katie echoed, her eyes widening. "Is there any way to make it come back faster?"

He hesitated. "Possibly. If you see something familiar or experience something that triggers a memory, that could hasten the process. But it's important not to push yourself to remember—stressful situations will only delay the healing."

When they arrived at the hospital, Mary waited until they took Katie away for her CAT scan before she walked outside and dialed the police station.

"Ivy Bay Police," a young man answered. "May I help you?"

"This is Mary Fisher. Is Chief McArthur in?"

"I'm sorry, Mrs. Fisher, but the chief already left for the day," the man replied. "This is Deputy Wadell."

She smiled. Deputy Wadell was a young but earnest cop. "Hi, Deputy. I was wondering if you could tell me if there are any reports of a missing person in Ivy Bay or anywhere else on Cape Cod."

"A missing person?" he asked, sounding surprised. "Let me take a look."

Mary heard the sound of computer keys tapping on the other end of the line.

A moment later, the officer said, "No reports have come in today. I've looked at both the local and statewide bulletins."

"Okay," she said, disappointed. "If you do receive a report, could you give me a call at home?" Then she told him about finding Katie at her shop and the girl's amnesia.

"She doesn't remember *anything*?" he asked when she'd finished her story.

"No," Mary replied. "So I'm hoping someone she knows is looking for her—or will be soon."

"I'll keep an eye on the bulletins," he said, "and give you a call if I see or hear anything."

"Thanks, Deputy." Mary hung up the phone, praying that someone was looking for the girl and would contact the authorities soon.

A short time later, a pretty young nurse wheeled Katie back to the waiting room.

"I told them I didn't need a wheelchair," Katie said, looking a little embarrassed as the nurse parked it in front of Mary.

"I told her just to sit back and enjoy the ride," the nurse told Mary with a smile lighting her face. "After the day she's had, she could use a little pampering."

"You're right," Mary agreed. "And I know just where she can find it."

THREE

⬦◆⬦

"Y̶ou're coming home with me," Mary told Katie as they left the hospital.

"I can't impose on you like that," Katie said.

"Nonsense," Mary replied. "Where else would you go?"

That was a question neither one of them could answer. Katie grew quiet, gingerly touching the bandage on the inner crook of her left arm as they walked to Mary's car. Between the CAT scan and blood draw, they had been at the hospital for a good two hours. Fortunately, Dr. Teagarden had called ahead so the hospital staff was prepared for their arrival.

As they climbed into the car and began the drive to the house on Shore Drive, Mary considered the possibility that Katie's amnesia might have been caused by some kind of drug—even an illegal drug. Tiny prickles of doubt began to plague her during the short drive.

Had she made a mistake inviting Katie into the home she shared with Betty? Should she have called her sister first to talk it over? Katie certainly seemed like a nice, sweet girl, but was that the real Katie or the one who had no memories of her life?

She glanced over at her passenger and was thankful that Katie seemed unaware of Mary's concern. Katie's gaze was fixed on the passing scenery—so breathtaking this time of year. Red and yellow leaves floated from the trees, landing along the trails leading to the sand dunes and marshes. As the sun moved toward the western horizon, it cast a lovely purple haze through the clouds dotting the sky.

A few minutes later, Mary pulled into the driveway. "This is it."

"Your home is beautiful," Katie said softly. "The flowers are gorgeous."

"My sister has the green thumb in the family," Mary said as they emerged from the car and started up the front walk. Betty had recently planted some asters along the front foundation, the rich purple blooms brightening the entrance to the house.

Katie's step faltered. "Does your sister live here too?"

"Yes," Mary told her, slowing her pace a little. "It's just the two of us and my cat, Gus."

"Are you sure she'll want me here?" Katie asked. "Are you sure *you* do?"

Despite some of her doubts, Mary couldn't turn Katie away now. Where would she go? "I'm sure," she said gently. "We'll just take this one step at a time, okay?"

"Okay," Katie agreed, following her up the front steps and into the house.

Gus greeted them at the door, his tail flicking behind him.

"Hello there," Mary greeted the cat. She'd left him home from the bookshop today when she'd found him curled up in

Betty's lap this morning in the sunroom, both of them taking a nap. Now he seemed wide awake.

"Katie, this is Gus," Mary said as the cat began to brush up against Katie's ankles and meow.

Katie smiled as she bent down to pick him up. "He's gorgeous and such a big boy."

A loud purr emanated from Gus as Katie stroked his head and neck.

Mary chuckled. "It looks like Gus approves of our new guest. Now we'll have to introduce you to Betty."

But as they made their way from the living room into the kitchen, there was no sight or sound of Betty. Mary called out for her a few times and even looked out the window into the backyard before concluding that her sister wasn't home.

"I'm sure she'll be here soon," Mary told Katie. "In the meantime, I can show you to your room."

"That would be wonderful," Katie said, still holding on to Gus.

Mary led her upstairs to the second bedroom that served as a guest room. The sage-green walls and the vintage nine-patch quilt that covered the bed made it a cozy place for visitors. "The bathroom is this way." Mary led the way down the hall and opened the door to the bathroom, the light scent of citrus disinfectant still lingering from last Saturday morning's cleaning spree. "There are towels in the cupboard and a clean robe in the closet, if you'd like to clean up before dinner."

"I'd love a shower," Katie said. "Maybe it would help clear my head."

"Of course," Mary told her. "If you'd like, I could bring some soup up here when you're done with your shower. Then you can just relax the rest of the night."

A wistful sigh escaped Katie's lips. "That sounds heavenly."

Mary reached out for Gus. "I'll take him with me so he doesn't get in your way. Let me know if there's anything you need."

"I will," Katie told her as she handed over the cat.

Gus purred all the way down the stairs, then waited patiently near his food dish until Mary fed him. She washed her hands at the kitchen sink and then retrieved the container of chicken soup from the refrigerator. Betty had made the soup yesterday, telling Mary that there was nothing better than a pot of homemade soup simmering on the stove while the rain pattered against the roof.

Mary knew the soup would taste even better today now that the flavors had mingled overnight. She set the pot on the stove and set the burner just high enough to warm the soup without scorching it. Above her, she could hear the sound of the shower running in the upstairs bedroom.

"Mar?" Betty's voice called out from the living room.

Both Gus and Mary looked up expectantly, then headed toward the living room. "Here I am," Mary said as she entered the room to see Betty holding the front door wide open.

Excitement gleamed in Betty's blue eyes. "Have I got a surprise for you!"

Before Mary could reply, she heard a man's voice call out from the front stoop. "Careful there, Frank. Let me get a handle on this end before you start pushing."

Intrigued, Mary moved closer to the door. "What's going on?"

"Eleanor and I went to an estate auction in Falmouth today, and I found something I couldn't resist!"

"Got it, Frank," the man's voice called out. "We're almost there."

"Bets...," Mary began, but her mouth gaped when she saw a large covered item slowly making its way through the front door. "What in the world?"

Betty grinned. "It's a piano! A beautiful antique piano in perfect condition."

"A piano?" Mary echoed as the first man entered, his back facing her and the words *Mayhew Moving Company* printed on the back of his gray coveralls.

"You know how much I loved to play before I married Edward," Betty explained. "I've always wanted to get back to it, but time just kept slipping away from me. But when I saw it, I just knew it was the one for me."

Mary smiled at the excitement in her sister's voice. "I can't wait to see it."

"Are you through the door, Ed?" another man's voice called out.

"I'm in," Ed replied. "You can bring her the rest of the way."

Betty beamed as the moving men slowly rolled the covered piano all the way through the front door. "I didn't intend to be so late getting home, but once I bought the piano, I had to arrange to have it moved here. And these nice men made time in their schedule to bring it today."

"Happy to be of service," the man called Ed told Betty. He was completely bald except for a few wisps of gray hair that he'd slicked back on his forehead. "Now, where would you like it?"

Betty made a slow turn in the room. "I've been thinking about that ever since I left Falmouth. Maybe in between those two windows on the west wall." She turned to Mary. "Do you think it will fit there?"

"Maybe," Mary replied, a little doubtful. Betty had a great eye for design, but the piano looked too big for the room.

Betty pointed out the spot to the movers. "Let's try it there, please."

Ed and Frank carefully rolled the piano in that direction and placed it between the windows.

"That's not too bad, I guess," Betty said, and her brow furrowed as she watched Ed and Frank remove the padded cover.

"Oh, Bets," Mary said when the cover was off. "It's really nice."

The piano was much darker than the furniture in the rest of the room, but Mary couldn't deny the beauty of the carved scrollwork on the legs and along the front panel. She walked over to lift the keyboard cover, and the wood smoothly rolled back to reveal the ivory and ebony piano keys.

"I have all my old sheet music up in the attic," Betty said. "I can't wait to bring it down and look through it again." She turned toward the movers. "Thank you so much. Would you like me to pay you now, or will you send me a bill?"

"Our bookkeeper takes care of all that," Ed told her. "She'll send you an invoice in the next day or two."

"Wonderful," Betty said, walking over to the front door and retrieving the purse that she'd set behind it. She reached inside and drew out some bills, handing each man a generous tip. "Thank you again."

"Thank you," Frank replied with a grin. He tipped his hat to both Betty and Mary, then headed out the door.

"You ladies have a good evening," Ed said, tucking the bills into his front shirt pocket, then followed his partner outside.

Betty closed the door behind them, then hurried over to the piano. She ran her hand over the top, caressing the smooth wood surface just as Mary had been longing to do.

"Does it have a bench?" Mary asked.

"No," Betty replied as Gus gingerly sniffed a claw-shaped piano foot. "But I thought we could use Grandma's old piano bench that's up in the attic."

"That might work."

"I know the wood won't match," Betty told her, "but I could refinish it someday." She reached out and tinkled some of the keys.

Gus let out a yowl at the sound and scampered from the room.

Mary chuckled. "I guess Gus isn't a fan of piano music."

"It's just badly out of tune," Betty said. "I'll have a piano tuner out this week to get it into shape. I can't wait to start playing again."

"It's been a long time, hasn't it?"

"At least thirty years," Betty told her. "After I married Edward and then Evan came along, I just didn't have the time I needed to devote to my music. But when I saw my rheumatologist last week, he mentioned that I should find a hobby to improve my fine motor skills. When I saw the piano today, I thought it might be just the right therapy."

"I hope it is," Mary told her.

Betty sniffed. "Is that chicken soup I smell?"

Mary had almost forgotten about the soup on the stove—and the woman in the shower. "It is, and I have a surprise for you too."

Mary told her sister about finding Katie in the bookshop and everything that had happened since that moment.

"So you're telling me that you invited a strange woman to stay with us?" Betty said, her voice low as she watched Mary ladle soup into a bowl. Betty didn't seem upset about their unexpected houseguest, just a little perplexed.

"She seems very nice," Mary said. "And I just wanted to help her. She doesn't have any money or anyplace to stay—at least nowhere that she remembers."

"Surely someone has missed her by now."

Mary set the steaming bowl of chicken soup on a tray, then added a small plate of crackers. "I thought about that while we were at the hospital, so I called the police station when Katie was having her CAT scan. They don't have any reports of a missing person so far, but they'll call if one comes in tonight."

"And what about the person who wrote that note?" Betty asked. "Why aren't they looking for her?"

"That's what I've been wondering ever since I saw it," Mary admitted. "And why meet at 1:12? Doesn't that seem strange?"

"Very strange."

Mary walked over to the refrigerator and pulled out a carton of milk. "Maybe the person who wanted to meet Katie there knows me. Maybe it's one of my regular customers—and that's why he or she wanted to meet her in the bookshop."

"Then why did no one show up?"

Mary shrugged. "The person could have called Katie and canceled, but with her amnesia, she wouldn't remember the call. Now that I think about it, there's really no way to know how long that note has been in her pocket."

"Oh, that poor girl," Betty murmured, then frowned. "Are you sure she's not faking it? You hear so much about scams and such these days."

"Her injuries were real," Mary told her sister. "And Dr. Teagarden diagnosed her with amnesia." She added a glass of milk to the tray, then picked it up. "Do you want to come upstairs with me and meet her? Then you can judge for yourself."

Betty didn't come upstairs often, due to issues with her rheumatoid arthritis, but she nodded and headed toward the stairs. "I would like to meet her."

Mary followed her sister up the stairs, not minding the slow pace. Betty hung on to the railing but seemed to have little trouble negotiating the steps. When they reached the second bedroom, Mary was surprised to see Gus already there, waiting by the closed door.

"Gus seems to like her," Mary whispered to her sister, considering that a point in Katie's favor.

Betty just smiled as Mary moved in front of the door. "Katie, if you're ready, I have your soup."

A moment later, Katie opened the door, the white terry-cloth robe wrapped snuggly around her. "Thank you so much," Katie said, brushing her wet bangs off her forehead. Then her gaze moved to Betty.

"I'm Mary's sister, Betty Emerson." Betty reached out to shake the young woman's hand.

Katie clasped it gently. "Thank you for letting me stay here. I appreciate it so much and promise not to overstay my welcome."

"Don't you worry about it," Betty assured her. "We're happy to have you."

"Here's your soup," Mary said, making her way inside the room. She set the dinner tray on top of the dresser. "Along with some crackers and a glass of milk. If you don't like milk, I can get you something else to drink."

"I like milk," Katie replied. "At least I think I do."

Gus padded into the room and slid his furry body against Katie's bare ankles.

"Gus," Mary chided, picking up her cat, "leave the poor girl alone."

Katie chuckled, reaching out to pet him. "It's all right. I think he's a sweetie." Then tears filled her eyes. "I wonder if I have a cat or dog at home. One that's waiting for me to come back." She inhaled deeply, blinking back her tears. "I'm sorry. I think the day is catching up with me."

"That's perfectly understandable," Mary said gently. "We'll leave you alone so you can eat and then get some rest. I'm sure you'll feel better tomorrow."

Betty moved toward the foot of the bed, where Katie's crumpled clothes were piled. "Why don't we wash these for you so you'll have clean clothes in the morning? We could let you borrow some of ours, but you're so slender and tall that I'm afraid they wouldn't fit at all."

"Please don't go to any trouble," Katie began.

"It's no trouble at all," Betty said, gathering up the clothes in her arms. "I'll go downstairs and just throw them in the washing machine."

Betty headed out the door before Katie could protest any further.

Mary turned to follow her sister. "I'll be right down the hallway if you need anything during the night."

"Thank you again," Katie said, her voice growing tight with emotion. "You've been so kind to me. I don't feel quite so scared anymore."

"There's no reason to be afraid. We're going to find out your identity." Mary hoped she could keep that promise. "In fact, I know just the place to start tomorrow."

FOUR

◆◆◆

The next morning, Mary sat in the sunroom with a cup of coffee in her hands. She'd just finished her morning devotional and reflected on the simple but powerful verse: *Love never fails.*

She loved the uplifting message in 1 Corinthians about love. The love of her family and friends hadn't failed her when she'd lost John, and neither had the love of the Lord. Love had lifted her up in her darkest moments, and she prayed that it might do the same for Katie.

Mary gazed out the window, watching the tree branches dance in the gentle morning breeze. Several red maple leaves fluttered gracefully to the ground. Gus lay purring at her feet, and she couldn't imagine a more serene moment. It was the perfect way to start the day.

A few minutes later, Betty peeked her head inside the doorway. "Is Katie up yet?"

"I haven't seen her," Mary replied, turning toward her sister. Betty wore a lovely dove-gray silk blouse and a pair of black slacks. A single strand of pearls circled her slender neck, matching the pearls in her ears. "Going somewhere?"

"I have a meeting with my stockbroker this morning. Then I have a few errands to run." She reached up to adjust one of the pearl earrings. "But I did manage to reach the piano tuner, and he's able to squeeze me in tomorrow afternoon."

"Perfect," Mary said. "I can't wait to hear you play again."

"I'm sure I'll be a little rusty," Betty said, "but I'm anxious to get started."

Gus stretched his legs in front of him, then hopped into Mary's lap. She reached out to pet him. "I'm going to leave Gus home today since Katie and I have a few errands of our own to run."

"Oh, that reminds me," Betty said. "I just put Katie's clean clothes on the kitchen table so she could find them."

"Thanks again for doing her laundry." Mary sighed. "Let's hope the new day brings some new hope in finding her identity."

"Well, if anyone can figure it out," Betty said with a smile as she turned around to leave, "you can."

"Have a good day," Mary called after her, then turned her attention back to Gus. He purred in her lap, and part of her wished she could just stay in the sunroom all day and enjoy the peace and quiet.

"Love never fails," she told Gus, stroking his head. She was so blessed by the love of her sister, her children and grandchildren, and all the friends she'd made through the years, both in Ivy Bay and in Boston.

Her heart ached to think of the friends and family who might be missing Katie right now, and she worried about her. Mary closed her eyes, praying for peace and comfort for them and for a speedy reunion with their lost loved one.

"Good morning," said a soft voice from the doorway.

Mary opened her eyes and saw Katie standing there, wearing the white bathrobe and holding her folded clothes in her arms. Her bangs were brushed to the side, and her pretty face looked freshly washed.

"Good morning," Mary greeted her. "How did you sleep?"

Katie smiled. "Much better than I expected, actually. My headache is completely gone."

"Glad to hear it," Mary told her, setting Gus aside as she began to rise from her chair. "How about some breakfast?"

Katie held up both hands. "You stay put," she insisted. "You and Betty have already been kind enough to let me stay here and also do my laundry. I'd feel less like I'm intruding on your hospitality if you'd let me fend for myself."

"Of course," Mary said with a smile as she settled back into the chair. Gus resumed his spot on her lap, obviously not holding a grudge. "There's oatmeal on the stove and bowls in the cupboard to the left of the stove. You'll find a spoon in the drawer next to the sink."

"Thank you," Katie said with a smile. "May I get you some?"

"I've already eaten, thanks. But there's coffee brewing on the counter and dried cranberries, walnuts, and honey on the table, so please help yourself."

"I will." Katie took a step away from the doorway and then turned back. "You mentioned last night that you knew a good place to start the search for my identity."

Mary nodded. "I thought we'd start at the police station. I know Chief McArthur, and he'll do his best to help us."

LOST FOR WORDS ～ 39

Katie's brow furrowed. "But I thought the police hadn't received any reports of a missing person."

"They haven't—at least not when I called last night. But there could be other clues about you out there. Perhaps an abandoned car or some item belonging to you, like a purse or wallet, that might come to their attention. This way, at least they'll know your story and where to find you."

Katie nodded. "You're right. That probably is the best place to start."

Mary glanced at her watch. "Shall we leave in about an hour?"

Katie gave another nod, her expression both apprehensive and excited. "I'll be ready."

Chief Benjamin McArthur sat behind his black steel desk and pulled out a pencil from the front pocket of his beige shirt. His silver badge gleamed under the fluorescent beam of the long ceiling light. "What brings you here today, Mary?"

Mary sat next to Katie, who hadn't said a peep since they'd been escorted into the chief's office. "I found this young woman in my bookshop yesterday, and she's lost her memory. We were hoping you might be able to help us figure out her identity."

His bushy gray eyebrows rose about an inch as he peered at Katie through his wire-rimmed bifocals. "Lost her memory? You mean she has...amnesia?"

Mary nodded. "Dr. Teagarden said it's due to a head injury, but Katie doesn't know where or how it happened."

Mary told him the rest of the story, starting with Katie's appearance in the shop yesterday and ending with their arrival at the police station this morning.

Chief McArthur sat forward in his chair, his burly forearms resting on his desk. "Did you bring this note with you?"

Katie dug into her pocket. "I have it right here." She handed it to him and watched him intently as he read it.

He looked up from the note and stared at Katie. "And you have no idea who wrote it?"

"None," Katie said. "I waited in Mary's shop, but no one ever showed up. If she hadn't helped me, I don't know what I would have done."

He handed the note back to her. "So the last thing you do remember is walking around on the beach."

Katie nodded. "I had a slight headache, but have no memory of falling or hitting my head."

He leaned forward, sliding a yellow pad toward him across the surface of his desk. "Can you describe the beach?"

She frowned, looking puzzled. "Well, there was sand."

One corner of his mouth tipped up in a smile. "Sorry. I should have been more specific. Was there anything that stood out to you? A building or a sign? Some kind of landmark?"

Katie pursed her lips as she considered his question. "There was a shed just off the beach, near a wooded area."

Mary sat up straighter. "Can you describe it?"

"It was small," Katie said slowly. "And I think there was a sign on it once, because there was a square area of the wood siding that was much darker than the rest of the building."

Mary met Chief McArthur's gaze. "Any ideas?"

He shook his head. "Not offhand."

Then Katie turned to Mary. "The roof had this metal fish thing on it that twirled around."

Mary's pulse quickened. "You mean like a weather vane?"

"Yes." Katie's eyes widened with relief. "That's it! A weather vane."

Mary smiled as she looked at Chief McArthur. "That has to be Ned Simpson's old bait shop."

"Sure sounds like it," he said, swiveling in his chair toward the map of Ivy Bay posted on the wall behind him. He tapped a thick finger near one section of Little Neck Beach. "Which means that Katie must have been right about here."

While Mary was thrilled that they'd figured out part of Katie's story, it still wasn't enough to identify her. "There aren't any rental cabins in that area," Mary said. "In fact, there's not a lot of foot traffic on that area of the beach."

"So how did I end up there?" Katie asked, looking between the two of them. "Any ideas?"

The police chief turned his chair around to face them. "Not yet, but I'll canvass the area and see what I can find. If there are any cars around, I'll run the plates and see what turns up."

Mary rose to her feet. "I think we should go with you, if you don't mind. Maybe it will spark a memory for Katie."

Chief McArthur nodded. "That's fine with me." Then he turned to Katie. "Before we leave, I'd like to have a photograph taken of you and get your fingerprints."

Katie blanched. "My fingerprints? Do you think I might be a criminal or something?"

He smiled. "I doubt it, but you could still be in the fingerprint database. Some employers require a fingerprint background check before they hire someone, so that's one possibility."

"That's right," Mary concurred. "A friend back in Boston has a daughter who is a speech therapist. She had to go through a background check before she was allowed to work with children and the disabled."

He cocked his head to one side as he looked at Katie. "I'd say you're somewhere in your midtwenties, which means you were a child back in the late eighties. That was a time when fingerprinting children had started to become popular with parents, just in case their child was ever abducted. If your parents used one of those kits, your name would be in the database and so would the names of your folks."

Katie's shoulders relaxed. "So there are legitimate reasons you might find my fingerprints in a database somewhere."

"There sure are," Chief McArthur said. "The fingerprinting process is a little messy, but it might save us a lot of time in finding out your identity."

Katie stood up. "Then let's do it."

———

Twenty minutes later, Mary and Katie followed Chief McArthur's police cruiser to Little Neck Beach. Mary parked behind the cruiser. Then they all made their way to the beach. A flock of seagulls flew overhead, and a large boat cruising in the bay blew its horn.

Katie walked slowly toward the water, looking around her with each step. Mary could only imagine how desperate Katie must be to remember something. Like looking for a key to the past, but not knowing what form that key would take.

Chief McArthur moved beside Mary. "It's pretty deserted around here today."

Mary nodded as she watched Katie wander through the sand. "Even if there were witnesses who saw Katie yesterday, we have no way of finding them, short of posting her photograph on the evening news."

"Hopefully, it won't come to that," Chief McArthur said. "The last thing we need is false leads or people claiming they saw Katie when it was really someone else."

Mary assumed there would be a flood of phone calls from people missing someone in their lives who matched Katie's description. Her heart ached for the lost people in the world, and she breathed a silent prayer asking the Lord to watch over them.

Mary stepped toward Katie. "Does anything look familiar?"

"Yes and no," Katie said, moving toward her. "I remember the beach from yesterday, but nothing else. I was only here a few minutes before I found that note in my pocket and headed downtown to look for Mary's bookshop."

Chief McArthur pointed to the shed a few yards away. "And that's the shed you remember?"

"Yes," Katie said as the chief started walking over to it.

Following him, Mary looked around for clues that Katie might have missed, but there was nothing but sand and seashells on the beach.

When they reached the shed, Chief McArthur turned the handle and opened the door. "Looks like Ned wasn't too worried about vandals."

Mary looked through the open door into the barren shed. There was nothing inside but a few broken shelves and a couple of old buckets that had once held earthworms. "Well, Katie, it doesn't look like this is where you were staying," Mary said with a smile.

Katie chuckled. "If it was, I have bigger problems than amnesia."

Chief McArthur closed the door and then turned to them. "There doesn't seem to be anything here, but we'll keep our eyes open. I'll show your photograph around at the local inns and hotels to see if they recognize you or have a missing guest."

"And you'll let me know about the fingerprints?" Katie asked him.

He nodded. "I have an officer checking the database now. If we get any matches, I'll let you know immediately."

"Thank you," Mary told him, sensing that he was as determined to find Katie's identity as they were. "You can call my shop or my cell at any time, day or night."

"Will do," the police chief said, then turned to Katie with a reassuring smile. "And you may not know it, but you met just the right lady to help you out. Mary is known around here not only for owning a mystery bookshop but also for solving local mysteries."

Katie glanced at her and smiled. "That's good to know."

He winked, said good-bye, then headed out to his cruiser.

Mary watched him drive off, wondering if he'd have any luck at the inns or hotels. Surely someone in Ivy Bay knew Katie. So why hadn't that person gone to the police when she'd disappeared?

"I guess this was a dead end, wasn't it?" Katie said, sounding a little dejected.

Mary reached out to give Katie's arm a gentle squeeze of encouragement. "Don't give up; we'll find something."

"I hope so," Katie said, rounding the car to the front passenger door. "Since I don't know anything about myself, maybe I should just assume I'm an optimist."

Mary smiled. "That's the right attitude." She opened the car door, and they both climbed inside. "Now how about a little shopping to lift our spirits? You could use some more clothes, and I know that Cape Cod Togs has a wonderful clearance sale happening this week."

"But I don't have any money," Katie told her, "and I simply can't let you buy me anything. You've done so much already."

"Then consider it a temporary loan," Mary said as she started the engine. "You can pay me back later."

"When I finally get my life back," Katie said, a small smile on her face. "All right; it's a deal."

Mary pulled the car away from Little Neck Beach and headed for Main Street. She'd called Rebecca earlier and told her that she'd be in the shop before lunch, which gave them a good hour to shop for clothes.

As they turned the corner, Mary could see the high school marching band about a block away and heading right toward them.

"What's going on?" Katie asked, laughing a little at the sight in front of her.

"It must be a special marching band practice," Mary said as she slowly steered the car over to an empty parking space on the side and shut off the engine. She rolled down her window so they could enjoy the music. The band was playing the school fight song, with the drum major leading the way with her large baton.

"I heard they were going to have a street practice this week," Mary told her, "in preparation for marching in a big parade next week in Falmouth."

Mary and Katie stepped out of the car to watch the impromptu parade. Mary waved to several band members as they passed by, and Katie also seemed to be enjoying the show.

"Who's that guy waving to me?" Katie asked her, pointing across the street.

Mary looked over and saw a group of men standing under the awning of Jimmy's Hardware store. "Which one?"

"The guy in the sunglasses," Katie said. Then she shook her head. "No, wait. I think he was waving to the kid with the trombone." She emitted a nervous laugh. "I guess I'm a little paranoid. Someone I know could wave to me on the street, and I wouldn't even recognize them."

Mary could only imagine how unsettling that would feel. They resumed watching the impromptu parade, but it only lasted a few minutes before the band made its way past her car and down the street.

"That was fun," Katie said as they returned to the Impala. "I wonder if I ever played in a marching band."

It was a question that had no answer—not yet anyway. But since Katie had decided to be an optimist, Mary thought they might as well have fun guessing Katie's life during their short trip.

"Maybe you played a trombone," Mary said playfully, slowing her car as they neared the shop.

Katie laughed. "No way! Too heavy for me, especially if I have to walk a long distance. I think I'd choose the flute, or even better, the piccolo."

"Then the piccolo it is." Mary pulled in front of the shop. "Now we get to see what kind of clothes you like. Are you ready?"

"Sure," Katie said, following her to the door of Cape Cod Togs. A bell dinged as they walked through the door, and Mary inhaled the delicate scent of eucalyptus mingled with mint. She saw the clerk Carolee Benson behind the cash register.

"Hello, Mary," Carolee greeted her, stepping away from the counter and walking across the gleaming cherry floor to greet them.

Carolee looked at Katie, her green eyes widening with recognition. "Well, hello! It's so nice to see you back again."

FIVE

— ◆◆◆ —

Mary's mouth gaped as she stared at Carolee. "You know her?"

"You know me?" Katie echoed, taking a step toward her.

Carolee blinked as she took a step back, appearing bewildered by their reaction. "You were in here on Monday," she told Katie. "Don't you remember?"

"No," Katie told her, a smile spreading across her face. "I have amnesia. But you remember me!" Then she turned and gave Mary an impromptu hug.

Mary was smiling too, thrilled that they'd found someone who recognized Katie, even if that someone still looked perplexed. Mary decided to explain before Carolee made an escape out the nearest exit.

"Katie was injured and lost her memory," Mary told the store clerk. "She doesn't remember anything about her life or why she's in Ivy Bay."

"Oh dear," Carolee said, her hand fluttering to her chest. Carolee was older than Mary by about five years and, according to Betty, loved suspense novels. But this real-life mystery seemed to have caught her off guard.

Carolee cleared her throat. "I thought amnesia only happened on television."

"Unfortunately not," Mary said, eager to learn what Carolee knew about Katie's situation. "Can you tell us what time she was in the shop on Monday?"

Carolee thought for a moment, the effort furrowing her forehead. "I think it was around four o'clock or so. I remember because I'd just washed the windows and wiped them dry with the sports section of Monday's *Wall Street Journal*." She wrinkled her nose. "I don't like sports. Anyway, the newspaper usually arrives between three and three thirty." She held out her clean hands. "My fingers still had newsprint smudges on them."

Mary glanced at Katie. "Does any of that sound familiar?"

Katie shook her head. "No, but I wish it did."

Carolee cocked her head to one side as she looked at Katie. "You had your hair in a ponytail that day, and you wore jean shorts and a yellow peasant blouse." Her hand moved toward her collarbone. "And you had on a lovely silver necklace. The pendant was shaped like a small compass, and you showed me the words etched on it."

Mary's heart quickened. "What did it say?"

"Oh, what was it...?" Carolee hesitated for a long moment. Then she smiled. "I remember now. It said: 'There are no shortcuts to anywhere worth going.'"

The sentiment made Mary smile. She liked the message, which spoke about life as much as it did about traveling. She hadn't traveled much since opening her shop, although she still enjoyed visits to Lizzie in Melrose and Jack in Chicago. But opening her bookshop had been a journey in itself.

She enjoyed surrounding herself with books and meeting people from so many different places. Living in Ivy Bay often felt like a vacation—there seemed to be something new to experience almost every day, and the scenery, which changed with each season, was always spectacular.

"What else can you tell us?" Mary asked, hoping that Carolee might remember something that would actually lead to Katie's identity. "Did she come here with anyone? Did she use a credit card for her purchases?"

Carolee sighed. "She came in alone, and I'm afraid she didn't buy anything. She just tried on a few dresses and then left."

Katie's shoulders sagged. "Did I say anything? Tell you why I was in Ivy Bay or where I was staying?"

"I'm sorry," Carolee said, shaking her head. "We didn't talk much. When I asked if you needed any help, you told me that you were just browsing."

Katie forced a smile as she looked at Mary. "I guess there aren't going to be any shortcuts for me today. At least someone recognized me."

Mary nodded. "And Carolee might not be the only one. If you were in the area on Monday, there might be other people who will recognize you too."

Katie brightened. "That's true."

Mary's gaze moved over the well-spaced clothing racks as string music played a peaceful adagio from discreetly placed speakers. "Why don't we find some things for you to try on first? Then we'll take a stroll around to the different businesses to see if anyone else saw you on Monday."

Carolee clapped her hands together. "That sounds like a good plan." She walked over to one of the wall racks and began pulling out some capri pants and shorts, along with several summer tops. "These all look about your size, and we've just reduced the price again." She glanced over at Katie. "Do you have a favorite color?"

Katie grinned and shrugged. "If I do, I don't remember it."

"Oh dear," Carolee said. "That was a silly question, wasn't it? Well, with your fair complexion and cute figure, almost anything will look good."

Mary and Katie sorted through the other racks, each picking a few pieces before Carolee led Katie back into the dressing room.

Cape Cod Togs was known for its high-end prices, but Mary found a couple of tops for herself on the clearance rack that were real bargains and just her size. She walked over and set them on the counter as Carolee returned from the dressing room area.

"Did you find something?"

"I did," Mary told her. "I'll take these, along with whatever Katie selects."

Carolee picked up the first item and began typing the information from the tag onto the computer register. "Why do you call her Katie if she can't remember anything about herself?"

Mary briefly explained about the note in Katie's pocket, without going into too much detail. She also mentioned that Katie would be staying with her until this mystery was solved.

"So you're like her guardian angel," Carolee said with a smile, now taking down the information from the other top.

Mary chuckled. "I don't feel very angelic most of the time, but I do want to help her. She's a sweet girl." Then she wondered if Carolee might know more than she realized. Maybe a few more questions would spark *her* memory. "So what was your impression of her when she came in the store on Monday?"

Carolee slipped the light blue polo shirt off the hanger and began to fold it. "Well, she was nice enough, but she seemed in a bit of a hurry. Although, she did come out of the dressing room to show me the black-and-white cocktail dress she tried on." Carolee smiled. "She looked amazing in it. I told her it was made for her."

"But she didn't get it?"

Carolee breathed with a disappointed sigh. "No. I think she got a case of sticker shock when she looked at the price tag. Unfortunately for her, that particular dress wasn't on sale. She did love it though—you could see that by the way she kept looking in the three-way mirror outside the dressing room."

Mary looked toward the small rack of special-occasion dresses near the large window. Cape Cod Togs specialized in sailing apparel but carried a few nice dresses and a small stock of shoes, along with some jewelry and other accessories.

"Can you show me the dress?" Mary asked, hoping if Katie saw it, she might remember something.

Carolee frowned. "I'm afraid it's gone. It sold right after she left the shop." Then her frown turned quizzical. "It was rather strange, actually. There was a man outside—I saw him through the display window. As soon as she left, he just walked right into the store and bought the same dress she'd just tried on."

"Who was it?"

She shook her head. "I'd never seen him before."

"Can you describe him?" Mary wasn't sure the man who bought the dress had any connection to Katie, but it did seem odd that he'd purchased the same dress that Katie had just tried on.

Carolee pursed her lips. "He was in his thirties and dressed like a tourist. He wore sunglasses and a ball cap.

"Did he say anything?"

"Nothing of note," Carolee replied. "Although he did surprise me when he paid for the dress in cash."

Mary felt a thud of disappointment deep inside her. "So you don't have anything with his name on it?"

"I'm afraid not. So few people pay cash these days, especially for such an expensive item, that I simply asked him if he wanted it gift wrapped." Carolee leaned closer, a curious gleam in her eyes. "That's when it really got weird, now that I think about it."

"What do you mean?"

"I asked him if he wanted the dress gift wrapped, and he told me that he already had a special package for it." Carolee moved back. "Then he smiled."

Mary wasn't sure if the purchase was as creepy as Carolee made it sound, or if she was caught up in the mystery of Katie's amnesia and the stranger who had bought the dress.

Katie emerged from the dressing room and joined them at the counter. "I think I'm ready." She placed three tops, two pairs of denim shorts and a pair of khaki-green capris—all clearance items—on the counter.

"Are you sure you don't want more?" Mary asked her.

Katie met her gaze. "I'm assuming I won't need more and will find my way back to my real life soon." She took a deep breath. "I'm an optimist, remember?"

Mary smiled. "Then that makes two of us."

———

After placing their bags in the car, Mary and Katie spent the next thirty minutes walking up and down Main Street and popping into every business that Katie might have visited. They spoke to Sophie Mershon at the Tea Shoppe, Jayne Tucker at Gems and Antiques, and even Jimmy Shepard at his hardware store. While all the shopkeepers were happy to meet her, none of them remembered seeing Katie. And Katie didn't remember ever walking into any of their shops before.

Tess Bailey felt so sorry for Katie that she gave her a free double-dip ice-cream cone featuring Mary's special flavor of the month—raspberry ripple. Mary enjoyed a small cone too, unable to resist. She also promised Tess to have a new ice-cream recipe ready for her soon.

As they made their way back to the bookshop, Katie made a game of naming the new ice-cream flavor using an amnesia theme. "You could call it Retrograde Rocky Road," Katie joked.

"Or maybe Forgetful Tutti-Frutti," Mary suggested with a smile.

Katie wrinkled her nose. "Those don't sound very appetizing, do they?"

"At least you remember different ice-cream flavors," Mary said.

"You're right; I do." Katie smiled and then licked her cone as they passed the front window of the bookshop. "I definitely like this one."

"Thank you." Mary opened the door and then followed Katie inside. Rebecca stood on the rolling ladder, dusting the top of one of the bookshelves. There was only one customer in the store—Hazel Pritchard, who sat in the rocking chair in the children's section, her nose buried in a middle-grade novel. A former elementary teacher, Hazel still liked to keep up on the newest publications in children's literature and often bought books to donate to the elementary school library.

"Hello," Rebecca called out, sweeping the feather duster over the bookshelf. "I'll be down in a minute."

"Take your time," Mary told her. She walked over to the front counter and placed her handbag into one of the cubbyholes.

Katie popped the last bit of ice-cream cone into her mouth and then licked one of her fingers. She held up both of her hands. "I'm a little sticky. Is there someplace I can wash up?"

"Sure, I'll show you," Mary said, directing her to the sink in the back room.

When she returned to the counter, Rebecca was climbing down from the ladder. She walked over to Mary, brushing back a stray lock of her brown hair. "Is that the same girl from yesterday?"

"It is," Mary replied, then told her Katie's story. By the time she was finished, Rebecca's brown eyes had slightly welled.

"That poor girl." Rebecca set the feather duster on the counter. "Is there anything I can do for her?"

"Just keep your eyes and ears open," Mary said. "Someone in Ivy Bay must have seen her besides Carolee, and surely someone is looking for her. I'm hoping that Chief McArthur has some luck passing her picture around at the local inns and hotels, but we haven't heard from him yet."

Katie returned from the back room. She smiled at Rebecca. "Hello again."

"Hello," Rebecca said, holding out her hand. "I'm Rebecca Mason. Mary told me your story."

Katie shook Rebecca's hand. "It's a crazy one, isn't it?"

"Yes," Rebecca said bluntly. Then all three of them laughed.

Mary finished her ice-cream cone, wondering what she should do with Katie. She wanted to keep an eye on her, but there was work to do at the shop too. Before she could form a plan, Katie suggested one of her own.

"Do you mind if I just help out around here?" Katie asked Mary. "There's still a possibility that whoever was supposed to meet me here yesterday will still show up. And I'll feel better if I can be useful."

"Of course," Mary said. "We'd appreciate the help. Right, Rebecca?"

"We sure would." Rebecca picked up the feather duster and handed it to Katie. "I've dusted all the top shelves, but if you can do the lower ones, that would be great." She smiled. "And one of the perks of this job is reading between the shelves, so be sure to take time for that too."

Katie smiled, holding the feather duster in one hand. "Thanks, I will."

Katie headed off to dust as Rebecca grabbed her sack lunch from a cubbyhole in the counter. "It's such a beautiful day that I think I'll eat lunch on the patio out back. Let me know if you need me."

"We'll be fine," Mary assured her. "Enjoy your break."

After Rebecca left, Mary glanced over at Hazel, who was still engrossed in her book. Then her gaze moved to Katie, who had a serene expression on her face as she swept the feather duster over the bottom shelves.

She was grateful that Katie had such a good attitude given her difficult situation. "A cheerful heart is good medicine," Mary murmured, remembering part of the verse from Proverbs 17:22. Maybe Katie's decision to be optimistic would help her heal more quickly. Mary prayed that it might be so.

Her cell phone rang, and Mary reached for her bag and dug inside. She scooped it up, looking at the screen just long enough to catch Chief McArthur's name. "Hello?"

"Hello, Mary. This is Chief McArthur."

"Yes?" Mary said, her voice almost a whisper. "Did you find anything?"

"I'm afraid not," he replied. "I showed Katie's photo around all the hotels and inns, but nobody recognized her. We didn't find a match for the fingerprints either."

Disappointment shot through Mary. "Well, thank you for trying. I'll let Katie know."

"Keep me posted," Chief McArthur said. "I hope she finds her way home."

"So do I," Mary said before ending the call. She dropped the cell phone back into her purse, reluctant to tell Katie the bad news. Maybe she should have encouraged Katie to buy more clothes at Cape Cod Togs. Katie's situation might not resolve itself anytime soon.

Then she remembered the message from Katie's compass necklace: *There are no shortcuts to anywhere worth going.* It seemed there were no shortcuts to finding Katie's identity either.

But that didn't mean Mary intended to give up. She believed the journey would be worth the destination. She just had to figure out the right path.

SIX

The next day, Mary walked along Main Street on her way to Grace Church. The morning air was a little cool and damp, making her wish she'd worn one of her favorite sweaters. Instead, she'd opted for one of her new polo shirts from Cape Cod Togs, along with a light jacket. Gray clouds still filled the sky, but the church was only a block away from her shop, and she enjoyed the short stroll.

Mary always looked forward to meeting with her prayer group, and this morning was no exception. She stifled a yawn as she headed down the sidewalk. The storm last night had kept her awake, and Gus hadn't taken refuge from the thunder in her room as he usually did, preferring to hide out in Katie's room instead.

Mary didn't mind. Gus had taken quite a liking to Katie, and the feeling seemed to be mutual. He'd stayed in Katie's lap during the length of their Scrabble game last evening, perfectly content to let her cuddle him. Katie had beaten both Mary and Betty by more than fifty points and seemed to enjoy the game as much as they did.

The girl's loss of memory certainly hadn't affected her vocabulary. The fact that Katie was smart and a good competitor revealed little puzzle pieces to her personality. Maybe if they could put enough of those pieces together, it might help them figure out her identity.

Mary had left both Katie and Gus at the bookshop with Rebecca this morning, along with a steady flow of customers. Mary knew Rebecca appreciated the extra help. Katie caught on quickly, and while she wasn't running the cash register yet, she helped shelve books and do other little chores that made her nice to have around.

Katie was adamant about working at the shop every day until her memory returned, still holding on to the hope that someone she knew would find her there. But Mary knew that with each passing day, that hope would diminish.

Something told her that Katie knew it too. While the girl did her best to put on a happy face and act optimistic, Mary could see the shadows of fear and apprehension in her eyes. It was a wonder the girl didn't walk around terrified all the time—not knowing what the future, or the past, held for her. All Mary and Betty could do was reassure Katie that her memory would eventually return—and pray that it was the truth.

Mary walked into the prayer chapel and found Jill Sanderson, Millie Russell, and Amy Stebble already there. She greeted them as she settled into a comfy stuffed chair next to Jill. "No folding chairs today?" Mary asked, referring to the circle of folding chairs where they usually sat.

"Not today," Jill replied, reaching up to tuck her blonde hair behind her ear. "All the folding chairs were commandeered for a bridal shower luncheon that's being held in the church basement."

"This is cozier anyway," Mary said. "How are the boys?"

Jill smiled, always happy to talk about her two rambunctious sons, Luman and Benjamin. "Happy to be back in school, I think—not that they'd ever admit it. I can't believe Benjamin will be in middle school soon."

"They do grow up fast," Mary said, thinking of her own two children, Jack and Lizzie, and her grandchildren. "Daisy will actually be graduating high school in a couple of years."

Bernice Foster and Tricia Miles walked into the room and greeted them, settling into the nook.

Dorothy arrived next and frowned as she looked around the room. "The folding chairs are downstairs already? I was promised they'd be here for our prayer group."

"We can make do here," Bernice said, patting the empty chair beside her. "We just have to squeeze in a bit."

Dorothy pursed her lips but didn't argue as she made her way to the seat beside Bernice. She set her purse on her lap and pulled out a sheet of folded paper. "I wrote down the prayer requests from the bulletin last week and added a couple more. Strom Engle tripped, spraining his ankle at Seafarers' Hall."

"Oh, poor Strom," Bernice murmured. "Will he be all right?"

"I believe so," Dorothy said, "although I was told he's limping quite a bit. The man's almost ninety and shouldn't be gadding about so much. He's lucky he didn't break his hip."

"He's a tough old bird," Millie Russell said, chuckling.

Tricia's eyes widened. "Speaking of birds, I'd like to offer a praise." She smiled, glancing at Mary. "Some of you have already heard the news, but I was offered a flute solo at the Wildlife Rescue Foundation concert."

Amy clapped her hands together. "That's wonderful, Tricia."

"I feel so blessed," Tricia told them. "I love playing the flute, and now I get to share that passion for a good cause."

"Matthew and Madeline Dinsdale are on the organizational committee this year, aren't they?" Amy asked.

"Yes, along with the board of directors of the foundation. It should be a great time."

They chatted for a few minutes about the concert and then took turns sharing their individual joys and concerns. Amy asked for prayers for the students and staff at the school as they started a new year. Lynn shared that her daughter was taking a trip to Toronto with a friend next week and asked for prayers for them. Jill expressed hope that her son Benjamin wouldn't need braces, even though their dentist referred him to an orthodontist.

Millie asked for prayers for a dear cousin who had just been diagnosed with a thyroid condition, and Bernice shared the good news that a dear friend who she hadn't seen since high school was planning a visit to Ivy Bay soon.

Then it was Mary's turn. She told them about Katie and her amnesia, asking for their prayers. Then she passed around a photo of Katie that she'd taken on her cell phone this morning, hoping that one of them would recognize her.

"She doesn't look familiar," Amy said, gazing at the cell phone photo. "We should pray for her family too; they must be frantic with worry."

When it was Dorothy's turn, she cleared her throat. "I don't have any personal news to share," she told the group. "But I wasn't quite finished with the prayer requests when Tricia shared her news."

"Oh, I'm sorry," Tricia said, quick to apologize. "I didn't mean to interrupt you before."

"Not at all," Dorothy said with a polite smile. "You were excited, and it's nice to have some good news in between the bad."

"Oh dear," Bernice said. "Does that mean you have more bad news?"

"I'm afraid so," Dorothy said. "Anthony Cantuccio was mugged last night."

Mary gasped, along with several others in the room. Anthony owned the Pizzeria Rustica on Water Street. She didn't know much more about him, although whenever she saw him at the restaurant, he always had a smile on his face. "Mugged?" Mary said. "In Ivy Bay?"

"I'm afraid so." Dorothy sighed. "Apparently, he was thrown to the ground and his belongings stolen. He was hurt as well, although I don't know the extent of his injuries."

Jill leaned forward. "Oh no. Is he in the hospital?"

"I believe he's recovering at home," Dorothy told them. "I wasn't given a lot of information. Just a request for prayers for him and his family."

Mary barely heard her. *A man was mugged in Ivy Bay.* Could the same thing have happened to Katie? It would explain the bump on her head and her skinned knees. And the mugger would have taken her purse with all her identification. It fit.

Mary turned to Dorothy. "Do you know where it happened?"

"On one of the trails near Little Neck Beach," Dorothy said. "Or at least that's what I heard."

Goose bumps prickled over Mary's forearms. The same beach Katie had found herself before coming to the bookshop.

Mary looked around the group, knowing Katie needed their prayers now more than ever. "Shall we pray?"

They bowed their heads and prayed for their concerns, gave thanks for their joys, and asked God's guidance for the challenges in their lives. They prayed for Strom and Anthony and Katie, and for the people near and dear to them.

The fellowship they shared and the prayers they spoke gave Mary peace and hope. God would lead the way, just as He always had.

Jill closed the prayer time, followed by a heartfelt chorus of "Amens." Then Mary lifted her head and smiled. The sun might not be shining outside, but she felt the warmth of God's love all around her.

The clouds had parted when Mary left the church, letting a few rays of sunshine warm the air around her. As she crossed the street and walked in the direction of the bookshop, she pulled her cell phone from her purse and dialed the direct line to Chief McArthur.

The police chief answered on the second ring. "McArthur."

"Chief, this is Mary. I wanted to ask you about the mugging last night."

"How much do you know?" he asked carefully.

"I heard that Anthony Cantuccio was mugged on a trail near Little Neck Beach and that he was injured but recovering."

"There was an apparent mugging," the chief told her. "Unfortunately, we don't have a suspect in custody. Anthony wasn't able to give us much information."

As a trio of laughing tourists approached her from the opposite direction, Mary slowed her step and moved off the sidewalk and under the shade of a large maple tree. "Do you think the same thing might have happened to Katie?"

"That thought did occur to me," the chief said. "Especially since the incident happened fairly close to that old bait shop."

Mary sucked in a deep breath. "It did?"

"Just a few yards away," the chief said. "Now, that could just be a coincidence, but I increased the patrol in that area, just in case. If something like that happens again, we'll catch the culprit."

His tone told Mary that he meant business. But what if the mugger didn't attack again? Then any possible connection to Katie might be lost. "Will you let me know if you catch him?"

"I will," the chief promised.

Mary ended the call, dropping the cell phone back into her purse before continuing on her way. Patches of blue sky now grew wider between the gray clouds, promising another nice, sunny day. The peacefulness that had filled her at the prayer group meeting stayed with her as she walked down the block. She waved to Kip and Heather Hastings as they emerged from Meeting House Grocers, each holding a bag in their hands.

Mary turned into her bookshop, happy to see that it was filled with customers. Ashley was behind the counter, showing Katie how to work the cash register. Rebecca stood at the new book display, assisting a woman who Mary recognized as Roger Foley's new wife, Diana. Roger had moved to town about a year ago and worked as an electrician. Mary and Betty had hired him to fix a minor problem with their fuse box and had been impressed by his work. The fifty-year-old former bachelor had a quick wit and a good work ethic, making him a good fit in the community.

Folks around town had ribbed Roger when he'd recently brought home a bride from Boston, certain that he'd miss his bachelorhood. The good-natured electrician had taken it all in stride, appearing very happy whenever Mary saw him around town. She'd heard that Diana had a son and daughter from a former marriage, but she hadn't met either of them yet.

Mary turned and waved to Pastor Miles, who sat in the children's area, reading a book to his grandson Trevor. The little boy's wide eyes and rapt attention told her that he was enjoying the story.

Sophie Mershon's younger sister Giselle sat cross-legged in one of the chairs by the fireplace, reading a book in her lap. Gus sat curled up in the opposite chair, sound asleep despite the activity around him. Mary smiled to herself, certain that he was tired from last night's thunderstorm too.

"Hello there," said a familiar voice behind her.

Mary's smile widened as she turned around and saw Henry standing behind her. They'd known each other since childhood and had rekindled their friendship when she'd moved to Ivy Bay. His smile lit up his sea-green eyes, and his silver hair looked shorter than the last time she'd seen him. "Well, this is a nice surprise! I thought you'd be out on the boat today."

"I was earlier," he said, "but I came into town for a haircut, so this seemed like the perfect time to stop in and buy a birthday gift for Karen. And to see you, of course."

His daughter Karen lived in Richmond and was an avid reader. She usually stopped in the bookshop whenever she visited Henry.

"And what about Kim?" Mary asked with a smile, referring to Karen's twin sister. Kim lived in Boston and kept busy with her two boys. "Do you need a book for her too?"

He chuckled. "Not this time. Kim already let me know that she wanted a pair of slippers for her birthday. Seems the last pair were a snack for my grandsons' new puppy."

Mary laughed. "Puppies do like to chew on things. Let's just hope she's able to keep the new pair out of the puppy's reach."

"If not, I'll know what to get her for Christmas," Henry said, an amused twinkle in his green eyes. "Now, Karen likes mysteries," he continued, then nodded in Katie's direction. "And from what Ashley told me, you've got a real-life mystery right here in the shop. She introduced me to Katie, who seems like a nice young lady."

Mary smiled, not surprised to see that Ashley had already taken Katie under her wing. "Katie is nice. She's staying with us until her memory returns—or until someone can identify her."

He shook his head. "It's hard to imagine that no one's missed her yet."

"I know," Mary said, more bothered by that fact than she'd wanted to admit to Katie. "Especially in light of the note. Did Ashley tell you about it?"

"Katie did," Henry replied. "Said she waited here all afternoon, but nobody ever showed up."

At least no one that she and I could identify, Mary thought to herself. It was possible that the person who was supposed to meet with Katie had been here, but Mary and Katie just didn't know it.

"I just think it's strange," Mary mused, "that someone would write her that note and not show up." She shrugged. "On the other hand, that note could have been in her pocket for days. There was no date on it, and the time of 1:12 didn't specify AM or PM, although I guess it's obvious since we're not open at 1:12 AM." She smiled. "It's strange all around, isn't it?"

"Very." Henry's brow furrowed. "And you don't remember seeing Katie in the shop before?"

"No, and neither does Rebecca. I know we have a lot of tourists in the summer, but I think I'd remember her."

Mary's gaze moved to Katie, who was still taking instructions about the cash register from seven-year-old Ashley.

"So do I press this key next?" Katie asked the little girl, her finger poised over the old-fashioned cash register.

"No. You press the one just to the left of it. But that was a good try," Ashley said patiently. "This cash register is tricky. Even my mom has trouble sometimes."

Katie smiled at her. "You're a good teacher."

"Thanks," Ashley said. "I've been working here quite a while." She reached up to pat her shoulder. "Don't worry, Katie. You'll catch on."

Mary smiled as she watched the interaction between them and then looked at Henry, who was listening to their conversation as well.

"Katie seems like a sweet girl," Henry said, leaning toward her so no one could overhear. "Is that note the only clue you have?"

"Well, something else did come up today." She told him about the mugging and how it had happened near where Katie found herself on the beach.

Henry nodded. "I heard about that at the dock today. Terrible thing." Then his gaze narrowed as he looked at Mary. "You think it might be connected to Katie?"

"It's possible. She has a head injury, and the last place she remembers was walking around on Little Neck Beach near Ned Simpson's old bait shop."

"So if Katie was mugged by the same person..." His voice trailed off.

"Then he might still have her purse with her driver's license inside or something that can identify her." Chief McArthur had told her that he didn't have any suspects in the mugging, but he hadn't mentioned what Anthony had told him about it. Maybe if she talked to him herself...

Henry's chuckle broke her reverie.

"Looks like you're planning something," he said.

"I am," she admitted. "And I'm going to tell you all about it. But first let's find the perfect mystery novel for Karen's birthday."

SEVEN

——◆◆◆——

This pizza smells heavenly," Katie said, carrying a takeout box from Pizzeria Rustica in her hands as they walked to the front door of the house that evening.

"Just wait until you taste it," Mary said. She'd kept the shop open twenty minutes later than usual due to a sudden influx of customers right at closing time, but she did find a few minutes to tell Katie about Anthony Cantuccio. Then they stopped in at Pizzeria Rustica and learned from the restaurant manager that Anthony was feeling better but was still recuperating at home for the next few days.

While Mary was anxious to talk to Anthony, she decided to wait until tomorrow. She could take him some food and, hopefully, ask him some questions about his mugging that might help Katie.

"Does Betty like pizza?" Katie asked her.

"Who doesn't?" Mary said with a smile. "Actually, Betty makes a delicious crust herself, but Anthony's is better." As she reached for the doorknob, she smiled and whispered, "Don't tell her I said that."

Katie laughed as Mary opened the door. When they walked inside, Mary saw a man kneeling near the piano and Betty standing nearby.

"Hello," Betty greeted them. "This is Dell Damico, a piano tuner from Falmouth. He was kind enough to make time in his schedule for me today."

Dell was about fifty, with thinning brown hair and a round belly hanging over his belt. He turned to them and waved. "Hi."

"Hello," Mary said, wondering if she should have bought more pizza. "How's it going?"

Dell tested the middle foot pedal, then used a tool to adjust something on it. "I'm just finishing up." He rose to his feet, hitching his belt up. The light green T-shirt he wore had the words *Dell's Piano Tuning* spelled out in piano keys on the front.

He sat down on the piano bench and played a series of scales up and down the keyboard. The sound was true and pure, filling the room with melodic notes. Then he looked over at Betty. "What do you think?"

"It sounds wonderful," Betty said, one hand caressing the top of the piano. "So much better than it did before."

"Well, it's a fine instrument," Dell said, as he began packing up his tools.

Gus meowed in his carrier, and Mary let him out. He made a beeline for Katie's ankles, weaving himself in and out between them until she handed Mary the pizza and then leaned over and picked him up.

"He's really taken a liking to you," Mary said with a smile.

Katie nuzzled her face against his. "I like him too." Then she held one of his paws in her hand and looked at it, running her finger over one of the pads on the bottom side of his paw.

"Is something wrong?" Mary asked.

Katie shook her head. "I thought I felt something strange, but it was just a tiny pebble."

Mary headed for the kitchen, and Katie followed her, still holding Gus. "I'll put this in the oven on warm until Betty's ready to eat. Do you want to get the salad out of the fridge? There's some dressing in the door."

"Sure," Katie said, making herself right at home.

Mary was delighted with how well Katie had adjusted to her situation. The old saying that houseguests and fish both stink after three days didn't seem to apply to the girl. Although, this was only the third day that Katie had been staying at the house, Mary reminded herself. She just prayed, for Katie's sake, that she'd soon find her way home.

Mary took the pizza out of the box and placed it in the oven while Katie retrieved the salad and dressing from the refrigerator and then began to set the table.

"Do you want to come with me to see Anthony tomorrow?" Mary asked, realizing that the girl might not feel comfortable inviting herself.

Katie hesitated, her hand still on the dinner plate she'd just placed on the table. "I don't think so," she said at last. "Since you already know him, he might feel more comfortable talking to you alone. I should probably stay at the bookshop."

Mary had noticed before that Katie's connection to the bookshop was almost like a security blanket for her. It was the one place in Ivy Bay that had some sort of connection to the life she couldn't remember. "That's totally fine." She peeked down the hallway and saw Betty still talking to Dell. The spicy aroma of pizza filled the air, and Mary couldn't wait to dig in.

"So what should I take for Anthony tomorrow?" Mary asked, hoping to distract herself until it was time to eat. "A tuna casserole, maybe, or a dessert?"

"How about some of your ice cream?" Katie suggested as she placed a knife and fork at each table setting.

Mary sighed. "That's a great idea, but I don't have all the ingredients I need on hand to make it for tomorrow." She walked over to the refrigerator and opened it, spying an unopened package of her favorite commercial pie dough. "I could make him a cranberry-apple pie," Mary said. "Apples and cranberries are in season now, so we've got both in the crisper." She turned to Katie. "What do you think?"

"It sounds scrumptious to me."

"Then cranberry-apple pie it is," Mary announced, taking the box of pie dough out of the refrigerator and setting it on the counter. It worked best at room temperature, so she'd start putting the pie together after supper.

Betty walked into the kitchen. "Did you say pie?"

Mary smiled. "I did." Then she told her sister about Anthony and her plan to pay him a visit tomorrow. "We've got one of his roasted vegetable and goat cheese pizzas in the oven, if you're ready for supper."

"That's one of my favorites." Betty walked over to the table and pulled out a chair. "My mouth started watering as soon as you walked in the door with that pizza. I didn't think Dell would ever finish. He's quite the perfectionist."

Mary pulled the pizza from the oven and brought it over to the table, setting the pan on a cast-iron trivet. Katie joined them, carrying a pitcher of iced tea. "Well, the piano sounds marvelous. I can't wait to hear you play again."

"I'm excited," Betty said as Katie took her seat. Then they bowed their heads. Betty said grace, thanking the Lord for their blessings and asking for His healing power to surround Anthony during his recuperation.

When she finished the prayer, Betty dished up the first slice of pizza onto her plate and then handed the spatula to Katie.

Mary reached for the salad. "So, Bets, what do you know about Anthony? When did he move to Ivy Bay?"

Betty chewed thoughtfully on her pizza, then swallowed. "About four years ago, I believe. His wife, Rosa, is in the garden club with me, and we've talked quite a few times. She said Anthony's parents owned a pizzeria in Chicago and both he and his brother decided to branch out and open their own restaurants."

"Does she work at the restaurant too?" Mary asked. "I don't think I've seen her there."

Betty licked a string of melted cheese off her finger. "No, she's a respiratory therapist and works the night shift at the hospital."

Now Mary knew why she didn't see Rosa very often. She'd always admired night-shift workers who could turn their sleep schedule upside down and still manage to stay involved in community activities like the garden club.

"And they have a son, don't they?" Mary asked, spearing a salad leaf and a cherry tomato with her fork.

"Yes, Anthony Junior. He's sixteen and he goes by AJ." Betty sighed and took a sip of her tea. "AJ's been a handful for them lately, according to Rosa. Getting in trouble at school and breaking his curfew."

"Kids can be tough at that age," Mary said, remembering Jack's youth. Her son had never been too much trouble, but he'd definitely challenged Mary and John a few times during his teen years. The most harrowing time for Mary had been when fifteen-year-old Jack had questioned his faith. She'd prayed for God's guidance and trusted Him with Jack's journey, aware that she couldn't force her son's faith against his will. But Proverbs 22:6 had sustained her and proven to be true for Jack: "Start children off on the way they should go, and even when they are old they will not turn from it." Today, Jack and his wife, Christa, were faithful churchgoers and had raised Daisy in a home filled with faith and love.

Katie reached for a second slice of pizza. "Just think how much fun it would be to have parents who owned a pizza place. I'd probably eat there every night."

Betty smiled. "According to Rosa, AJ hates spending time at the restaurant and has ever since he was little. But his father insists he work there and learn the family business."

"So that may explain part of their troubles," Mary said, sympathetic to both father and son.

Mary wished she knew the Cantuccios better. They might find it a little odd when she showed up at their door. "Any chance you want to go with me tomorrow?" she asked her sister. "I'm planning to stop by their house after lunch."

"I wish I could, but our book club is meeting tomorrow afternoon." Betty set down her fork and placed her napkin on top of her empty plate. "But don't worry; they love having company and will welcome you with open arms."

"I believe it," Katie said, her voice wistful. "I've only been in Ivy Bay for three days." She paused and gave a small shrug. "Well, three days that I know about, and everyone is so friendly. A big part of me is hoping that I actually live here, although if that were true, I'm sure *someone* would have recognized me by now."

"I think you're right," Mary said gently. "So far, Carolee is the only person who's recognized you. But you might have a connection to Ivy Bay we don't know about yet."

"I hope I do." Katie looked between Betty and Mary. "I already have you two for friends, as well as Rebecca and Ashley." She grinned. "I may have lost my memory, but something tells me I haven't met another seven-year-old like her."

They all laughed just as the doorbell rang. Mary glanced over at her sister. "Are you expecting someone?"

"No," Betty said, pushing her chair back. "I'll go see who it is."

As Betty got up from the table and headed for the front door, Mary added some dressing to her salad and scooped up a piece of pizza.

Katie sat with her fork poised above her pizza. "Should we wait for Betty to come back?"

Before Mary could reply, Betty walked into the kitchen with Eleanor on her heels.

"I'm so sorry to interrupt your dinner," Eleanor began, looking as refined as ever in an ivory cashmere sweater and camel-brown slacks. "But I just told Betty that I have some wonderful news to share, and I couldn't wait another minute."

"Have a seat," Betty said to her. "Would you care to join us for dinner?"

Eleanor wrinkled her nose at the pizza. "It looks delightful, but I have dinner plans for later this evening, so I'd better pass." Her gaze fell on the iced tea pitcher. "But I'd love some tea."

Katie scooted back her chair. "Coming right up." She walked over to the cupboard and retrieved a glass.

Mary noticed Eleanor's gaze on the girl and decided that she'd better make the introductions. "This is Katie," Mary told Eleanor. "She's staying with us for a few days and helping out at the bookshop."

"Well, isn't that nice?" Eleanor said as Katie poured a glass of tea and placed it in front of Eleanor. "Betty mentioned your predicament, dear girl. It must be awful for you."

Katie gave her a faint smile. "Well, Mary and Betty have helped tremendously. I don't know how I'll ever thank them."

"We enjoy having you," Betty assured her, then glanced at her sister-in-law. "Do you mind if we eat while you share your news?"

"Please do," Eleanor said, "because you may be too excited to eat, Betty, after you hear what I have to say."

Mary had rarely seen the snooty Eleanor this excited. "What is it?"

"Well," Eleanor began, reaching into her black designer handbag. "I came over here to give you some free tickets to the Wildlife Rescue Foundation fund-raiser." She set them on the table in front of Mary. "I'm sure you'd like to see your sister perform."

"Perform?" Mary and Betty echoed at the same time.

Eleanor's eyes glittered as she looked at Betty. "That's right. I got you a piano solo in the concert. A prime spot too, right before the headline act."

Betty gaped at her. "You what?"

Eleanor smiled like a cat that had just found a bowl of cream. "I knew you'd be surprised. I got the idea as soon as you won the bid for that piano on Tuesday."

"S-surprised," Betty stuttered. "I'm shocked. How is this possible when I didn't even audition?"

Eleanor's smile widened. "Well, it helps when your sister-in-law is on the foundation committee. Heather Hastings had auditioned a piano solo and won a spot in the concert, but she had to back out after a conflict with her job. The committee was reluctant to hold more auditions, and that's when I thought of you."

Mary knew she shouldn't be surprised by Eleanor's pull in the community, but this power play even caught her off guard.

"But I haven't played in years," Betty said, looking half terrified and half thrilled. "I won't be ready to play in front of an audience in time for the concert."

"Nonsense," Eleanor said, waving away her concern with one manicured hand. "Talent like yours just doesn't disappear. I'm sure that once you start practicing, it will all come back to you. Like riding a bicycle."

Betty laughed. "I haven't done that in years either."

Mary could tell the idea was growing on Betty. "It might be fun."

"Oh, I'm sure it would." Betty looked at her hands, opening and closing her fingers. "But I'm not as limber as I used to be. I just don't know...."

"The musical piece you select for the concert doesn't have to be difficult," Eleanor told her. "This is a night for fun. We're all just getting together for a good cause. As an Emerson, you belong on that stage, and I'll be there cheering you on."

"I appreciate your support," Betty said with a smile, "as well as your incredible power of persuasion that convinced the board to give me this opportunity. I think . . . " Her voice trailed off, and Mary found herself holding her breath in anticipation of her sister's answer. "I think I'll take it!" Betty exclaimed.

Eleanor clapped her hands together in delight. "Excellent. I knew you wouldn't disappoint me."

"I can't believe I'm going to do this!" Roses bloomed in Betty's cheeks, and her eyes shone with delight. "And you were right, Eleanor. I'm much too excited to eat now."

Mary laughed, thrilled to see Betty so happy about this concert opportunity. Betty had been a teenager the last time Mary had seen her perform in front of an audience. Now Evan and his family would be able to see Betty play.

"How fun," Katie told Betty. "It looks like you got the piano tuned just in time."

"Oh, there's one more surprise," Eleanor announced. "The headline act will be Adam Sullivan, from the Boston Grand Opera Company."

Mary blinked. Adam Sullivan was Lizzie's favorite performer and one of the most popular men in Boston. His strong tenor voice drew raves from fans and music critics alike.

"Who is Adam Sullivan?" Katie asked.

Eleanor looked perplexed by the question for a moment, and then her face cleared. "Well, of course you wouldn't know, given your condition. He's a famous Boston opera singer and quite a catch for our fund-raiser. We'll have a packed house." She turned to Mary. "Would you mind selling tickets at your store? We want to make them as available as possible."

"I'd be happy to," Mary told her, certain she and Betty would be buying quite a few to give to family and friends.

"Wonderful," Eleanor replied, rising to her feet. "I'll make sure a packet is dropped off at your shop tomorrow." Then she pointed at Betty. "And I'll let you know the rehearsal schedule as soon as I get it."

Betty leaned back in her chair. "I hadn't even thought about rehearsals."

"Don't worry," Eleanor told her. "They'll basically just be run-throughs to get the timing down and make sure the evening goes off without a hitch."

"Then I'd better start practicing," Betty said, standing up to walk Eleanor to the door.

After they left the room, Katie helped Mary clear the table and put the leftovers away.

"I'll take care of the dishes," Katie offered, "so you can start on the pie."

"It's a deal." As Mary walked over to open the box of piecrust, she could hear the notes of the piano from the other room. But the sound wasn't quite as melodious as when Dell had played earlier. In fact, from the sound of it, Betty was hitting quite a few wrong notes.

Gus yowled at the noise and bounded up the stairs to escape. Mary hated to admit it, but she almost wanted to follow him.

EIGHT

◆◆◆

The Cantuccios lived in a lovely colonial-style house just west of the high school. It had white siding with dark green shutters and beautiful red geraniums in the window boxes. *The colors of Italy*, Mary thought to herself as she carried the foil-covered fruit pie up the steps to the front porch.

Betty had given Mary a quick overview of directions to the Cantuccio home that morning, anxious to start practicing the piano before her book club meeting that afternoon. Betty was already sitting down on the piano bench, paging through her sheet music, when Mary and Katie left the house.

Mary had been busy at the shop all morning and into the afternoon, so she didn't make it to the Cantuccio house until well after two o'clock. She rang the doorbell and then heard the shrill yap of a dog from inside. If Anthony was resting, he wouldn't be for long with all that noise. The dog kept barking until the door opened and Rosa Cantuccio stood on the other side.

"Mary Fisher," Rosa said, opening the door wider. "This is a nice surprise."

"Hello," Mary greeted her. "I tried to call earlier to let you know I was coming, but there was no answer. I hope you don't mind that I just stopped by."

"Not at all," Rosa said, standing aside so Mary could enter the house. "Please come in."

Rosa was shorter than Mary by at least two inches, and rounder by at least four inches. In her late forties, Rosa's dark brown hair didn't show a thread of gray, and her brown eyes sparkled with delight at Mary's arrival. She wore a pair of black yoga pants and a blue fleece sweatshirt, a comfortable outfit that could serve double duty as pajamas.

"I hope I didn't wake you," Mary told her. "Betty told me that you work the night shift."

"I do, but I've taken a few days off while Anthony is on the mend, so I'm wide awake today."

"I was so sorry to hear about his ordeal." Mary spotted a small Yorkie directly behind Rosa. "Betty and I were both heartsick that such a thing could happen in Ivy Bay." She held out the pie. "I hope this might help him feel better."

"That's so sweet," Rosa said, taking the pie from her as the dog moved forward and began sniffing Mary's shoes. "Pete," Rosa said, her voice gently scolding the little dog, "go lay down."

To Mary's surprise, Pete turned around, his toenails clicking on the hardwood floor as he made his way to the small doggie bed in the corner of the cozy living room. "He's certainly well behaved."

Rosa laughed. "He's the only one who listens to me in this house. If only my husband and son obeyed me half as well." She took a peek under the foil. "This looks delicious. What kind is it?"

"Cranberry-apple."

Rosa nodded. "Anthony will love it." She turned and headed toward the dining room. "Come with me, Mary. He's out on the deck, and I know he'll want to see you."

Mary followed her through the dining room to the double French doors leading to the large covered deck. Potted flowerpots still decorated the redwood floor, and Anthony sat in a lounge chair, his right ankle encased in a black foam cast and propped on a round sofa pillow. Classical piano music emanated from a CD player on the patio table next to him.

"You have company," Rosa announced after she walked through the door.

Anthony sat up and turned down the volume on the CD player. His face brightened when he saw Mary. "Well, this is a nice surprise."

Despite their hospitality, Mary sensed that they were both curious about her visit, given that she'd never been to their house before. "I come bringing pie, sympathy, and a few questions," Mary said with a smile.

Anthony arched a quizzical brow. He had dark hair and eyes like his wife, along with an olive complexion that the summer sun had deepened into a golden tan. "Now I'm intrigued and grateful, since I've been bored out of my mind." He motioned to the empty chair beside him. "Please sit down and ask me anything."

Rosa turned to Mary. "May I get you something to drink?"

"No, thank you," Mary told her, taking a seat at the table. "I'm fine."

Rosa looked at her husband and held up the pie in her hands. "Mary brought over a cranberry-apple pie." She turned toward the French doors. "I'll go put it in the kitchen. We can have it for dessert tonight."

"Find a good hiding place," he called after her, "or AJ will find it when he gets home from school and there won't be any pie left!"

Mary smiled. "Your son must have quite an appetite."

Anthony sighed. "I've never seen anyone eat so much, and he's still as thin as a reed. The boy can eat two pizzas in one sitting."

"Well, your pizzas *are* delicious. We had one for supper last night."

His eyes widened. "What kind?"

"Roasted vegetable with goat cheese. I think it's my new favorite."

He chuckled. "That's the only kind of pizza that AJ *won't* eat. He hates vegetables." Anthony leaned back in his chair, propping his ankle on the cushion again. "But you didn't come here to talk about pizza. You said you had some questions."

"I do," Mary affirmed. "I felt so bad when I heard what happened to you." She looked at his ankle. "Is it broken?"

"No. It's just a sprain." He reached down to gently pat the thick brace. "A bad one, according to the doctor at the emergency room. I got a few scrapes and bruises too. Never saw it coming."

"A friend of mine was injured, near that same area, on Tuesday." Mary told him about Katie's amnesia and her search for her identity.

Anthony gave her his full attention, his eyes softening with sympathy at the story. "That poor girl. Do you think she was mugged too?"

"I don't know." Mary watched a ruby-throated humming-bird flutter at a special feeder hanging from one of the deck beams. "But it's the only available lead we have so far. *If* she was mugged by the same person and *if* he can be tracked down, then we might find her purse and some form of identification." She gave him a wry smile. "It sure sounds like a long shot, doesn't it?"

He shrugged. "Sounds like it's worth pursuing to me. I just wish I could help you. I didn't see the mugger, so there's no way I can identify him."

That's what Chief McArthur had told her, but Mary wanted to hear the story for herself. "Do you mind telling me what happened?"

"No, I don't mind at all, especially if it would help your friend."

Rosa returned to the deck and sat down at the table.

"I've told the story a few times already," Anthony continued, "so my wife can let us know if I leave out anything."

"You know I will," Rosa said with a playful smile.

Mary sat back in her chair as Anthony began to recount the story of his mugging.

"There's not much to it, really," Anthony said. "I put in a full day at the restaurant, and it was a doozy. One of the ovens quit working, and the health inspector showed up for a surprise inspection. We passed with flying colors, but it was still a crazy day." He shook his head, as if reliving it in his mind. "Then AJ was supposed to pick up some parts for the oven at Jimmy's Hardware, but when the boy showed up for work, he claimed that he forgot."

"He did forget," Rosa said in defense of their son. "He had two big tests at school on Wednesday, and you know how stressed he's been about his grades."

"He's not the only one," Anthony quipped, then shook his head. "Anyway, I made it to the hardware store right before it closed and bought the parts I needed. I was tired from the long day at work by then and still irritated with my son, so I decided to go for a walk. It was dusk and the sunset was beautiful. I thought a walk might help me relax before heading back to the restaurant."

One corner of his mouth tipped up in a wry smile. "It turns out my walk wasn't as relaxing as I'd hoped. All of a sudden, I heard footsteps behind me...."

Rosa lifted her hand to her throat as her husband recited the story, and Mary could see the distress in her eyes.

"But before I could turn around," he continued, "someone rammed into me. The impact was so sudden and so hard that it pushed me to the ground. My ankle twisted as I fell, and I think I bounced on the ground a couple of times."

"You should see his knees," Rosa interjected. "Both of them are scraped raw."

Just like Katie, Mary thought to herself. "Did the mugger hit you in the head?"

"No," he replied. "But the guy literally ran right into my back. I did hit my head when I fell, but there was only a small bump. The doctor checked it out and said it was nothing serious. Now that I know what happened to your friend Katie, I'm counting that as a blessing."

"Katie?" Rosa asked, looking between the two of them for clarification.

Mary filled her in, explaining that Katie might have been mugged too, although she had no memory of what happened to her.

"Oh dear," Rosa said. "It's bad enough that one person was mugged in Ivy Bay. But two?"

"We don't know if that's what happened," Mary said quickly. "It's just speculation at this point, but Katie also suffered a bump on her head and scrapes on her knees. The doctor thinks the head injury is what caused her amnesia."

"Was anything stolen?" Rosa asked. "Because the man who attacked Anthony stole the shopping bag right out of his hand."

"It actually wasn't in my hand anymore," he clarified. "I dropped the bag when I fell. I didn't even realize I'd been mugged until I saw that the bag was missing. I thought the guy just ran into me by accident, but he must have done it on purpose. Not sure what he plans to do with oven parts, but I let Jimmy know in case anyone tries to return them for a refund."

"Are you sure that you never saw the mugger before?" Mary asked, already knowing the answer.

"There's no way for me to know," Anthony said, "because I didn't see him Wednesday night. Not his face, anyway."

"By the time Anthony recovered from his fall, the mugger was running away," Rosa said. "He disappeared in the trees before Anthony could get a good look at him."

Disappointment washed over Mary, even though she'd prepared herself for it. "Was there anything distinguishing about him? His size or his clothes…anything at all?"

"Not really," Anthony said with a shrug. "He had black jeans and a black hoodie. The hood was up, so I couldn't see his hair color."

"You said he was young," Rosa interjected. "And skinny."

"How could you tell his age?" Mary asked, curious about this detail. "There are skinny older guys."

He smiled. "Yes, I wish I was one of them." Anthony thought about her question for a long moment. "I guess it was his shoes—or rather, his shoelaces. They were bright green and almost glowed in the dark. I don't know too many older guys that wear glow-in-the-dark shoelaces."

Mary nodded, thinking he was probably right but also aware that there was always an exception to every rule—especially fashion rules.

Rosa leaned forward in her chair. "The fact that he was dressed in all black makes it sound like it was planned to me. If he'd waited until it was pitch dark, Anthony wouldn't have seen anything except those shoelaces."

"Were his shoes black too?" Mary asked.

Anthony nodded. "I believe so. It all happened so fast I can't be sure. I mainly just noticed the laces."

It wasn't much to go on, but Mary appreciated the information he'd given her. She stood up. "Thank you so much for your time. I'd better let you rest now."

"Well, I appreciate your stopping by," Anthony said. "And especially bringing over that pie. I hope Katie gets her memory back soon."

"So do I," Mary told him.

Rosa escorted her to the front door, then waved good-bye as Mary stepped outside. "Thank you for stopping, Mary. I hope Anthony was able to help you."

Mary waved back and then headed down the porch steps. She now had a clearer picture of what Anthony experienced during his mugging. Maybe when she shared the story with Katie, it would trigger something in her memory.

"Shoelaces?" Katie said, standing in the children's nook of the bookshop. She and Ashley had been shelving new books and straightening up the area when Mary returned from her visit with Anthony. "Is that all he could tell you?"

Mary could see Katie struggling not to show her disappointment. She'd gotten her hopes up too, despite knowing that Anthony hadn't been able to describe the mugger to the police.

"That was the only thing that stood out to him and made him believe the mugger was fairly young," Mary said. "Like someone in his teens or twenties."

Ashley picked up some books left in the carpet-lined bathtub and began placing them back on the shelves. "I have neon pink-and-yellow shoelaces, but I've never found neon green."

"And it sounds like we won't be able to find the mugger." Katie sat down in the rocking chair. "At least Mr. Cantuccio remembers what happened to him, although I'm sorry that he got hurt."

"And he feels bad for you," Mary said. "But we still don't know for certain that you *were* mugged. So even if the mugger were caught, it might not make a difference."

"I know," Katie said. "But at least it was *something* to go on."

Ashley turned to her. "You can't give up, Katie. You have to keep trying to remember."

"Oh, I am," Katie said with a tender smile. "It's just hard sometimes. It's been four days now since I lost my memory and still...nothing."

Ashley walked over to the rocking chair and stood beside her. "Remember the story of *The Little Engine That Could*?" she asked, referencing a popular children's book. "Nobody thought such a little engine could pull that long train over the high mountain, but the little engine didn't give up. She just kept saying, 'I think I can. I think I can.' And then she did it!"

Katie smiled and reached out to give Ashley a hug. "That does make me feel better. Thank you, Ashley."

"Just keep telling yourself that you think you can get your memory back," Ashley told her, full of confidence, "and you will."

"I'll give it a try," Katie promised.

And so will I, Mary thought. She wasn't ready to give up helping Katie find her identity. She just had to trust that God would lead the way.

───

On Saturday, Mary, Betty, and Katie spent the morning cleaning the house and then shared a lunch of ham sandwiches and potato salad. For dessert, they enjoyed the last of the raspberry ripple ice cream in the freezer, reminding Mary that it was time to work on her next ice-cream recipe. Tess would be expecting it in the next few days, and Mary didn't want to make her wait.

"I love this," Katie said, licking the ice cream off her spoon. "I can't believe you created the recipe."

"It's one of my hobbies," Mary told her. "I'm planning to work on another recipe this afternoon, if you'd like to help me."

"That sounds fun," Katie said and then turned to Betty. "Are you in?"

Betty chuckled as she shook her head. "No. I usually leave the ice-cream making to Mary. She's the expert in that field." Betty flexed her fingers. "I think I'll practice the piano. We have rehearsals coming up soon, and I want to be ready."

Mary and Katie exchanged glances. Betty's piano playing last night had been rough. The notes seemed to jumble together at times, but Betty kept plugging along, practicing the same Beethoven sonata over and over again.

Her sister was tenacious when she set her mind to something, but Mary was a little worried that Betty was expecting too much of herself. She'd always been a perfectionist and seemed to think she could just pick up where she'd left off decades ago.

Mary opened her mouth to say something, then closed it again. Betty hadn't asked for her opinion, and she didn't want to discourage her. She was just a little rusty, after all. Time and practice should fix that problem.

"We'll clean up in here," Mary told her, "so you can go ahead and get started."

"Thank you." Betty got up from the table and headed for the living room. A few moments later, she began playing a series of scales to warm up, missing a few notes along the way.

Gus raced down the hallway from the living room and scampered upstairs, still not a fan of the piano.

"So what kind of ice cream do you have in mind?" Katie asked as she got up from the table and started picking up the plates and silverware.

Mary thought for a long moment. She'd made a fruit ice cream last month, so she should probably do something different, but she'd gotten the niggle of an idea when she'd made that cranberry-apple pie last night, and it just kept niggling. "Since cranberries are in season, I think I'd like to make a flavor with fresh cranberries and white chocolate."

Katie nodded. "That sounds interesting."

The more Mary considered the flavors, the more the idea appealed to her. "The trick will be to balance the tartness of the cranberries with the sweetness of the chocolate. I don't want to lose that cranberry kick."

Katie washed up the dishes while Mary sat down with a notebook and pen to put together the recipe. Piano music floated into the kitchen, and Mary soon realized that Betty had given up on the sonata and moved onto another song. "That sounds vaguely familiar," she said, listening to the melody, "but I can't place it."

Katie rinsed off a plate at the kitchen sink. "It's 'Come, We That Love the Lord.' That was one of my nana's favorite hymns." Then she froze and turned to Mary.

Mary stared at her. "You remembered something."

Katie carefully set down the wet plate, her hands visibly shaking. "It was the music. It made me remember the song. And I can see my nana's face in my mind and hear her singing the lyrics."

Happy tears gleamed in Katie's eyes. "I remember her, Mary!" she cried out. "I remember!"

NINE

◆◆◆

W hat's going on in here?" Betty asked as she walked into the kitchen. "I thought I heard someone shouting."

"That was me," Katie said, blushing a little. Her wide smile lit up her face. "I remembered something!"

Mary was smiling too, thrilled that Katie's memory seemed to be healing. *Thank You, Lord*, she prayed silently.

"You did?" Betty exclaimed, clapping her hands together. "Oh, that's wonderful! What did you remember?"

Katie stood next to the sink and covered her face with her hands, half laughing and half crying. She looked overwhelmed by the enormity of what had just happened.

"Let's sit down," Mary suggested, walking over to Katie and gently steering her toward the table. Mary was feeling a little breathless herself. In her opinion, all three of them needed to take a moment and calm down.

The table had been cleared, so they each took a seat. Gus suddenly appeared at the bottom of the stairs now that the piano music had ended. He peered into the room and then jumped off the bottom step, hesitating for a moment before turning and heading for his food dish.

Katie sat silent in the chair for several long moments. Then she placed one hand on her chest. "My heart is racing."

"This is such good news," Betty said, reaching out to squeeze Katie's hand. "How did it happen?"

Katie smiled at her. "It was your music."

Betty blanched. "I'm not sure I would call that music. Not yet, anyway."

"It was the hymn you were playing just now," Mary told her sister. "Katie recognized it."

Katie nodded. "My nana used to sing it all the time. I can picture her standing in the kitchen, rolling out some cookie dough on the counter and singing that song." She paused for a moment and then began to sing:

> Come, we that love the Lord,
> And let our joys be known;
> Join in a song with sweet accord,
> And thus surround the throne.

Katie had a soft, sweet voice, and the tune matched the one that Betty had played just moments ago. Mary thanked the Lord again for this blessing.

"That *is* the name of the song I just played," Betty said, her tone full of wonder. "I picked it out because it was fairly short, so I figured it wouldn't take me long to learn it."

Mary wanted to believe that it was God's hand that led Betty to select that particular song. She turned to Katie. "That memory came back when you weren't even trying to remember."

"I know," Katie said wryly. "Here I've been struggling for the last five days to bring up some memories, and this one just came to me out of the blue. As soon as I heard the music, the memory was there."

"I've read that our memories are often tied to the senses," Mary said. "And I think it's probably true. Every time I smell lilacs, I think of my grandmother. Her backyard was filled with them."

"Lilacs do the same for me," Betty said, nodding. "In this case, it was Katie's sense of hearing that unlocked a memory."

Mary leaned forward. "So what exactly do you remember, Katie?"

The girl took a deep breath, calmer now than she'd been when the memory first returned. "I can see my nana's face in my mind. She has blue eyes and wears glasses. Her hair is short and curly and mostly gray."

Just the way Katie spoke about her made it apparent how precious this memory—and this grandmother—was to her. But even more apparent was the resemblance Katie's grandmother had to Mary. Blue eyes and glasses? Check. Short, curly, and mostly gray hair? Check. *Maybe that's why she trusted me*, Mary thought to herself. *Maybe I remind her of her nana.*

"Do you remember her name?" Mary asked gently.

Katie nibbled her lower lip. "I can't...place it. I'm trying; I really am. It's like her name is on the tip of my tongue, but I just can't say it."

"Don't try to force it," Mary said. "The memory is there. It will grow with time."

"That's right," Betty agreed. "You know what they say: 'A watched pot never boils.' Just try to let it go for now and relax. The harder you try to remember, the more frustrated you'll become."

Katie nodded even as her hands curled into fists on the table. "I know you're right. I just need to be patient. It will happen. It has to happen." Then her hands relaxed and a small smile quivered on her lips. "I think I can. I think I can."

The words caught Mary off guard, and she began to laugh.

Betty smiled as she looked between them. "Am I missing something?"

"Ashley gave me some wise words of advice from a children's book yesterday," Katie explained. "I was frustrated then, too, and she quoted the Little Blue Engine from *The Little Engine That Could* and suggested I have the same can-do attitude."

Betty chuckled. "That is good advice. I may take it myself, since my piano playing isn't up to par yet." She heaved a deep sigh. "I think it's the music. It's decades old, and the paper is yellow. Maybe if I buy some new sheet music that I'm passionate about, it will help."

Mary glanced at her watch. "Strings & Things closes early on Saturdays, so you may want to scoot if you want to buy any today."

"You're right." Betty rose from the chair and grabbed her handbag from the counter. "I'm off to Strings & Things to find the perfect music for the concert." As she walked toward the door, she said, "I think I can. I think I can."

Mary and Katie both laughed. "I'll have to tell Ashley how popular that mantra has become," Mary said as she reached for her notepad. "Now how do you feel about making some ice cream? Maybe an afternoon of cooking and recipe building will spark another memory."

"I hope so," Katie told her. Then she folded her hands together in front of her, a shimmer of happy tears in her eyes. "I'm just so happy to have a memory of someone I loved— and who loved me. I don't feel so alone anymore."

Mary walked over and hugged her. "And I'm happy for you." She thought about the verse from 1 Corinthians she'd read the other day: Love never fails. Katie's love for her grandmother had sparked that memory. She prayed that same love would sustain Katie until her full memory returned.

"Okay," Katie said, wiping the tears from her eyes. "Let's make ice cream!"

———

"Are you sure you want to do this?" Mary whispered.

She looked over at Katie, waiting for her answer. They sat in a pew at Grace Church for the Sunday morning service, listening to a harp solo by Dorothy Johnson's visiting cousin. Betty sat on the other side of Katie, a hymnbook in her lap. She kept massaging her fingers, which told Mary that the hours of piano practice were taking their toll.

"I think so," Katie said after a long pause. She'd styled her hair in a neat braid and worn her khaki-green clam diggers and a white peasant blouse to church this morning, along with a pair of khaki-green sandals that she'd borrowed from Rebecca.

"Okay," Mary whispered to her. "Just let me know if you change your mind. We still have a few minutes."

Katie nodded, but didn't respond. Mary didn't blame the girl for being a little nervous. It wasn't fun to stand up and talk in front of a crowd—especially a crowd of virtual strangers.

Although, now that Mary thought about it, Katie did know some of the congregation members. Dr. Teagarden was here with his wife, Lynn, and so was Henry, whom Katie had met at the bookshop the other day. Carolee Benson sat near the back and had waved to them when they'd come in. Katie had met Pastor Miles at the shop too, along with Trevor, although they hadn't gotten to chat very long.

That was why Mary had talked to him before the service today, making sure he agreed to their plan to talk to the congregation shortly before the worship service ended.

Katie sat stiffly beside her, and Mary could feel the waves of tension emanating from her. They'd had fun making ice cream together yesterday afternoon, and the cranberry with white chocolate chunks had been delicious. She was sure Tess was going to love it. But there had been no more memories for Katie, and as the evening had worn on, she'd grown quieter. That was when Mary had suggested that they ask the congregation for help.

Katie had hesitated at first, not sure she wanted to involve them in her problems. She'd asked to sleep on it, and this morning, to Mary's surprise, Katie had agreed that it was a good idea.

The harpist ended her performance with a flourish, expertly plucking several strings on the harp. Pastor Miles had given a wonderful sermon about the parable of the talents, and the service was now coming to a close.

"Before I give the benediction," Pastor Miles said, "Mary Fisher has a special request." His gaze found her in the pew, and he raised one hand to wave her forward.

Mary stood up and looked over at Katie, who gave a small nod, and then rose to follow her to the front of the sanctuary. Pastor Miles had taken a seat in the chair to the left of the podium, leaving enough room for both of them to stand there.

"Good morning," Mary began. "Pastor Miles has been kind enough to allow me to speak to you during the service." She turned and motioned toward Katie. "This is Katie. I'm afraid I don't know her last name, and neither does she. As some of you are already aware, Katie has amnesia. I found her in my shop last Tuesday, and she has no memory of how she got to Ivy Bay or who she is."

Small gasps sounded across the sanctuary. Mary paused a moment to let the noise die down. "I'm sure you can imagine how hard it's been for her. She's staying with Betty and me until her memory returns, but it's been a difficult week. If there is anyone here who saw Katie before last Tuesday or knows anything about her, please don't hesitate to come to us." Mary sensed Katie moving closer beside her. "There's no detail too small," she told the congregation. "And we also ask for your prayers that Katie may soon heal enough that her memory returns."

Katie leaned over and whispered, "May I say something?"

Mary was surprised by the request given Katie's earlier nervousness. But she nodded and turned to make more room for Katie at the podium.

Katie cleared her throat. "I just wanted to say thank you to the people of Ivy Bay. You've been so kind to me, even the strangers that I've met, and it's made this unusual journey a little easier for me. I'd especially like to thank Mary and Betty for welcoming me into their home and making me feel like a part of their family." Her voice cracked on the last word, and Katie took a moment to collect herself. "The hardest part of this for me is not knowing who my family is or where to find them. Thanks to Mary and Betty and the people of Ivy Bay, I don't feel quite so alone."

As Katie stepped back from the podium, Mary saw more than one congregant wipe tears from their eyes. They returned to the pew as Pastor Miles gave the benediction, and then the church service was over.

Several people came up to Katie before they were even outside, offering their sympathy and promising to pray for her. Katie graciously thanked them, but each time someone approached her, Mary could see the hope flare in Katie's eyes and then disappear when it became clear that no one recognized her.

Mary, Katie, and Betty lingered on the lawn after the service with the other members of the congregation. It was a gorgeous autumn day with the sun shining through the burnished red maple leaves overhead. After several minutes, Betty drifted away to talk to Eleanor, while Mary looked for Henry in the crowd.

A few fallen leaves crunched under Dr. Teagarden's shoes as he made his way over to them. "Hello," he greeted them. "I was happy to see you in church today, Katie. You've been on my mind. How are you feeling?"

"I'm fine, physically," she told him. "No more headaches. But the amnesia is still mostly there."

Dr. Teagarden arched a brow. "Mostly?"

Katie told him about recovering the memory of her nana yesterday.

He smiled. "That's good to hear. I'd expect for you to recover more and more of your memories in the coming days and weeks."

"Weeks?" Katie said, her shoulders slumping. A moment later, she straightened them and said, "I think I can. I think I can."

Dr. Teagarden looked perplexed. "What?"

Mary chuckled. "It's just a little joke we share," she told him. "It keeps our spirits up."

"Well, I have some news that may help," Dr. Teagarden said. Then he lowered his voice a notch as he looked at Katie. "Would you like to talk about this in private?"

Katie circled her arm around Mary's waist. "You can say anything in front of Mary. I don't mind."

The doctor took a step closer to them. "I received the results of your lab tests yesterday, Katie. I'm sorry I wasn't able to call you right away. I was out on my boat all day and didn't get home until quite late."

"So what did the tests say?" Katie asked in a soft voice.

"There was no evidence of any medications or toxins in your blood work," Dr. Teagarden told her, "and of course, the CAT scan was clear."

"And that's good news, right?" Katie asked him.

Mary smiled. "Very good news, I'd say. Right, Doctor?"

"That's right. It means you don't have any medical conditions that we don't know about—at least none that require medication. And it also means your amnesia wasn't the result of drugs or alcohol."

Katie blinked. "I never thought of that." She suppressed a shiver. "You're right. That is good news. So it's all due to this bump on my head?"

"It appears so," Dr. Teagarden said. "Especially given the fact that your headache hasn't returned and part of your memory has."

"A very small part," Katie clarified. "But an important one."

He nodded, then reached out to pat her shoulder. "Don't worry. You'll get there." Then he glanced behind him. "Looks like my wife is searching for me." He turned back to them. "Promise you'll give me a call if you have any questions or concerns."

"I promise," Katie told him.

They watched him walk off, and Mary couldn't help but feel disappointed that no one had approached them with information about Katie. How could her presence in Ivy Bay be such a mystery? It was a small, close-knit community. Even the tourists felt at home here and often commented on how friendly everyone was. Surely there was at least one person who'd bumped into Katie before she'd received that bump on her head.

Mary looked up to see Henry walking toward them. His smile made her heart lighten, and she found herself smiling back at him.

"Good morning, ladies," he said. "Isn't it a beautiful day?"

"It certainly is," Mary replied. "What did you think of our little speech?"

Henry looked at Katie. "I think you both did a fine job. I can't imagine it was easy to get up there."

"I was so nervous," Katie admitted. "A little embarrassed too, since part of me feels that it's my fault that I don't remember anything."

"Oh, nonsense," Mary said, wondering how long Katie had felt that way. "None of this is your fault."

"It might be," Katie said, looking between the two of them. "I'm not down on myself—I'm just looking at all the possibilities. Maybe I did something to cause the bump on my head. Maybe I wasn't being safe or responsible. That's the problem with not knowing what really happened to me. My imagination goes a little wild."

Henry smiled. "There's nothing wrong with a wild imagination. That's where great stories come from. Maybe you should imagine the best about yourself instead of the worst. You never know—you might have a great story waiting for you when your memory returns."

"You're right," Katie said, laughing. "Every time I start feeling a little blue, someone comes along to cheer me up. First Mary, then Ashley, and now you, Henry."

He grinned as he performed a little bow. "Glad to be of service."

Mary was laughing along with them when she felt a tap on her shoulder. She turned around and saw April Whittaker standing behind her. April had just started working as a part-time teller at Ivy Bay Bank & Trust. "Hello, April."

"Hi," April said, her voice soft. She was twenty-three years old and a recent graduate of business college, according to her mother, Brenda, who stopped in the bookshop to browse through the shelves but rarely bought any books.

April had long blonde hair that hung to her waist and eyes the color of moss. She kept looking at Katie as if waiting for something.

Mary didn't know if it was just curiosity or if April had some information for them. She'd been in church often but had never approached Mary before. "April," she began, "do you know Katie?"

April gave a little shrug of her narrow shoulders. "I don't really *know* her, but I did see her last Monday at the bank."

Katie reached out and grabbed Mary's arm, her short fingernails biting into the skin. Mary reached out to loosen her grip a little, trying not to get her own hopes up too high. "That's wonderful, April," Mary said. "What can you tell us about her?"

April nibbled her lower lip as she looked around the lawn, acting like a deer that might spook at any sudden movement. "Do you really have amnesia?" she asked Katie.

"Yes," Katie said without hesitation. "What can you tell me about that day?"

"Well," April said slowly, "you came into the bank on Monday afternoon...." Then she shook her head. "I don't know how much I can tell you. We're supposed to keep the customer activity confidential. They really emphasized that in business school. There was even an exam question on it."

Now Mary understood the girl's reticence, even though she thought it was misguided. "I'm fairly certain you can talk to a customer about their *own* bank activity."

"I suppose so," April said. "But maybe I should talk to someone at the bank about it first. I could call you tomorrow...."

Katie reached out and grabbed the girl's hand. "Please," she told her, "just tell me. I promise I won't get you in any kind of trouble. Please."

Mary and Henry exchanged glances, both moved by the emotion in Katie's voice. At first, Mary thought April was going to refuse, but then Mary saw April's face soften.

"You cashed a check," April told Katie. "A big one—over eight thousand dollars. That's why I remembered you—because that was the biggest check I'd processed since I started working there."

"Who was it from?" Katie asked.

April winced. "I'm sorry to say that I don't remember that part. I'm sure the bank has a copy of it though. I can check with the manager tomorrow and—"

"What time does the bank open in the morning?" Katie asked her.

April blinked. "Nine o'clock."

Katie looked at Mary, a new hope shining in her eyes. "We'll be there when the doors open."

TEN

❖◆❖

Today was the day.

Mary and Katie arrived at Ivy Bay Bank & Trust a full five minutes before the doors opened. Even from a block away, they could smell the aroma of fresh-baked cinnamon rolls emanating from Sweet Susan's Bakery. Tourists emerged from the Chadwick Inn just past the brick bank building. They wore sunglasses, and sunscreen glistened on their skin under the warm September sun. Even though the weather was a little cooler in September, visitors still enjoyed the beach and other attractions around Ivy Bay. Many of them preferred to visit Cape Cod after the rush of the tourist season was over.

One older couple had rented a tandem bike and rode past them, a wicker picnic basket attached to the back.

"That looks like fun," Katie said, watching them ride in the direction of Little Neck Beach. She glanced at the bank entrance and began to pace in a small circle. "What time is it now?"

"Two minutes till nine," Mary told her.

Time had moved as slow as molasses ever since they'd talked to April Whittaker after the worship service yesterday. Mary and Katie had spent Sunday afternoon taking a long walk around town, while Betty stayed in, planning to try out her new sheet music. When they'd returned from their walk, they found Betty reading on the deck in the backyard, saying her fingers needed a rest.

Mary had suggested the walk in the hope that Katie might recognize something that would trigger her memory. But she'd also wanted to calm the girl's nerves. She'd even called the president of the bank, Owen Cooper, at his home yesterday to ask if he could open the bank on Sunday just long enough to show them the check. But the call had gone to voice mail, forcing her to leave a brief message, and Owen hadn't returned her call. Mary hadn't really expected him to go out of his way on a Sunday, but she'd still been disappointed.

Mary had spent a sleepless night in anticipation of this moment, and judging by the shadows beneath Katie's blue eyes, Mary wasn't the only one.

"I see someone," Katie said, staring at the glass door. A moment later, Mary heard the sound of a bolt turning, and April pushed open the front door.

"You *are* here early." April smiled. "I talked to Mr. Cooper a few minutes ago, and he's ready to see you, so come on in."

They followed her into the bank. Not surprisingly, they were the first and only customers. The other teller looked up as they entered and watched April lead them to Owen's large office. Something told Mary that April had probably shared Katie's condition with the other tellers, along with the reason why they were at the bank this early.

The butterflies that had been fluttering in Mary's stomach all morning went into full flight now. She'd barely been able to finish her oatmeal and was beginning to wish she'd skipped breakfast. Whatever the outcome, she reminded herself, the Lord would be with them.

April tapped on the open door to Owen's office, and he looked up, smiling when he saw Mary. "Good morning. Please come in."

Owen Cooper had grown up in Ivy Bay and taken over the job of bank president from his father. His short dark hair was threaded with silver and starting to thin a little. Now in his early fifties, Owen had encouraged his daughter to major in finance at the University of Massachusetts so the torch could eventually be passed on again.

Owen nodded to April. "Thank you. I can take it from here."

April left the office, closing the door behind her. Then Owen rounded his desk and reached out to shake Mary's hand. "Mary, it's a pleasure to see you again. I'm sorry I didn't return your call yesterday. We were out on the boat and didn't get back until late."

"That's no problem," Mary said, appreciating his firm handshake. "I just called on the off chance you might be home."

"I wish I would have been there," he said as he turned to Katie, a hint of curiosity in his kind green eyes. "And you must be the young woman that Mary mentioned in her telephone message. April filled me in a little bit more this morning."

"I'm Katie," she said, shaking his hand. "I know this must seem strange. April was afraid of breaking some kind of confidentiality code if she spoke to me. I hope she's not in any trouble."

"Oh, not at all," he hurried to assure her. "Although, you're right—this is a little strange. I don't think anything like this has happened in all the years I've been in the banking business." Then he took a step back and motioned to the two brown leather chairs opposite his desk. "Please, sit down. It sounds like we have a lot to talk about."

Mary and Katie each took a seat as Owen rounded his desk and sat down. She appreciated the fact that he'd made time for them this morning, but it didn't surprise her. A levelheaded businessman, Owen was also a devoted family man and invested a lot of volunteer time in the community.

"Now," Owen said, moving a folder on his desk, "April tells me that she saw you in the bank last Monday and that you cashed a large check."

"Yes," Katie said and then frowned. "Well, actually, I *don't* remember any of that, but April seemed fairly certain that it was me."

"Actually, I pulled the bank security tape from last Monday and reviewed it," Owen said, "just as a precaution."

"And?" Katie asked.

He smiled. "And it was definitely you. The tape showed you interacting with April at approximately four thirty that afternoon."

Katie leaned forward. "Do you have the check?"

He opened the folder in front of him. "It's right here. I made a copy from our electronic files of both the front and the back of the check." He cleared his throat, his gaze flicking to Mary and then back to Katie again. "The check was made out to cash and came from the account of Matthew Dinsdale."

"Matthew Dinsdale?" Mary echoed and then glanced over at Katie. There were no signs of recognition on the young woman's face. Mary sat back in her chair, a little baffled. Matthew was one of the wealthiest men in Ivy Bay, so the amount of the check didn't surprise her. But why had he given it to Katie? And why make it out to cash?

Mary hadn't expected the check to be from someone local. In fact, she'd been hoping that the check had come from Katie's own checkbook, since it would have her full name and address printed on it and possibly her phone number.

"Who is Matthew Dinsdale?" Katie asked, looking between Mary and Owen.

"A well-known local businessman," Owen told her. "He owns several rental units here in Ivy Bay and manages vacation properties all over the world."

He was also the husband of Madeline Dinsdale, a prominent local artist and a member of Betty's book club. Matthew was gone on business so often, sometimes weeks and even months at a time, that Mary had never met him.

Owen handed the paper in his hand to Katie. "Here's a copy of the check you cashed, along with your endorsement."

Mary leaned over so she could see Katie's name. But the name on the back of the check was an indecipherable scrawl.

"Wow, I guess I really do have bad penmanship," Katie said, staring at the paper. "I was blaming it on my sore hand, but I can't make this out." She looked over at Mary.

"Well, I recognize the K and the t in your first name," Mary said, studying the signature.

"Yes, so do I." Katie pointed to the first letter of the last name. "And that's a B, followed by what looks like an a."

Mary nodded. "And the last letter is either an r or an s, but I can't make out any of the letters in between." She looked up at Katie, trying to lighten the moment. "Maybe you're a doctor in real life."

Katie smiled. "I sure write like one, don't I?" She looked up at Owen. "I don't suppose you can make it out?"

He sighed. "I didn't have any better luck than you did. Our policy is for the tellers to check the customer's driver's license to make certain that the endorsement matches the name and, when applicable, the photograph. The security tape shows you handing your driver's license to April, but I already checked with her, and she simply can't remember it."

"At least we know you had a driver's license at that point in time," Mary told her. "It narrows down the time frame when the amnesia happened."

Katie nodded. "I suppose. But why does this have to be so hard? I'm no closer to finding out who I am than I was before."

"Yes, you are," Mary countered. "We now know the check is from Matthew Dinsdale. I doubt he'd give $8,300 to a total stranger."

"That's true," Owen confirmed. "He's a very careful businessman. Frankly, I was surprised that the check was made out to cash. I've never seen him do that before."

Mary had wondered about that too. They'd need to ask Matthew Dinsdale that question to learn the answer. She stood up, and Katie followed her lead. "Thank you so much for your help, Owen. We really appreciate it."

He rose to his feet and walked toward the door. "It was my pleasure." He looked at Katie. "I hope everything turns out for you."

"Thank you," she told him, then held up the paper in her hand. "Do you mind if I keep this? Maybe if I stare at it long enough, I'll be able to figure out the letters in my last name."

Owen smiled. "Of course. You don't need to return it. We've blacked out Matthew's account information, so there's nothing confidential on that paper."

When they walked out of the bank, Mary headed toward the crosswalk on Meeting House Road. "It seems we're getting closer," she told Katie.

"This almost feels like a scavenger hunt. But the end is in sight, right? I mean, this Mr. Dinsdale has to know my name if he gave me that much money."

"Absolutely," Mary said as she and Katie crossed the street and headed to the bookshop. The outside entrance had been recently swept clean of fallen leaves, and the wooden sign overhead swayed and creaked ever so gently in the warm morning breeze.

Rebecca was standing behind the front counter sorting receipts when they walked into the shop. She looked up expectantly and said, "Well, how did it go?"

"Good and not so good," Katie told her with a smile.

Mary had called Rebecca last night and told her that she and Katie were headed to the bank first thing in the morning. Rebecca had agreed to open the shop and was as excited as Mary that Katie might finally know her identity.

"What happened?" Rebecca set the receipts aside as they moved closer to the front counter.

Katie placed the copy of the check on the marble countertop so Rebecca could see it. "The good news is that we know the check came from the account of Matthew Dinsdale.

The not-so-good news is...well, just look at my signature on the back of the check."

Rebecca squinted down at the paper. "That's awful," she said bluntly. "It looks like a doctor's signature."

Mary smiled as she reached over to pat Katie's back. "We know. We made out a few letters. The first name is Katie, judging by the *K* and the *t*, but the last name is still a mystery."

Rebecca rounded the counter and reached out and grabbed Katie's shoulders, giving them a gentle shake. "Oh, Katie, my dear," she teased, "who taught you to write like that?"

Katie chuckled. "I'll blame my nana, since she's the only person I actually remember."

"A grandmother would never do such a thing," Mary said with a smile, relieved that Katie was taking this delay so well. She'd been so sure they'd find out her identity at the bank and this almost week-long mystery would be over.

Instead, they needed to keep digging. Only Mary was going to use a phone instead of a shovel. "I'm going to call Matthew Dinsdale right now and get this settled once and for all."

Mary could feel Katie's and Rebecca's eyes on her as she retrieved her cell phone from her purse. Then she looked over at Rebecca. "I don't suppose you know his number?"

"Not a clue." Rebecca walked behind the counter and opened a drawer. "But I can look it up." She pulled out the Ivy Bay phone directory and paged through it until she reached the Ds. "Damico, Denton, Dill," Rebecca began, reading off the listings as her index finger trailed down the page. "Here it is: Dinsdale, Matthew and Madeline." Then she told Mary the number.

Mary punched it into her phone and took a deep breath as it began to ring. She counted eight rings before a click sounded in her ear. "What's going on?" she said, looking at the viewing screen. It read "Call Ended."

"What's wrong?" Katie asked, taking a step closer.

"It rang eight times and then disconnected." She pushed the redial button. Another eight rings and then a click. "It happened again," Mary told them, holding out the phone.

"My mother-in-law's phone does that when her voice-mail box is full," Rebecca said. "That might be the problem."

Katie sighed. "Now what?"

"I'll call Betty," Mary told her. "Maybe she has another number for Madeline. Don't worry. We'll find him."

Rebecca and Katie headed over to the coffee station, and each poured themselves a cup of hot coffee while Mary dialed her home phone number.

Much to her relief, Betty answered on the second ring. "Hello?"

"Bets, it's Mary," she said. "I need to reach Madeline Dinsdale, but there's no answer at her house. Do you have another number?"

"Whoa. Hold on," Betty said, sounding confused. "Why do you need to talk to Madeline? What's going on?"

Mary took a deep breath, realizing that she needed to slow down a little. The Dinsdales were well established in the community—they weren't going to disappear if Mary didn't locate them immediately. *Lord, give me patience.*

"Mar?" Betty asked, breaking the silence. "You still there?"

"Yes, I'm here," she said. "Sorry, Bets." She told her all about their meeting at the bank and the check from Matthew Dinsdale.

"Well, that's interesting," Betty said when Mary had finished the story. "I wonder how he knows Katie."

"I've been wondering the same thing. We'll find out as soon as we can track him down. That's why I was hoping you had a cell phone number for Madeline or something. There's no answer when I call their home phone."

"I wish I could help," Betty said, "but I don't have another number for her. She wasn't at book club last week either. She and Matthew were planning to take a trip out of town."

That was the last thing she wanted to hear, but Mary knew it was a possibility. "Okay, thanks," she said. "I'll figure something out." Then she ended the call.

When she turned around, Rebecca and Katie were at the front counter. Rebecca handed her a cup of coffee. "You look like you could use this."

Mary smiled as she took the cup. "Thanks." The steamy aroma curled around her face as she took a sip, and she felt some of her tension drain away. "Betty doesn't have another number for Madeline."

Katie pulled a face. "Now what should we do?"

Mary thought for a long moment. Then she remembered that Lori Stone, the real estate agent who sold her the bookshop, also managed some local rental properties. Maybe Lori could help them reach Matthew.

"Well, we're not going to give up," Mary said. "Let's go for a drive."

The fragrant scent of fresh flowers filled the air when Mary walked through the front door of Stone Realty. A bouquet of yellow roses and carnations, accented with purple hyacinths, filled a milk-glass vase on top of the Early American pine sideboard. On either side of the vase were flyers featuring rental homes and properties for sale.

Lori looked up from her cluttered desk. "Hello, Mary. This is a nice surprise."

"Hi, Lori." Mary and Katie walked toward her. A laptop computer sat in the center of the desk, surrounded by color brochures advertising various rental properties around Cape Cod. There was also a framed photograph of Lori's miniature schnauzer Bitsy. "We need your help."

Lori peered at them through her designer glasses. Her pecan-brown hair was pulled back in a loose bun. She folded her hands on top of her desk as she looked between the two of them. "What can I do for you?"

"We're trying to reach Matthew Dinsdale," Mary said, deciding to cut to the chase. "Betty told me he and his wife were on a trip, and I really need to contact him."

Lori frowned. "Oh, Mary, I'm sorry. I wish I could help, but Matthew goes off the grid whenever he and Madeline take a vacation. Otherwise, his phone would never stop ringing."

Katie took a step closer to the glass desk. "But what if there's an emergency? There has to be some way to reach him."

Lori brightened. "Oh, I know! You can leave a voice mail at his home number. I believe he checks it periodically."

Mary stifled a groan of disappointment and saw Katie's shoulders slump at this newest obstacle in their path. Why did this have to be so hard? "I already tried that number, and his voice mail is full."

"I'm afraid that happens a lot," Lori admitted. "You can keep trying to call him in case he checks his voice mail and makes room for new messages." She gave a small shrug. "I'm not sure what else to tell you."

"Do you know when they'll be back?" Katie asked her.

"I don't," Lori said. "It might not be for another week or two."

"Another week or two?" Katie squeaked and reached out to grab the edge of the desk as if to steady herself.

Mary closed her eyes, trying to figure out what to do next. There was some kind of connection between Matthew and Katie, or else he wouldn't have written her that check. But what? And why would she be here when he was gone on vacation? When she opened her eyes, her gaze landed on the brochure on Lori's desk.

Maybe that was the key to finding out the truth about Katie.

ELEVEN

"The Dinsdales own several rental cabins around here, don't they?" Mary said, as an idea began to form in her mind.

"Yes." Lori swiveled in her chair and pointed to the map of Ivy Bay behind her. "See those green dots? That's where their cabins are located. They've got some prime spots."

Mary glanced at Katie, who arched a quizzical brow in her direction. Then Mary turned back to study the map. There were at least twelve green dots scattered across it, most of them on or near the beach. "Have you rented any cabins recently to a woman with the first name of Katie?"

"Or it could be under Katherine," Katie said, picking up Mary's train of thought, "or even Katrina."

Lori stared at them for a long moment. "We usually don't reveal the names of tenants without their permission. May I ask what this is about?"

Katie turned away from the map to face Lori. "I'm Katie, but I don't have any memory of anything that happened before last Tuesday."

Lori's ginger-colored eyes widened at this announcement, but she didn't interrupt.

"The doctor says I have amnesia," Katie continued, "so I'm looking for clues to my identity. We found out today that one of those clues is Matthew Dinsdale. I'm connected to him somehow. Maybe I rented one of his cabins."

"If she did," Mary added, "her belongings are inside. Things that could help identify her."

"I had no idea," Lori said breathlessly. She pulled a larger binder toward her and opened it. "All the rental contracts are in here, but I don't remember opening a cabin for anyone named Katie. I suppose it's possible Matthew might have done it earlier last week."

That brought up another question Mary wanted to ask. "When did he and Madeline leave for their trip?"

"A week ago last Monday," Lori replied. "Their plan was to drive to the airport in Boston that afternoon and take a flight from there."

"And what was their destination?" Mary asked, hoping to narrow down where to find Matthew. If, by chance, it was a small resort town or even an island somewhere, then maybe she could try to track him down. It wouldn't be easy, but it might be worth a shot.

"I'm afraid I don't know that either," Lori told her. "Sometimes, they just take off without a final destination in mind. Sometimes, they don't even get on the plane and just rent a car or hop on a ship. They always say that spontaneity is half the fun when they travel."

That sounded like something Madeline would say, Mary thought to herself. The artist's carefree spirit would relish venturing into the unknown. It might even inspire some of her artwork. Mary didn't know enough about Matthew to gauge his personality, other than the fact that he didn't check his voice mail often enough.

Mary sighed. There was no use trying to locate them even if she did discover the destination on their airline tickets. They could land at an airport anywhere in the world and then take another flight out or rent a car and drive hundreds of miles in any direction. With today's technology, it wasn't so easy to vanish into thin air anymore, but Matthew and Madeline Dinsdale seemed to have done it.

Lori flipped through several typed contracts in the binder. "I'm sorry, but no one with the name Katie or any derivative of it has rented one of the Dinsdale cabins in the last thirty days."

Katie rounded the desk and hovered close behind Lori's right shoulder so she could see the binder too. "What if someone else rented it," Katie asked, "like a friend or family member? Then I could be staying in one of those cabins, but my name wouldn't be on the rental agreement."

"Yes, it would," Lori countered and then turned in her chair to face Katie. "Our insurance policy dictates that every rental agreement includes the names of all the occupants of the cabin, even minors and pets. It's a safety measure in case something happens."

Something had happened to Katie, but they didn't know what. And judging by the little progress they were making today, they weren't about to find out. Mary's gaze went to the map again and those little green dots. Then she noticed something else. There were two orange dots, both fairly close together and in walking proximity of the old bait shack on

Little Neck Beach. It would be a long walk certainly, but doable.

"What do those orange dots mean?" Mary asked.

Lori closed the binder in front of her. "Oh, those are the Dinsdales' private cabins. They make them available to friends and family when they come to visit Ivy Bay."

Mary turned and looked at Katie. Giving someone over eight thousand dollars just *might* be something you'd do for a friend or a family member. "Do visitors have to sign a rental agreement for those properties?"

"No," Lori said, "because they're private property, not commercial." Then she looked up at Mary. "Are you thinking that Katie might have stayed in one of them?"

"It's possible, isn't it?" Mary asked, looking over at Katie. "Are they currently occupied?"

Lori shook her head. "I don't believe so."

"But it's possible I could be staying in one of them, right?" Katie moved toward the map. "It would explain a lot. Both of those orange dots are close to where I found myself on the beach. And if Matthew Dinsdale is the only one who knew me and he's not in Ivy Bay, that explains why I'm a stranger to everyone else."

Lori rose from her chair and joined them in front of the map. "He never told me anyone was staying in one of his cabins." Then she smiled. "But then, he's so busy that there are a lot of things he forgets to tell me. Besides, the only duty I have for those two private cabins is to arrange for a cleaning crew after the visitors leave and, half the time, Madeline usually takes care of it for me."

The butterflies in Mary's stomach started fluttering again. It made sense. This could be why none of the innkeepers or hotel staff had recognized the photo of Katie when Chief McArthur had shown it to them. Maybe Katie had arrived in Ivy Bay just before her injury. Or perhaps she was a writer, or an artist like Madeline, and had holed up inside the cabin to work, emerging only after she was injured and disoriented.

Mary knew she could stand there and speculate all day. There was only one way to find out the truth. "Do you have keys to those two cabins?"

Lori blinked. "Yes, I do . . . but I can't just waltz in there without Matthew's or Madeline's approval. That would be almost the same as just walking into their house while they're off on vacation."

"Please," Katie implored. "I can't stand the thought of waiting one to two more weeks to find out who I am."

Lori looked at her for a long moment, then heaved a sigh of surrender. "All right. We'll take a peek. I have to come with you though."

Mary wanted to hug her, but she restrained herself. "That's fine," she said with a relieved smile. "We'll follow you in my car."

Lori nodded. "Just give me a few minutes to finish up things here. Then we'll be on our way."

"We'll wait outside for you," Mary told her as she and Katie headed toward the front door.

Once they were outside, Katie turned to her. "What if this is another dead end?"

The same question had been plaguing Mary. Each time they thought they were close to finding more information about Katie, their hope was dashed. "We've just got to stay positive."

Katie sucked in a deep breath. "I think I can...." Her voice trailed off, and she bit her lip.

Mary reached out to hug her and prayed for the Lord to give them both strength on this difficult journey. "You *can* do this," Mary assured her, giving her an extra squeeze before stepping out of the hug. "We're already so much further than we were last week. We know you have a connection to the Dinsdales, and you've remembered your nana."

A shadow of a smile flitted over Katie's mouth. "You're right. I need to look at the big picture. The Dinsdales have to come home sometime, right? And Dr. Teagarden expects my memory to return eventually." She cocked her head to one side as her smile widened. "I wonder if I'm always this impatient in my real life. Do you think people's personalities change if they can't remember anything about themselves?"

Mary held up one hand. "That's an intriguing question, but too difficult for me to answer. Our experiences shape us, but I'm not sure what happens if we can't remember those experiences."

Katie gave a slow nod, looking deep in thought. "Well, I hope I like the person I really am. And I hope there's a really, *really* good reason that I'm in Ivy Bay by myself and that no one seems to be missing me."

Mary gave her a tender smile. "I'm sure someone misses you. But he or she might not know that you are missing—or at least not aware of what you're going through."

Katie breathed a wistful sigh. "Then I should have a good story to tell at the family Thanksgiving table. Let's just hope I can find it when the time comes."

"I have no doubt you will," Mary said as Lori emerged from the building.

Lori closed the door behind her and locked it and then looked over at Mary and Katie. "Let's go."

———

Mary and Katie climbed into the silver Impala and then followed Lori's midsize SUV onto Route 6A. They drove a short distance on Route 6A before the SUV pulled off onto a long gravel drive. A thick grove of trees blocked their view of the cabins until they rounded a bend and came upon them.

The Dinsdales' private cabins sat about sixty yards apart and had been designed in the Frank Lloyd Wright style. The lush landscaping around them was pristine, using native plants, shrubs, and flowers in a way that gave a natural, rustic appearance to the setting.

"These are really nice," Katie said as she opened her car door to get out. She turned in a slow circle, taking in everything around her.

"Does it feel familiar?" Mary asked.

Katie hesitated. "I'm not sure. I think I want it to feel familiar, but..." Her voice trailed off as she turned around again, her gaze taking in the cabins and their surroundings. Finally, she shook her head. "It's not triggering any memories for me. At least not yet."

Lori waited for them by her SUV. Then the three of them walked toward the front door. Mary was a little disappointed not to see any other cars in the area, but she told herself not to borrow trouble.

When they reached the door, Lori knocked loudly on the wood. She waited several seconds and then knocked again. No one answered. No one called out from the inside. Mary didn't even hear footsteps on the other side of the door.

"All right," Lori said, squaring her shoulders as she pulled a key ring out of her pocket. It held several silver keys. They were color coded, and each one was marked with a number.

Lori turned the key in the lock and then opened the door just far enough for her to peek inside. "It doesn't look like anyone is here." She pushed the door all the way open and walked into the foyer.

Mary and Katie followed her inside. The cabin was small but had an open-space concept that made it seem bigger. A wood fireplace was the centerpiece of the snug living room, with two creamy leather love seats on either side of it and a coffee table in the middle. A large oil painting of a lighthouse at dusk hung above the wooden mantel and had Madeline Dinsdale's signature in the bottom left corner.

High-gloss oak hardwood covered the floor, including the cozy dining area that seated six and the small chef's kitchen with its stainless-steel appliances and white granite-topped island.

"This is lovely," Mary said as she looked around. It was just as pristine as the exterior and showed no signs of anyone staying there. The counters and appliances were spotless, the dish drain empty, and the chairs lined up perfectly at the dining room table.

"Can you show us the bedrooms?" Katie asked the Realtor. "Maybe I have something in there."

"Of course," Lori said, leading the way.

Mary followed them, her pulse picking up as they made their way into the first guest room. But when they opened the door, there were no suitcases on the floor, no brochures or toiletries on the dresser, and the bed was perfectly made.

Lori strode over to the closet and opened the door. Empty hangers hung from the clothes rod, and the wood floor was bare.

"I guess this wasn't my room," Katie said, forcing a smile.

When they checked the other bedroom, they found it in the same condition. There was no sign that Katie, or anyone else, had been there recently.

Another dead end. Mary tamped down the disappointment welling up inside of her. She could only imagine how Katie must feel.

"Let's try the other cabin," Lori said, closing the door of the second guest room behind them.

They made their way out of the first cabin and took the walking path to the second one. It only took a few minutes, and the birds in the trees serenaded them along the way. Mary looked out into the bay, dotted with colorful sailboats, the water shimmering under the autumn sun.

The second cabin was a similar design to the first one, although it had black shutters instead of green and a pair of green double doors at the front entrance.

Lori knocked and, as with the first cabin, there was no answer. She used another key to unlock the door and walked inside, Mary and Katie right on her heels.

The layout of the cabin was the same as the first, with an open-concept design, a fireplace displaying Madeline's artwork above the mantel and a chef's kitchen. Everything was in place. There were no shoes or sandals piled near the back or front doorways, no dishes in the sink, and no towels hanging from the hooks on the back door that led out to the beach.

But something in the dining area caught Mary's attention. She walked over to the table and then gasped. "Katie, look at this!"

Katie and Lori both joined her at the table. A small white envelope lay in the center with the name Katie handwritten on the front.

Mary watched as Katie reached out to pick it up. "Thank You, Lord," she murmured under her breath. She'd been praying every step of the way from the first cabin to the second, hoping that they wouldn't find another dead end.

"It's empty," Katie said, showing Mary and Lori the torn white flap in the back.

"Your note!" Mary exclaimed, as the pieces started falling together for her. "The note you found in your pocket telling you to come to my bookshop. Maybe it was in that envelope."

Katie reached into her pants pocket and pulled out the note. Mary knew she always carried it with her. It was the one piece to her past that Katie could actually touch.

She folded the note along the crease marks, then slipped it into the envelope. It fit perfectly. Katie smiled at Mary. "I think you're right. So I must have opened this envelope Tuesday morning—since the note said I should come to your bookshop at 1:12 but didn't specify a date."

"I think you're probably right," Mary said. "It's possible that the note was there Monday, but we know you didn't have amnesia at the bank on Monday afternoon at four thirty, and that was well after 1:12 PM."

Lori looked between the two of them. "This is fascinating. I never realized that trying to find someone's identity would be so difficult. I'm so sorry that I hesitated to show you these cabins. I really had no idea that anyone was staying here."

"Don't apologize," Katie told her. "You were just doing your job." Then she flashed a smile and waved the envelope in her hand. "But now we have this! Which means I was staying at this cabin." She turned to Lori. "Can we look in the bedrooms?"

"Go right ahead," Lori said, still looking a little stunned. She took a seat at the table while Katie and Mary headed down the hall to the bedrooms.

"I'll take the one on the right," Mary told her. "You can look in the other one." They parted at the end of the hallway, each opening a different door. Mary stepped into the guest room. It was spotless, with no signs of occupancy. She checked the closet just to make sure, then took one more good look around the room.

A cry emanated from the other bedroom. Mary turned and hurried out of the guest room, rushing into the room across the hall.

"Look!" Katie said, kneeling in front of an open suitcase on the floor. "Clothes!" She plucked a cute yellow top from the pile and held it up in front of her. "What do you think?"

Mary chuckled. "It looks like your size. Is there anything in there besides clothes?"

"I don't think so." Katie sorted through the suitcase, removing clothes until she got to the bottom. "Just a couple of pairs of sandals." She kicked off one of the sandals she was wearing and tried on one from the suitcase.

"How does it fit?" Mary asked.

Katie grinned as she held her foot in the air. "Just call me Cinderella."

"You remember the story of Cinderella?" Mary asked.

Katie blinked, and then her grin widened. "I guess I do!"

Mary had never seen the girl so happy. Katie was actually glowing as she raked the clothes into a pile on her lap and then hugged them to her chest. "These are mine, Mary. They're a part of me."

Tears stung Mary's eyes. If Katie felt that way about a few clothes, how would she feel when she finally found her family?

"Look what I found," Lori called from the hallway. A moment later, she walked into the bedroom carrying a small valise. "This was in the bathroom." She handed the bag to Katie, who opened it to reveal cosmetics and toiletries inside.

"This is my stuff too?" Katie asked, a note of wonder in her voice.

Mary knelt down beside her, helping her sort through the items in the valise. "It sure looks like it." She was hoping to find a prescription bottle or anything that might have Katie's full name on it but came up empty.

"I looked through the rest of the cabin," Lori told them, "including all the cupboards and drawers, but I didn't find anything noteworthy."

"So no purse or bag of any kind?" Mary asked.

Lori shook her head. "Not that I saw. In fact, the only other evidence of Katie's presence in the cabin is the bottled water, apples, and cheddar cheese in the fridge." She slipped a key off her key ring and handed it to Katie. "Here you go. It looks like this place is yours for a while, at least until Matthew returns or you get your memory back."

Katie didn't say a word as she took the key from her. She just held it in her hand as tears formed in her eyes and began to slide down her cheeks.

Lori's eyes filled with sympathy. As she took her leave, she whispered to Mary, "Call me if you need anything."

"I will," Mary said, walking to the door with her. "Thank you so much."

"It was my pleasure." Lori reached out to squeeze her arm, then headed outside.

When Mary returned to the guest room, Katie was still sitting beside the suitcase. She looked up at Mary and said, "What do we do now?"

TWELVE

◆ ◇ ◆

"We need to keep searching for clues about your life." Mary's gaze fell on the clothes that Katie had dropped back in the suitcase. "And this seems like an excellent place to start."

Mary picked up a pair of black capri pants and checked the label. "St. John's Bay," she said, reading the brand name. Then she looked at Katie. "That's a brand that's carried in a lot of stores, like Sears and JCPenney. But if we can find one that was bought at a local shop, that might give us a clue where you're from."

Katie sat up on her knees. "Great idea!" She began pulling clothes from the suitcase and examining the labels as Mary continued to do the same.

They sorted through the remaining clothes, but they either came from a national chain or only had a label with the size and the care instructions. Mary folded the last pair of shorts and set them back in the suitcase. "Okay, so what does that tell us about you?"

Katie took some time to ponder that question. "That I shop at the same place most of the time," she ventured. "Maybe I'm too busy to do a lot of shopping."

Mary nodded. "Those are both valid theories. Or you might live somewhere small and fairly remote, where there isn't a lot of shopping available, so you order these clothes online."

"That could be true too." Katie reached for the valise and pulled it toward her. "Maybe I can learn more about myself in here." She began pulling out cosmetics that comprised a variety of name brands, such as Maybelline, Revlon, and Almay.

Katie picked up a bottle of lotion and squeezed some into her palm. She lifted her hand to her face and inhaled. "*Mmm*, this smells good." As she rubbed the lotion into her hands, the scent floated in the air toward Mary.

"Lavender," Mary said, identifying the fragrance. She picked up the bottle. "An expensive lotion judging by the brand name." She looked at Katie. "This tells us that you may have a good income. Or very generous friends or family members, if it was a gift."

"So how do I know Matthew Dinsdale?" Katie asked her.

That was the question of the day. "It's possible you could be a business acquaintance," she ventured. "Or perhaps a cousin or some other relative."

Katie looked around the bedroom, which featured high-end decor and a plush queen-size bed. "The Dinsdales must like me if they're letting me stay in one of their private cabins. But if I'm on vacation, why am I here by myself? And if Matthew and Madeline are friends or even family, why would I plan a trip when they're going to be gone?"

"I don't know," Mary answered truthfully. Both of those questions had occurred to her also. They were making progress in determining Katie's identity, but at the moment, it felt like baby steps. She glanced at her watch. "And I hate to say it, but we probably need to get back to the shop."

Katie got on her feet. "Would you mind terribly if I stayed here for the rest of the day? Maybe if I'm here a while longer, the cabin will trigger some memories."

"Oh, of course you should stay." Mary headed for the living room, laughing at herself for forgetting for a moment that Katie was not obligated to the shop like she was. "In fact, it's a good idea. But what about lunch?"

"You heard Lori," Katie said with a smile. "There's cheese and fruit in the refrigerator, so I won't starve. Besides, I'd like to take another look around the cabin, just in case I did stash a purse here somewhere."

Mary reached in her own purse and pulled out her cell phone. Then she handed it to Katie. "I want you to take my cell phone until I come and pick you up after I close the shop."

Katie held up both hands. "Oh, I couldn't."

"Yes, you can," Mary insisted. "I got along perfectly well for over fifty years without a cell phone, so I think I can manage for a few hours." She pressed the phone into Katie's hand. "If you need to reach me, the bookshop number is in there, along with Rebecca's phone number and Betty's."

Katie curled her fingers around the phone. "Thanks, Mary. I'm sure I'll be fine." She looked at the artwork above the fireplace. "It does feel a little strange, though, to know that I've been here before but have no memory of it."

"Just enjoy yourself this afternoon," Mary suggested, hoping a little relaxation might loosen some of those memories. "Take a walk outside or nap on the sofa. Pamper yourself a little. You're still healing, you know."

"I know." A mischievous grin tipped up one corner of Katie's mouth. "Are you sure you can get along at the shop without me? I've become pretty invaluable there."

Mary smiled. "I'm sure Rebecca and I will both miss you, but we'll try to manage."

Katie walked her to the door. "I'll see you in a few hours."

"Have fun!" Mary said, before making her way to the Impala. It was still parked by the first cabin, giving her time during the walk to talk to God about the events of the day so far. "We're getting closer, Lord. I can feel it. And I can feel Your presence too. Thank You for never letting us walk these paths alone."

An hour later, Mary stood behind the cash register at her shop and rang up a sale for Tess Bailey.

"I hope the book is as good as Joe told me," Tess said, speaking of her eldest son. "He's been hounding me for weeks to buy it, but I just haven't had time to do a lot of reading. Now that the summer season is over, I plan to enjoy some relaxation time."

Mary placed the mystery novel in a bag, along with the receipt. "I'm with Joe; it is a good read. It's set in World War II, and the characters are fascinating. I can't wait to hear your review."

Tess grinned. "Speaking of reviews, your raspberry ripple ice cream received rave reviews from my customers. Paige's boyfriend ate the last of it."

"I didn't know she was dating anyone."

"They just started dating," Tess explained. "It's Roger Foley's new stepson, Josh Durant. He's from Boston and likes to act tough." Tess rolled her eyes. "Paige is smitten, of course, and thinks he hung the moon."

Mary smiled. "Well, if he likes my ice cream, he can't be all bad."

"Oh, he's fine," Tess said with a wave of her hand. "So will the next ice-cream recipe be ready soon?"

"Very soon," Mary promised. "The flavor is cranberry with white chocolate chunks, and I just want to tinker with a few of the ingredients before I hand it over."

"Sounds yummy. And it's perfect timing with the cranberry harvest. I can't wait to taste it."

They chatted for a few more minutes. Then Tess took her leave. Mary looked around the shop, realizing she was all alone. She'd stopped by the house for an early lunch and updated Betty on Katie's situation before heading to the shop with Gus. Rebecca had taken the afternoon off to run some errands, and the dark gray clouds gathering in the sky seemed to be keeping most of her potential customers away.

Mary walked over to the window and looked up at the ominous sky, wondering if she should call Katie just to make sure she was all right.

"Don't be silly," Mary said out loud. "Katie is a grown woman, and she's just fine."

Her voice caused Gus to emerge from the back room and pad over to her. He looked around for a moment, as if to see who she was talking to, and then flicked his tail and sat down at her feet.

She bent over and scooped him up. "So what shall we do now, Gus?" she asked, cuddling him against her shoulder. There were new books to inventory and mail to open, but Mary couldn't stop thinking about the check that Matthew Dinsdale had written to Katie. "I know," she told him. "Let's do a little research."

Mary walked over to the computer and set Gus on the pearly white marble top. Then she perched herself on a stool and opened a search engine on the computer. She typed in the words Matthew Dinsdale Ivy Bay.

It only took a moment for several links to appear. She clicked on the top one, and it opened to a newspaper article, along with a photograph of Matthew and Madeline in formal attire. The headline of the article read "Dinsdales Donate to Diabetes Research."

Mary quickly scanned the article and learned that the Dinsdales had made a major contribution to diabetes research. They'd also sponsored a gala to raise more funds, which explained the fancy clothes. Between their donation and the gala, more than half a million dollars had been collected.

In the article, Matthew was quoted as saying, "I have loved ones who have suffered from diabetes and loved ones who have worked to find a cure. My wife and I have decided it is time to contribute to a cause that's near and dear to our hearts."

One sentence stood out to Mary. "Loved ones who have worked to find a cure." Was it possible that Katie really was a doctor, or possibly involved in medical research? A *loved one* of Matthew Dinsdale who was invited to stay in his cabin and had been given a large amount of money? Perhaps that eighty-three-hundred-dollar check was another donation for research.

It was just speculation at this point, but certainly a theory they could consider. Mary printed off the photo from the article, intending to show it to Katie that evening. Perhaps it would trigger her memory. If nothing else, Katie could see what the Dinsdales looked like since they played such a pivotal part in her life at the moment.

As the printer whirred into action, the door opened, setting off the tiny bell above it. Henry ducked inside just as a heavy torrent of rain began to hammer against the front window. "Whoa," he said, closing the door behind him. "I almost got soaked."

"Looks like perfect timing," she told him. "I just put on a pot of coffee."

"Perfect," he said. "I just wanted to tell you how much Karen liked her birthday present. She told me she read it in less than a day."

"I'm glad to hear it." A flash of lightning lit the sky outside. "Do you have time to stay for a while?" Mary asked. "I've got hot coffee brewing and an update about Katie."

"I have all afternoon," he said. "There's no way I'm taking the boat out in this weather. But maybe we could plan a ride for Sunday afternoon and take Katie with us. She may see something that jogs her memory."

Mary smiled. "A boat ride would be the perfect medicine. Let's just hope Sunday is warmer than today." She rubbed her hands over her bare arms, feeling tiny goose bumps erupt on her flesh. "It's a little chilly in here too, don't you think?"

Henry nodded. "Why don't I turn on the fire while you get the coffee? Then we can sit and have a nice cozy chat until the next customer comes in."

"That sounds like a fine idea." Mary peered out the window again on the way to the coffee station. The rain was still coming down in sheets. She didn't anticipate a customer anytime soon. Her mind drifted to Katie again, and she hoped the girl hadn't taken her advice to go for a walk.

But Katie was smart and would have watched the sky. Perhaps even smart enough to be a doctor, if Mary's theory was correct. She couldn't wait to tell Henry all about it.

When Mary returned home that evening, she was surprised to see a red bicycle parked near the front of the house. "Who could that belong to?" she murmured to Gus as she parked the car in the driveway and then started up the walk.

When she opened the door, she found Katie seated on the sofa with a magazine open on her lap. "I didn't expect to see you here," Mary said with a smile. She set down Gus's carrier and opened it to let him out. "I was just going to drop off a few things and head over to the cabin to pick you up."

"I rented a bicycle so you wouldn't have to drive me around anymore," Katie said, placing the magazine on the table beside her. "You and Betty have done so much for me already."

As Mary watched Gus disappear down the hallway, she sensed that Katie had more to say. "Is everything all right?"

"It's good." Katie smiled. "I decided to take your advice and just relax at the cabin for most of the afternoon. There's nothing like snuggling under a blanket for a light nap in a rainstorm while a fire crackles in the hearth." She breathed a wistful sigh. "It was heavenly."

"That does sound nice." Mary had enjoyed her time by the fire with Henry. They'd sat in the bookshop and talked about Katie and fishing and the upcoming concert, among several other subjects. Henry had stayed for almost two hours, until the rain had finally stopped and the sun peeked through the clouds. Then customers had started to find their way inside, and Henry had taken his leave.

"After my nap, I ate lunch," Katie continued, "and searched the cabin again, but I didn't find anything significant." A flash sparked in her eyes. "Oh, except this." She dug into her pocket and pulled out two one-hundred-dollar bills.

"Where did you find those?" Mary asked, surprised that Katie would take money she found in the cabin.

"In my shampoo bottle, along with an additional hundred. Or should I say, the container that was supposed to look like a shampoo bottle. It's actually made for hiding money when you travel."

"I'm sure that was a surprise."

Katie grinned. "It was. Especially since I decided to take a shower after my nap and discovered there wasn't any shampoo in that bottle."

Both the nap and the time in the cabin had done her some good, Mary thought to herself. Katie looked rested and happy—and probably relieved to have some spending money. Both Betty and Mary had offered her some cash to use for incidentals, but Katie had refused to take their money.

"So how was your afternoon?" Katie asked. "Were you busy?"

"Not really," Mary said, taking a seat in one of the antique wing chairs. "The rain kept customers away most of the afternoon." Then she reached into her purse. "Although there is something I want to show you." She pulled out the photograph of the Dinsdales that she'd printed off and leaned over to hand it to Katie. "Do you recognize either of these people?"

Katie stared at it for a long moment. "No. Should I?"

"They are Matthew and Madeline Dinsdale," Mary told her. "I thought they might look familiar."

Katie studied the photograph some more. "He's very distinguished looking. And Madeline is lovely. She wears her clothes like art too."

Mary could see what Katie meant. In the photo, Madeline wore a long, flowing silk blouse with a pattern of bright colors along with a black skirt and chunky gold jewelry.

"But I don't recognize either of them," Katie said at last, handing the photograph back to Mary. "I wish I did."

"I know," Mary said softly. A savory scent drifted from the kitchen. "Is that clam chowder I smell?"

Katie grinned. "It is. Betty told me it's her secret recipe. She even kicked me out of the kitchen, nicely of course."

Betty walked into the living room, a dish towel slung over one shoulder. "I did no such thing," she said with a smile. "I simply suggested that she sit down and relax." She smiled at Katie. "After all, you've had an eventful day."

Katie breathed a happy sigh. "I know. I still can't believe we found the cabin where I was staying and all my clothes. And the money, of course. I decided to spend it on a few things to make all our lives easier. So I rented the bicycle, and I also bought a prepaid cell phone." She pulled Mary's cell phone out of her pocket and handed it to her. "Thanks for letting me use yours. I hope you don't mind, but I already added my cell number to your phone in case you want to call me."

"I'm glad you did," Mary said, taking the phone from her.

Betty perched herself on the arm of the sofa. "She also made a stop at Meeting House Grocers on her way over here and restocked our cupboards."

"Oh, Katie," Mary said, her voice gently chiding. "You didn't have to do that."

"I want to," Katie said. "And I have enough money left over to repay you for the clothes you bought for me at Cape Cod Togs."

"Nonsense," Mary said kindly. "You've more than repaid me by all the work you've done in the bookshop."

"And around the house," Betty added, turning toward Katie. "Besides, we love having you here."

"And I love staying here." Katie looked at them gratefully. "But I think it's time for me to leave."

"Leave?" Betty cried, rising to her feet. "Where would you go?"

Now the bicycle and the prepaid cell phone all made sense. "She's going to the cabin," Mary said softly.

Katie nodded. "You've both done so much for me, and I hate to go, but the cabin is where I'm supposed to be. So I think I should stay there until my memory comes back or someone finds me."

Betty sank down into the other antique wing chair. "Are you sure you want to do this? I hate to think of you all alone there."

Katie nodded. "I'm sure. I feel like it's the right thing to do."

Mary didn't want to see her go either and shared Betty's concern about the girl staying alone, but she understood. Katie had been looking for home and, so far, that cabin was the closest thing to it. "We'll let you go," she said, a smile teasing her mouth, "but only if you let us see you every day."

Katie laughed. "Absolutely. I still intend to work at the bookshop, if you don't mind. It gives me something to do and makes the time go faster."

"I know the waiting must be hard," Mary told her. "I tried calling the Dinsdales again this afternoon, but their voice mail was still full."

Katie nodded, looking resolute. "I guess there's nothing I can do except wait for either my memory or the Dinsdales to return." She rose to her feet. "Would one of you mind giving me a ride? I can pick up the bike tomorrow."

"I'll drive you," Mary said. "And I'm sure the bike will fit in my trunk."

"Thanks," Katie said as Gus jumped onto her lap and placed both paws on her collarbone, his furry face looking into hers. "I think Gus is telling me good-bye."

Mary smiled. "Or trying to say that he doesn't want you to leave."

"Or that he wants you to take him with you," Betty chimed.

Mary looked at Katie. "You can," she said softly. "He loves you, and he'd keep you company at the cabin." She hated the thought of spending time away from Gus, but Katie probably needed him more at the moment.

"I appreciate the offer, and I'm very tempted...." Katie gave the cat a gentle hug and then set him on the floor. "But he belongs here. Cats can display behavior problems when adjusting to a new house. I don't want to cause him any stress."

"Spoken like someone who knows cats," Mary said, intrigued by the language she'd used. "No wonder Gus likes you so much. You probably have cats at your home."

"I hope so," Katie said wistfully as Gus sat at her feet and stared up at her. "I'll still see him at the bookshop, right?"

"Absolutely," Mary promised.

Betty moved toward them. "And you'll see him here too, when you come for dinner. In fact, you'll have dinner with us before you leave, right? You don't want to miss my clam chowder."

Katie smiled. "It smells so wonderful I can't resist. Yes, I'll stay for dinner." Then she looked over at Betty. "But don't you have rehearsal tonight?"

"It's tomorrow night." Betty rubbed her fingers together, wincing a little at the movement.

Mary sensed that the combination of the rain and the time she'd been spending at the piano had made Betty's rheumatoid arthritis flare up. "Will you be ready for it?"

"It's just a meet and greet, according to Eleanor," Betty explained. "So nobody will be playing. It's a good thing too—I still need a lot of practice."

Mary looked down at her sister's hands. "Maybe you should use some of that hand cream your doctor prescribed."

"Good idea. I think I still have some in my room."

Mary smiled. "You may want to dress up for the occasion too. Henry told me that he saw Adam Sullivan in town today, so you'll probably meet him tomorrow night."

"Really?" A spark of excitement lit Betty's eyes. "I can't wait. Why don't you come to the rehearsal with me, Mar?"

Mary knew Eleanor probably wouldn't be thrilled to have a party crasher at her rehearsal, but the chance to meet the handsome opera star was too tempting to resist. "Maybe I will."

Betty smiled as she turned to Katie. "You're welcome to join us tomorrow night too."

"Thanks," Katie said. "I'll think about it. Right now I should probably pack up my things in the guest room."

"And I should find that hand cream," Betty said.

Mary rose from her chair. "There's a duffel bag in the upstairs closet, Katie, that you can use to haul your stuff to the cabin."

"Thanks," Katie said, climbing off the sofa.

Mary led the way out of the living room. "I'll set the table while you two get ready."

"Sounds good," Betty said as she disappeared into her bedroom while Katie hurried upstairs, Gus following behind her.

It only took Mary a few minutes to set the table and pour them each a glass of iced tea to drink. But by the time Mary took the lid off the soup pot and began to fill three bowls, Katie was coming back down the stairs with the blue duffel bag in one hand.

"Just in time," Mary said with a smile. She carried one of the bowls over to the table and set it down. "I hope you're hungry."

"I am," Katie said, taking a seat at the table. "I had a light lunch, and soup just hits the spot on a day like this." She crinkled her brow as she looked at Mary. "Is that a memory? I mean, how else would I know soup tastes good on a rainy day?"

"I suppose it is. Although, Dr. Teagarden said you'd know general things, just not specific memories." Mary tilted her head to one side as she looked at Katie. "It's complicated, isn't it?"

"Very," Katie replied, a note of exasperation in her voice.

Mary carried the other two bowls to the table, fragrant steam rising from both of them. "I can't believe I'm going to meet a famous opera star tomorrow night. You really should come with us."

Katie smiled as she picked up her spoon. "It's tempting, but I think I'd feel a little out of place. Besides, I'm anxious to settle into the cabin."

Mary opened her mouth and then closed it again, deciding not to tell Katie that she planned to do a little snooping tomorrow night. The Dinsdales were one of the sponsors of the fund-raiser, which meant someone involved on the committee might know something useful. That someone could be Eleanor, Mary thought to herself.

While Betty ran in the same circles as the Dinsdales and other prominent families in Ivy Bay, Mary had noticed that

Eleanor often knew personal details about people that Betty did not. And, as the president of the Ivy Bay Chamber of Commerce, Eleanor might have insight into one of the most prominent businessmen in town.

The trick would be getting her to share that information with Mary. That's why Mary didn't want to say anything to Katie yet, not wanting to get her hopes up. She'd been disappointed too many times already.

After dinner, Mary and Betty took Katie to her new home. Mary parked the Impala in front of the cabin just as dusk descended on Ivy Bay. She shifted the car into park and switched off the engine. "Here we are."

Katie sat in the backseat for a long moment, making Mary wonder if she were having second thoughts about staying there. She was just about to ask her when Katie opened her door and climbed out.

Mary clicked the trunk button and heard it pop open behind her. She and Betty joined Katie outside and watched her lift her red bike out of the trunk. Then Betty grabbed her duffel bag from the trunk and set it on the porch.

Katie gazed at the western horizon. "Look at that."

Mary heard Betty's gasp of appreciation as they both turned to see the sky painted in an array of colors.

"Breathtaking," Betty said, her gaze fixed on the horizon.

"Now I know where Madeline got the inspiration for that painting above the fireplace," Katie said. "The sunset is so beautiful that mere words can't even describe it."

Mary agreed. They stood there in reverent silence for several long moments, just admiring God's handiwork and basking in the glory of it.

"What if I never remember?" Katie said, her voice almost a whisper. "What if Dr. Teagarden is wrong and my memory never comes back?"

"It will," Betty assured her. "It just takes time."

"And when the Dinsdales return next week," Mary added, "they'll be able to tell us who you are."

"I know," Katie said. "But if my memory doesn't come back, the people who know me will still be strangers—to me, at least."

Mary could hear the uncertainty in her voice and see the anxiety etched on her face. "The Bible says 'Therefore do not worry about tomorrow, for tomorrow will worry about itself. Each day has enough trouble of its own.'"

A tremulous smile reached Katie's lips. "Each day without my memory sure feels like trouble." Then she turned away. "Although, I have a lot to be thankful for too. You and Betty and all the folks in Ivy Bay who have made me feel so welcome." She squared her shoulders. "You're right. I shouldn't worry about tomorrow—at least not until it gets here."

"But you can still change your mind about staying here alone," Betty told her. "Are you sure you don't want to stay back at the house with us?"

"I'm sure," Katie said softly, turning to face them.

Mary reached out and embraced the girl, remembering how scared and alone Katie had been when Mary had first talked to her last Tuesday. *What a difference a week makes*, she thought to herself.

Katie stepped back so she could see both Mary and Betty. Her pretty blue eyes gleamed with unshed tears. "I don't know my mother, or even if I have one living anymore, but I feel like God gave me the two of you to take my mom's place until I find her."

Her words made Mary's own eyes sting with tears. The Lord moved in mysterious ways. Mary believed that He'd brought Katie into her bookshop for a reason. Maybe this was it.

Betty sucked in a deep breath, looking a little emotional as well. She reached out to give the girl a hug. "You can always come back if you change your mind about staying here."

"Thank you," Katie said, remaining in Betty's arms for several seconds before finally stepping away.

"Will I see you at the shop tomorrow?" Mary asked her.

"You can count on it," Katie said with a smile and then disappeared into the cabin.

THIRTEEN

---◆◆◆---

T he next evening, Mary drove her sister to the rehearsal
     meeting at the Ivy Bay Community Center. Although
Mary had once more tried to convince Katie to come along,
Katie had ultimately decided to spend the evening at the
cabin, reading a good book she'd found in the shop.

The community center was located on the west edge of
town and served as a popular venue for events, such as local
government meetings, wedding receptions, and craft shows.
The Cape Cod Wildlife Rescue Foundation concert was the
next big event at the community center, and volunteers were
hard at work to get it ready in time.

"There are so many committees for this concert that it's hard
to remember them all," Betty said as they arrived at the center.
"The decorating committee, the refreshment committee, the
talent committee, and even a seating committee."

"A seating committee?" Mary echoed. "So they're in
charge of where people sit?"

Betty laughed. "Something like that. That committee is
in charge of setting up chairs before the concert and taking
them down afterward. Eleanor thought giving it an official
committee name would entice more volunteers to join."

Mary chuckled, amused by Eleanor's leadership tactics. They seemed to work for her, though, judging by the bustle of people all around them.

She and Betty had arrived early, giving them time to mingle. Several of the participants were already there. Mary saw Tricia waving to her and started heading in that direction when Betty grabbed her arm and made a small gasping sound.

"Bets, are you okay?" Mary asked, concern welling inside of her. "What is it?"

"It's him."

Mary followed Betty's gaze to see Adam Sullivan stride into the community center. His frame was slight for an opera singer, although he had broad shoulders and stood about six feet tall. His hair was raven black and just slightly long, giving him the appearance of a knight of old. But it was his face that captivated audiences as much as his voice. The chiseled cheekbones and aquiline nose, along with his piercing blue eyes, had made more than one woman swoon over him.

Mary smiled to herself, remembering her daughter Lizzie's reaction the first time she'd seen him. They'd taken her to the Boston Grand Opera Company's production of *La Bohème* for her seventeenth birthday. John had managed to get them excellent seats so Lizzie had a close-up view of Adam in his debut performance with the opera company.

To Mary's surprise, Lizzie had been mesmerized by the twenty-one-year-old tenor. She'd admired her daughter's good taste and had helped Lizzie put up his poster in her room the next day. Lizzie's friends tolerated listening to *La Bohème* when they'd visit, although they hadn't been as impressed by the tragic opera tale of two ill-fated lovers.

Lizzie had always shown a maturity beyond her years, even in her choice of teenage crushes.

But like most things, time had eventually turned Lizzie's attention to other things, and Adam's poster was later replaced by another teenage heartthrob.

"Isn't he handsome?" Betty whispered beside her. "We were so lucky to snag him for the fund-raiser."

Mary watched as people started to flock around Adam, offering their greetings. "How exactly did that happen? He's a pretty big name, especially in this part of the country."

"Oh, you know Eleanor," Betty said wryly. "Once she sets her mind on something, she usually gets her way. Besides, I've read that he's a big advocate of animal rescue, so that probably played a part too."

Mary admired people who shared their time and talents for good causes. It was so easy for celebrities to get caught up in the bubble of fame and focus solely on themselves and their careers. It reminded her of a Bible verse from the twelfth chapter of Luke: "From everyone who has been given much, much will be demanded; and from the one who has been entrusted with much, much more will be asked."

Adam's presence here signified that he believed in giving back to the community. It heightened her opinion of him even more. She watched him make his way toward the makeshift stage that had been set up on one end of the large auditorium. A kitchen and hallway separated the auditorium from the smaller reception area on the other side of the community center, and she could see a few heads popping through the serving window of the kitchen to catch a glimpse of the star in their midst.

He'd dressed casually for the occasion, wearing a black knit polo shirt and a pair of khaki slacks. She judged him to be somewhere in his late thirties and in the prime of his career.

Eleanor hurried over to meet him and then escorted him onto the stage.

"Please take your seats, everyone," Eleanor said, standing in front of a podium and speaking into the microphone. "We don't want to waste Mr. Sullivan's time."

Mary and Betty made their way to the rows of chairs that had been set up in front of the stage. Everyone settled in fairly quickly, and soon a hush settled over the room. Mary knew this venue was far different than some of the famous opera houses where he'd performed, but he seemed perfectly at ease with his surroundings.

Eleanor stepped up to the microphone again. "It is my sincere pleasure to introduce our star for the Cape Cod Wildlife Rescue fund-raiser, Mr. Adam Sullivan. As many of you know, he's been the lead tenor of the Boston Grand Opera Company for the last seventeen years and has performed around the world. Let's give him a nice round of applause."

The crowd burst into applause. Adam smiled as Eleanor turned the microphone over to him and then waited for the applause to fade before he spoke. "Thank you so much, Eleanor, for that nice introduction. And I'd like to thank all of you for inviting me to participate in this important fund-raiser. I will do everything in my power to make sure it is a success, and I'm sure everyone in this room feels the same way." He stepped back as the small crowd gave him another enthusiastic round of applause.

Betty leaned toward Mary. "So far, so good. I was afraid he might be a bit of a diva—or whatever the male version of a diva is."

Mary was impressed as well. She sat back in her chair as Eleanor took control of the microphone once again. "Thank you, Adam." She pulled a clipboard from behind the podium and gave it a quick perusal. "Our meeting agenda is fairly short this evening. I thought this would be a good opportunity for everyone to meet Adam. We have members of the stage crew here tonight, as well as makeup artists, hairstylists, all the different committee members and, of course, the performers."

"Hair and makeup?" Betty whispered. "I wasn't expecting that."

Mary leaned toward her sister. "Sounds like Eleanor is pulling out all the stops. Have you thought about what you're going to wear?"

"I've been considering a couple of outfits in my closet, but now I'm thinking I should pay a visit to Dora's Dress Shop and get something a little more formal than I'd planned."

Eleanor read off the proposed schedule for the night of the concert and indicated that all the performers and volunteers would need to be there at least two hours in advance. Adam stood next to her as she spoke, his arms clasped behind his back and a patient smile on his face. He nodded a few times when Eleanor mentioned how important it was to raise as much money as possible for the Cape Cod Wildlife Rescue Foundation.

"This is Ivy Bay's chance to show the rest of Cape Cod how it's done," Eleanor told the participants. "We need to work hard and to devote all our time, energy, and resources to make this concert a success." She turned toward Adam. "Is there anything you'd like to add, Mr. Sullivan?"

He smiled as he leaned toward the microphone. "Well, first I'd like to ask everyone to call me Adam. And second, I'd like to quote Aristotle, who wrote: 'Pleasure in the job puts perfection in the work.' So if we all enjoy our roles in this concert, then the audience will enjoy the performance."

His words were met with another round of applause, and Eleanor had to wait a few moments before the noise died down enough for her to speak again. "Ladies and gentlemen, the concert will be held a week from today. That only gives us seven days left to prepare. The program should be done soon, so you'll know your spot on the schedule for the evening, but I encourage you to show up early for our rehearsals and prepare to stay late. Mr. Sullivan . . . I mean *Adam* may not be able to attend all of them due to his obligations with the Boston Grand Opera Company, but everyone else's presence at the rehearsals is mandatory."

"How many rehearsals are there?" Mary whispered.

Betty leaned toward her. "Three, including the one the day before the concert. I have to admit now that I see the stage and all the people involved, I'm getting a little nervous."

"That's only natural," Mary assured her as the meeting wound down. But Mary wondered if her sister had reason to worry. Her playing had improved, but it still wasn't perfect by any means, and she didn't have much time left to practice. She prayed that Betty's rheumatoid arthritis wouldn't flare up again and prevent her from playing.

Eleanor ended the meeting and then invited everyone to stay for refreshments. Then Eleanor and Adam left the stage and found themselves immediately surrounded by a crowd of people.

"I wanted to go up and introduce myself," Betty said, looking in their direction. "But it looks like I might have to wait."

"The line at the refreshment table is much smaller. Why don't we treat ourselves there first? Then maybe we'll be able to chat with him."

"Good idea."

The kitchen helpers were still putting platters of goodies on the refreshment tables. They'd gone all out with fancy finger desserts, like mini cream puffs and chocolate éclairs, a chocolate fountain with a platter of fruit on one side and bite-size pieces of angel food cake on the other, and a wide variety of miniature cupcakes decorated with musical notes made out of fondant.

"Wow," Mary said, picking up a paper plate and looking over the selection. "I wonder if they're rehearsing the food for the night of the concert. There's a reception afterward, right?"

"There is," Betty said, reaching for a miniature cupcake and placing it on her plate.

After they'd filled their plates and chatted with Bea Winslow and some of the other members of the refreshment committee, they made their way to one of the empty tables near the back of the room.

Mary glanced in Adam's direction and saw that he was still surrounded by a throng of admirers. She wondered if he enjoyed the attention or merely endured it. She imagined it would get tiresome after a while.

Betty plucked the black fondant musical note off one of her miniature cupcakes and took a small bite. "I think I overdid it with the refreshments. They just all looked so good." She popped the rest of the fondant note into her mouth. "Maybe I'll save the other cupcake to take home."

"I'll do the same with my chocolate éclair," Mary said, moving it to the side of her plate. "Unlike you, I've already picked out the dress I'm going to wear to the concert, but it might not fit if I eat everything on this plate."

Betty chuckled. "We're quite the pair, aren't we? Remember when Grandma used to say that our eyes were bigger than our stomachs?"

"I do. I guess some things never change."

Eleanor approached their table with a cup of coffee in her hand. "Do you mind if I join you?"

"Not at all," Betty said cheerfully, pulling out the empty chair next to her.

Eleanor sat down with an exasperated huff. "I wish people would stop mobbing poor Adam. It's rather unbecoming."

"Everyone is just excited to meet him," Betty told her. "I'm sure things will settle down once we all spend more time around him."

Eleanor took a sip of her coffee. "I hope you're right, because all our focus needs to be on this concert."

Mary leaned forward in her chair. "I heard the Dinsdales are on the foundation committee. Do you know when they're expected back from their trip?"

Eleanor frowned. "Not until the day of the concert, if you can believe it. I tried to tell Madeline that we needed all hands on deck for this event to be a success, but she told me Matthew had already made all their reservations and they couldn't be changed."

Mary's shoulders sagged. If Katie's memory didn't come back on its own, that meant she'd have to wait another week to find out her identity. She didn't look forward to telling her that, but there was apparently nothing they could do about it.

"I've told Eleanor a little about Katie's situation now," Betty informed her. "She doesn't know where they went on vacation or how to reach them."

Eleanor clucked her tongue. "I can't imagine going off somewhere and leaving no contact information. But it really doesn't surprise me. I adore Madeline, but she is a bit flighty. It's the artist in her, I suppose. I hear she's nothing like his first wife."

"First wife?" Mary echoed as she looked over at Betty.

Betty stared at her sister-in-law. "Matthew was married before?"

"Yes. Didn't you know?" Eleanor took a sip of her coffee. "It was before he moved to Ivy Bay. Apparently, his first wife passed away, and that's when he devoted himself to his business ventures. Five years later, he met Madeline and it was love at first sight."

Betty blinked. "I've heard Madeline say they fell in love quickly, but I don't think she ever mentioned that he was a widower."

"Well, as I said before," Eleanor chimed in, "she's a little flighty. She probably doesn't remember who she told. I thought you knew or I would have told you."

Mary chewed thoughtfully on a chocolate-covered strawberry. This added another element to the mystery surrounding Katie. Was is possible that her connection to Matthew was through his first wife?

"Well, what do you know about her?" Betty asked Eleanor, obviously intrigued by this new information. She glanced over at Mary, the curiosity in her blue eyes revealing that she was having the same thoughts about a possible connection to Katie.

"Not much," Eleanor replied, curling one manicured hand around her disposable coffee cup. "I believe she was killed in a car accident. Very tragic, of course. Madeline said that Matthew didn't like to talk about it."

Mary's heart went out to him. Even though she had never spoken to him, she knew how difficult it was to lose a spouse. She did know that he and Madeline had married about twenty years ago, so he'd been blessed with a second chance at love. Madeline was a warm and charming lady with a big heart, even if she was, as Eleanor described her, a little flighty.

Adam Sullivan walked up to their table. "I'm sorry to interrupt, ladies. I just wanted to let Eleanor know that I need to be heading back to Boston soon."

Eleanor rose to her feet, as did Mary and Betty. "Well, thank you so much for coming this evening. As you can tell, you're quite popular in Ivy Bay." Then she motioned toward Betty. "This is my dear sister-in-law Betty Emerson, and this is *her* sister Mary Fisher."

"Pleased to meet you," Adam said, shaking both of their hands. "Will you both be performing in the concert?"

"No," Mary said with a smile and pointed to Betty. "Just her. She's a wonderful pianist."

"Excellent." He looked at Betty. "What piece will you be performing?"

Mary held her breath, knowing that Betty had been debating that question for days now. She'd brought home a wide variety of sheet music from Strings & Things, covering a few different genres.

Betty paused for a long moment and then said, "'Rondo alla Turca.'"

"Ah," Adam replied, nodding his approval. "Mozart. That's an excellent choice. I'm sure the audience will enjoy it."

"Thank you," Betty replied, her cheeks turning a delightful shade of pink. "I hope so."

Adam turned to Eleanor. "I'll be seeing you soon. You have my cell phone number, right?"

"Yes, I do," she said, preening a little.

"Great. Just give me a call if you need anything."

Eleanor walked him to the door of the community center as Mary and Betty sat back down.

"So what do you think?" Mary asked her sister. Mary was still processing the information that Matthew had been married previously and what that might mean for Katie.

"I think all that sugar went to my head. I haven't even practiced 'Rondo alla Turca' yet. It just popped out."

Mary smiled, realizing they'd been thinking about two different things. "You can always change your mind."

"No, I do love the piece, and it was one of Edward's favorites," Betty said, speaking of her late husband. "It's just...difficult. I'll have to double my practice time."

Mary's gaze fell to Betty's fingers. "Are you sure you want to do that?"

"I'll take a lot of breaks," Betty promised, flexing her fingers. "And I can play through the pain, if necessary."

Mary nodded, not wanting to argue with her. "On another subject, do you think there's any chance that Matthew's first wife is connected to Katie?"

"It's certainly possible." Betty wrapped her untouched miniature cupcake in a clean napkin. "But we won't know until next week when Matthew and Madeline get back from their trip."

Mary nodded, knowing her sister was right. But in the meantime, it wouldn't hurt to do a little digging of her own.

FOURTEEN

A full moon lit the sky when Mary and Betty arrived home from the rehearsal meeting. It had been a long, busy day, and Mary couldn't wait to curl up on the sofa with Gus and a good book.

"Did you happen to pick up the mail today?" Mary asked her sister as she switched off the engine.

"No," Betty said, stifling a yawn, "but I can get it now."

"You go on in," Mary said, seeing her sister's fatigue. "I'll get the mail."

Betty didn't argue with her, heading for the house as Mary closed the driver's door. As Mary walked toward the mailbox, she heard the sound of a basketball hitting pavement. The sound was coming from the Walinski house next door.

Mary looked over and saw the silhouette of a tall, willowy boy in the neighboring driveway. She couldn't see his face in the darkness, but there was one thing she could see that made her gasp out loud.

Neon-green shoelaces on his feet.

She hadn't forgotten about the mugger, but with no new leads, she'd put him on the back burner. Mary headed straight for the Walinski house. As she drew closer, the porch light shone on the boy's face as he took a shot at the hoop. The basketball rounded the rim before it fell through the net.

"Nate?" Mary said.

The sixteen-year-old caught the basketball in his hands as it bounced on the ground and then turned to face her. "Hey, Mrs. Fisher. How are you?"

"I'm good." She looked down at his shoes, wondering how to start this conversation. It didn't help that he was wearing a black hoodie, just like the one Anthony Cantuccio had described. She certainly didn't want to accuse the neighbor boy of a crime, especially since Nate had never been violent. He was a responsible kid who took care of his little brother and helped out his single mom.

"Mom's not home yet," Nate said, obviously assuming that she'd come over to talk to Sherry. "She went shopping for groceries, but she should be home soon."

"Actually, I wanted to talk to you." She pointed to his shoes. "Did you know your shoelaces glow in the dark?"

He laughed. "Yeah, we planned it that way."

"We?"

"The cross-country team," he explained. "We all got the same shoelaces because it goes with the color of our team shirts."

"I didn't realize you ran cross-country."

"I didn't until this year," he explained. "I'm not really much of a runner, but it gets me in shape for basketball season." He spun and made a shot toward the hoop. The ball hit the backboard and bounced away from the net. He scowled as he chased down the ball. "Doesn't help me with my shooting though."

Mary debated whether to tell Nate about the mugging and the connection with neon-green shoelaces. While he might be able to help her, she didn't want to involve him if the evidence pointed to one of his teammates. Instead, she decided to ask him some careful questions that would give her some information while keeping him out of the mix.

"So tell me more about your cross-country team," Mary said. "My son Jack used to run cross-country in high school. He even placed second at the district meet."

"Wow, he must have been good." Nate took a step closer to her, cradling the basketball in his arms. "What do you want to know?"

"How many kids are on the team?"

He screwed up his face for a moment, thinking over her question. "There's twelve guys and eight girls."

"Do you all wear the same uniforms?" she asked. "Right down to the green shoelaces?"

"Yep. And the coach had to order the shoelaces online because we couldn't find that color anywhere in Ivy Bay."

That fact made it even more likely that the mugger had come from the cross-country team.

"Do you want to see our T-shirts?" he asked. "They're pretty cool."

"Sure."

He tossed the basketball toward the lawn. It bounced once and then settled into the plush green grass. Then he tugged at his black hoodie, pulling it over his head to reveal a neon-green T-shirt underneath. The words *Ivy Bay High Cross-Country* were printed in black on the upper right side of the shirt.

She smiled. "I guess your coach doesn't have to worry about losing one of you at a meet when you're wearing those shirts. They're very bright."

"Yeah, the girls picked the color," he said wryly. Then he turned around. "But the guys picked out the slogan for the back."

"'The Faster You Run, the Quicker You're Done,'" Mary said, reading the printed words on the back of his T-shirt.

"The slogans are supposed to be witty," Nate explained. "Every school has a different slogan on the back of their shirts. It's fun to read them during the meets."

"I'm sure it is," Mary said, remembering that Jack's team had done the same thing. "My son's cross-country shirts always had a slogan too." She glanced at the hoodie in his hand. "Does the team wear black hoodies?"

He nodded. "They're part of our warm-up uniform."

A car pulled into the driveway, the headlights illuminating both Mary and Nate. They moved out of the way so Sherry could drive her car all the way in. Nate pulled on his hoodie again and then walked onto the lawn to scoop up his basketball.

"Hello, Mary," Sherry said, carrying two canvas shopping bags. "Nice night, isn't it?"

"Very nice, especially after the rain we had this afternoon." Stars now glittered in the sky, and she could glimpse the lights on the boats bobbing out in the bay. "I saw Nate playing basketball, so I just came over to chat a minute."

Just like she'd debated telling Nate about the mugging, she weighed the decision to inform Sherry about the possible involvement of a young man wearing neon-green shoelaces like the ones on Nate's feet. But there were eleven other male members of the team who could also be suspects, and Mary knew in her heart that Nate wasn't guilty. Telling Sherry would only make her worry, and Mary didn't want to give her that burden. She'd wait to tell Sherry everything after she'd collected more facts.

"I was telling Mrs. Fisher about our cross-country team," Nate said.

Sherry smiled. "You should see the quote on the back of their T-shirts."

"I already showed it to her, Mom," Nate said.

"What's your brother doing?" Sherry asked her son.

"Watching television," Nate replied.

"He's supposed to be doing his homework." Sherry shifted the bags in her hand. "I guess I'd better go inside and supervise. Nice to see you, Mary."

"It was nice to see you both," Mary said, walking in the direction of her house. "Good luck at your next cross-country meet, Nate."

"Thanks, Mrs. Fisher," Nate called after her.

Mary picked up the mail and returned to the house. She could hear piano music before she even opened the door.

"There you are, Mar," Betty said, turning on the piano bench as Mary walked inside the house. "I was starting to wonder what was taking you so long. I was half hoping that Katie had changed her mind and decided to come back."

"I'm afraid not." She flipped through the thin pile of mail, noting that it was mostly advertisements, and then set the envelopes on the table by the door. "I stopped to chat with Nate when I got back. He was wearing neon-green shoelaces."

She watched her sister's expression. It took a moment for the meaning behind those words to sink in.

"What?" Betty's eyebrows knitted together. "You don't mean—" She shook her head. "Not our Nate."

"I don't think so." Mary walked over and sat down on the sofa, kicking off her shoes so she could wiggle her cramped toes. Gus was curled up on the other end of the sofa, right where Katie had been sitting last night before she'd left.

"In fact," Mary continued, "I'm almost positive he's not involved in the mugging. But he did tell me that the cross-country team all wears the same neon-green laces. They even had to special order them when they couldn't find that particular neon color in Ivy Bay."

Betty paged through the sheet music in front of her. "Well, that tells you something. I just hate to think of one of our high school kids involved in a crime like that."

"Me too." Mary leaned back against the sofa cushion. It had been a very long but eventful day. She wondered how Katie was doing at the cabin and was glad the girl had purchased a cell phone so she could keep in touch.

"What did Nate say when you told him about the mugging?"

Mary looked over at her sister. "I didn't tell him. I thought about it, but I didn't want to put him in the position of possibly pointing the finger at one of his teammates. You know how teenagers are. He might take a lot of grief from the other students if they found out."

Betty nodded. "I think that's a good call. There's no reason to get Nate involved in this. So what do you plan to do next?"

"I thought I'd call Chief McArthur in the morning." Mary stifled a yawn. "It's late tonight, and I don't want to bother him, especially when I don't even have a name to give him."

"And you're tired," Betty observed.

"A little," she admitted. "I just want to sit here and relax and listen to you play the piano."

Betty smiled. "I'm afraid you couldn't avoid it even if you didn't want to listen. I need all the practice I can get if I'm going to perfect 'Rondo alla Turca' by next week."

Mary leaned her head on the back of the sofa as Betty began to play some warm-up scales. They were much better than before. As she listened to the music, she let her mind drift to things she needed to do tomorrow. She made a mental note to drop off her ice-cream recipe at Bailey's and to check on that book order that hadn't come in yet.

She breathed a restful sigh as her gaze moved to the window. Mary could see the stars in the sky, far too many to count, glowing above the waters of the bay.

"Okay, here goes nothing," Betty said as she started to play the Mozart piece.

Gus, who had been sleeping during the scales, now scrambled off the sofa and out of the room. Mary winced as Betty hit a wrong note—and then another. Her timing seemed off too. "Rondo alla Turca" was a popular classical piece with a fast tempo. The more Betty played, the more Mary grew concerned. Should she say something? She didn't want to make Betty self-conscious, especially since she'd just started practicing this particular piece.

Besides, Betty could hear the music as well as she could. She just needed more time to get it right.

Mary reached over and picked up the Bible on the end table next to her. She turned to the book of Romans as Betty continued to play, looking for some soothing words after such a hectic day. She found them in chapter eight: "And we know that in all things God works for the good of those who love him, who have been called according to his purpose."

"Amen," Mary whispered.

The next morning, she arrived at the bookshop with Gus before either Rebecca or Katie. After she let Gus out of his carrier, she picked up the phone and dialed the police station, asking for the chief.

"I'm sorry, Mrs. Fisher," said the male officer who had answered the phone, "but Chief McArthur isn't here."

"Do you know when he'll be in?"

"Not for a while," the officer said. "He got called out to an accident on Route 6A, about ten miles out of town. A semitruck overturned in the middle of the road."

"Oh dear. I hope no one was hurt."

"The truck driver wasn't hurt, and he didn't hit anybody else," the officer replied, "but there are pumpkins all over the road."

"Pumpkins?"

He chuckled. "That's right. The truck was coming from a pumpkin farm and hauling them to Boston. Now all the traffic on Route 6A has to be diverted until the pumpkins are cleared off the road." He cleared his throat. "Would you like me to take a message?"

"No, I'll give him a call later," Mary said before ending the call.

She didn't want to wait until all the pumpkins were off the highway. Which meant that she'd have to talk to the cross-country coach herself.

FIFTEEN

———◆◆◆———

Mary had called ahead to the school to set up a meeting with Coach Darrin Stover. When the secretary asked what the meeting was about, Mary demurred, telling her it was a private matter. She wanted to be careful about accusing anyone of a crime, especially a minor.

She didn't know much about the coach, since he'd just accepted a teaching job at Ivy Bay High School and moved to town with his wife in August. Mrs. Stover had come into the shop once to buy some books by local authors. She was a quiet woman in her late thirties who worked at home as a medical transcriptionist.

When it was time for her meeting with the coach, Mary left the bookshop in Rebecca's capable hands, with Katie there to assist her, and made her way to the high school. She walked into school just as the students were moving between classes. The halls were full of laughing students and the sound of lockers opening and closing. She waited near the front entrance, trying to stay out of the way until a path cleared.

She saw several of the kids from Grace Church talking and laughing with their friends. Then Anthony Cantuccio Jr. sauntered out of the principal's office and headed toward the gym. The halls were almost clear when the second bell rang, indicating the start of the next class session. The secretary had told her that Coach Stover taught chemistry in room 8, so she started down the hallway checking the classroom numbers on the doors as she walked.

When she reached room 8, the door was open and the coach was seated at a desk in the corner. He was a stocky man with auburn hair shaved close to his scalp and matching beard stubble covering his jaw.

He didn't look up from the textbook in front of him until Mary tapped lightly on the open door. "Hello," he said. "You must be Mrs. Fisher. Please come in."

"Thank you." Mary stepped inside the room, which smelled faintly of sulfur. She'd disliked chemistry class in high school, confused by all the symbols and formulas. John had loved it and helped her study for the test so she'd managed to pass with a decent grade. It had been her one trepidation in going to nursing school because college chemistry was a required course, but her marriage and Jack's impending birth had led her to stop attending after her first year. The silver lining had been that she'd never had to take chemistry again.

Lab stations were set up around the room with Bunsen burners and test tubes and eye goggles. Nope, Mary thought as she approached Coach Stover's desk, she didn't miss chemistry one bit.

"I appreciate your taking the time to see me today," Mary told him, holding out her hand.

"No problem." He rose from his seat and shook her hand. "My wife loves your bookshop. I'm not much of a reader myself, except for my science magazines. And between teaching classes and coaching cross-country, I don't have much time to read those."

She smiled. "Well, I'll try not to take up too much of your time. I have an...unusual situation I'd like to discuss with you. Do you mind if I close the door?"

He arched a curious brow. "Not at all. We had an experiment go wrong last period, and it got a little stinky in here. I opened the door along with some of the windows, but the smell is almost gone now."

Mary walked over to close the door and then returned to the desk, taking a seat across from him. She'd rehearsed her story in the car on the way over, but now that she was face-to-face with the coach, she wasn't quite sure where to start. Should she tell him about Katie first? Tell him one of his team members might be a criminal? Then it occurred to her to start with the scene of the crime.

"I'm not sure if you heard that Anthony Cantuccio was mugged near Little Neck Beach last week. He owns Pizzeria Rustica."

The coach nodded. "Yes, I did hear about it. My wife and I eat at his restaurant quite often."

"Well, it's possible there may have been a second mugging done to a friend of mine. I happened to talk to Anthony about his experience, and he didn't see his mugger's face."

The coach nodded again. "Yes, that's what I've heard. It's quite disturbing to think there might be a mugger in our midst."

Closer than you think, Mary thought but didn't say out loud. "However, Anthony was able to identify one unusual aspect of his mugger's attire. He wore neon-green shoelaces."

The coach blinked. "Come again?"

Mary swallowed a sigh, hating to be the bearer of bad news. "I'm afraid it's true. I talked to one of your team members last evening when I saw him wearing neon-green laces. He told me that they had to be ordered through the Internet because no store in Ivy Bay carried that color. So when I heard that the mugger had the same type of shoelaces..." Her voice trailed off, letting him make the obvious conclusion.

"So you think one of my runners is a thief?" he said. "I can't believe it."

"I know," Mary said softly, understanding his distress.

Then he met her gaze. "So why are you telling me this instead of the police?"

"I was going to tell Chief McArthur this morning," she said, "since he's helping me with my friend's case and it might be related to Anthony's mugging. But when I learned he was busy with a traffic incident, I decided I couldn't wait. I hope you don't mind."

"No," he said without hesitation. "I'm actually grateful. If there had been a policeman in these halls, the word would have gotten around quickly, and the last thing I want is any false accusations made against one of my team members." He raked one hand over his scalp. "I'm sure you understand."

She thought about Nate and nodded. "I do. In fact, I think it's important to keep this as quiet as possible until the case is resolved."

"So how do you intend to resolve it?"

That was a good question and one she'd need his help to accomplish. "I was hoping you could give me a list of your male team members, and I would go from there. I know I could have asked the boy I spoke to yesterday, but I didn't want to involve him any further."

"May I ask who it was?"

She hesitated, then decided that trust was a two-way street. "Nate Walinski. He lives next door to me."

Coach Stover nodded. "Nate is a great kid. You don't think he had anything to do with it, do you?"

"No," she said unequivocally. "I've known him for a while now, and I just can't see him doing anything like that."

"I agree." The coach leaned forward, propping his elbows on his desk. "I just can't get over the fact that one of my kids could have done this. Is Anthony sure the shoelaces were neon green?"

"He seemed sure. He also told me the mugger was wearing a black hoodie."

Coach Stover emitted a deep sigh. "Like the ones we use for warm-ups."

Mary nodded. "Perhaps the boy was simply out training last Wednesday and the mugging was a spontaneous decision. We won't know until we identify him." While Mary wanted to believe that, it didn't fit in with her theory that Katie might have been mugged near the same spot and by the same person.

Coach Stover stared at her. "Did you say last Wednesday?"

"Yes, why?"

He pulled his desk calendar toward him. "What time?"

"Anthony said it was dusk when he was walking the trail where he was mugged. So that would make it about seven o'clock or so."

He sat back in his chair with a sigh of relief. "Then it couldn't have been one of my boys. The team had a race in

Hyannis. It started at four—so we left here at two thirty in the afternoon. When the race ended around six o'clock, we went out for pizza in Hyannis. We didn't get back to Ivy Bay until after nine."

Mary stared at him, not sure what to say. She'd been so certain those green shoelaces were the smoking gun. And now it appeared someone else in town had them. *Was that intentional?* The culprit could dress like one of the boys on the cross-country team. He could run on the trails around Ivy Bay and not look suspicious. Even better for him when someone is mugged, the suspicion falls on a member of the team.

It was almost too devious to contemplate, but Mary knew she had to consider all the possibilities.

"So none of the twelve boys could have been the mugger," Mary said, thinking out loud, "because they were all in Hyannis last Wednesday?"

"Yes," he said. Then his face paled. "Wait. I'm wrong about that. There was one boy who didn't make the trip due to some academic problems."

"Can you tell me his name?"

The coach took a deep breath, obviously fighting the urge to protect one of his own. "I can handle it from here, if you'd like. I'll even escort him to the police station for questioning."

Mary hesitated, trying to find just the right words to turn down his offer. "I appreciate that. I really do. But I need to talk to him about my friend first. You see, she received a head injury, possibly from a mugging, but we don't know the reason because she has amnesia. She doesn't remember anything about her past. She doesn't even know her last name."

"Wow," he said, shaking his head. "That's awful."

Mary leaned forward in her chair, silently imploring him to agree. "So I'd like a chance to talk to the boy before we bring in the police. I'm hoping that he'll open up to me. At least enough to help us figure out her identity. He may not even be involved with her injury, but I'm sure you understand it's a sensitive issue all around."

Coach Stover gave a slow nod. "I guess I do. All I ask is that you keep me updated and let me know what happens after you talk to him."

"I will." Mary sat there for a long moment, waiting for him to give her a name.

He picked up a yellow highlighter pen and then reached for a piece of paper on his desk. He carefully drew a line across the paper before handing it to her.

Mary looked down at the paper and saw a list of names. It was a team roster. Then her gaze landed on the highlighted name.

It was Josh Durant.

———

After Mary left the high school, she drove around town for a short while, trying to figure out what to do next. When she saw Josh Durant's name, she instantly thought of Paige Bailey. According to Tess, the girl was smitten with her big-city boyfriend. But how would Paige—or Tess—feel if they knew Josh might be the person who mugged poor Anthony Cantuccio? And possibly Katie as well.

Thoughts of the Baileys made her remember the ice-cream recipe she had in her handbag. So she turned her Impala in the direction of their shop, not even sure yet what she was going to say about Josh.

Tess was alone in the shop, chopping some nuts behind the counter, when Mary got there. "Good timing," Tess told her, wiping her hands on a towel. "I need a break."

"Well, I can't stay long," Mary warned, pulling the recipe out of her bag. "I just wanted to give you this."

Tess took the recipe from her. "So you did go with the cranberry and white chocolate chunk. I was afraid you might change your mind."

"Nope," Mary said with a smile. "The cranberry harvest inspired me. Of course, now that I know there are some smashed pumpkins along Route 6A that are probably free for the taking, I should have created a pumpkin recipe."

"I heard about that," Tess told her. "Blake ran into the roadblock after a trip to Falmouth this morning. Good thing that farmer has insurance, because Blake said most of those pumpkins could not be salvaged."

"I imagine that's quite a sight. Slippery too, since the inside of a pumpkin is so slimy."

"Slimy is never good." Tess looked at the recipe in her hands. "This, however, looks amazing." She began to read off the list of ingredients. "Fresh cranberries, sugar, heavy cream, milk, salt, egg yolks, and white chocolate chunks. Simple and delicious. I'm sure my customers will love it."

"I hope so," Mary said, lingering in front of the counter. Was now the time to tell her suspicions about Josh?

"Now, do you happen to have a recipe for a broken heart?" Tess asked her.

"Oh no," Mary said. "Paige?"

Tess nodded. "My poor girl is heartbroken. She liked Josh so much, and their breakup hit her hard."

Mary wondered if Paige was suspicious that Josh had mugged Anthony. Or maybe he'd even confessed it to her. Mary still didn't have any definitive proof, other than Anthony's eyewitness statement and the neon-green shoelace connection to the cross-country team. "What happened?"

Tess shrugged her shoulders. "Paige said that he just stopped calling her and avoided her at school. Now she alternates between blaming herself or stating that she's better off without him."

"It's possible the latter may be true," Mary said carefully, not wanting to reveal too much. Now that the couple wasn't together anymore, she didn't feel obligated to share her suspicions about him. She'd hate to start a rumor that later turned out to be untrue, even though her instincts told her that Josh was involved in Anthony's mugging.

"I tend to think so." Tess picked up a cleaning rag and began wiping down the counter around her. "They're both so young, and we really don't know that much about him. Besides, next week, she'll probably be madly in love with another boy and we can start the drama cycle all over again."

Mary chuckled. "I remember those days, but they grow out of it."

"Promise?" Tess said with a grin. Then she picked up the recipe. "I think I'm going to cheer myself up by making a sample batch of your cranberry ice cream with white chocolate chunks."

"Good idea. I'm anxious to hear what you think."

Mary left the ice-cream shop while Tess was gathering up the ingredients she needed to make her newest ice-cream recipe.

As she stepped outside, Mary pulled her phone out of her handbag, realizing that she should give Chief McArthur an update. She searched for the phone number to the police station in her contact list and was just about to press the dial button when she suddenly changed her mind.

The chief probably still had his hands full with roadblocks and smashed pumpkins. She could update him *after* she talked to Josh.

Mary was about to drop the phone back into her purse when it rang. Lizzie's name and phone number appeared on the screen. She smiled and answered it right away. "Hello there."

"Hi, Mom. How are you?"

"Good," Mary replied, stepping out from beneath a tree and into the sunshine. "Even better now that I'm talking to you."

Mary loved talking to her daughter and could do it every day of the week if Lizzie wasn't so busy with her children, Emma and Luke, and her husband, Chad. "What's new with you?"

"Well, I just found out that Adam Sullivan is going to be performing in Ivy Bay. Why didn't you tell me?"

Mary smiled into the phone. "I thought you'd gotten over your crush on him years ago. Does Chad know?"

Lizzie laughed. "Very funny, Mom. I love Adam Sullivan now for his talent, not his face, although he's still very handsome."

"I know. I got to meet him on Monday night."

"Are you still joking around or are you serious?" Lizzie asked.

"I'm completely serious. Your aunt Betty is going to perform at the concert, and I attended a rehearsal meeting with her. Adam was there, and we both got to speak with him."

"Wow, I'm so jealous." She chuckled. "But don't tell Chad."

Mary laughed, well aware that Lizzie only had eyes for her handsome and fun-loving husband.

"So what is Aunt Betty going to do at the concert?"

"Play the piano." Mary bit her lip. "Actually, I'm a little concerned about that. She's rusty after not playing for so many years, and that, combined with her rheumatoid arthritis, is causing some difficulty for her."

"Oh, you know Aunt Betty," Lizzie said. "She'll excel at this just like she does everything else. I wish I was half as talented as her."

Mary sensed that her daughter might feel differently if she'd heard Betty play. But Lizzie did have a point. Betty seemed to excel at everything she touched, from her flair for decorating to her green thumb to her taste in clothes. The piano would probably be no exception, especially since she'd perfected it in the past.

"And now that I know that my aunt is going to be performing," Lizzie continued, "as well as my favorite opera star, I *have* to be there. Can you get us two tickets? I'll reimburse you."

"Of course." Mary felt a thrill of anticipation at seeing her daughter soon. "And the tickets will be my treat. Will you bring the kids with you?"

"I don't think so. Chad's parents have been wanting to have them over, and it just hasn't worked out. I'm sure they'd be thrilled to watch them the evening of the concert. We may even have them stay the night there since we'll be getting home late."

"Why don't you and Chad stay with us?" Mary suggested. Now that Katie was staying at the cabin, the guest room was free again. "You know we have plenty of room."

"We just might do that. It's been a while since we've gone anywhere without the kids."

Joy rippled through Mary, thrilled at the prospect of spending time with her daughter. She wished her grandkids were coming too, but she knew how much Chad's parents would enjoy them. "If you come to the concert, you'll get to meet Katie."

"Who's Katie?"

The question made Mary realize how long it had been since they'd last talked. "Well, it's a long story." Then she began to tell her daughter all about the mystery woman in Ivy Bay.

SIXTEEN

———◆◆◆———

Later that afternoon, Mary made her way to Roger Foley's house. She'd sent him a wedding card shortly after his nuptials, so she knew the address. As she headed south on Water Street, she checked her watch. The high school had let out for the day, and she could see some kids walking along the sidewalks, backpacks slung over their shoulders.

Roger's house was a two-story bungalow with a wraparound porch and gray stone chimney. The front door was open, and she could see the glow of a television through the old-fashioned screen door. When she pulled up to the curb, Mary spotted Josh half reclined in the front porch swing, a pair of headphones in his ears and a green backpack under his feet.

She parked the car and then took a deep breath, knowing this conversation wouldn't be easy. She was a stranger to Josh, but she feared that if she didn't talk to him now, he might clam up—or even lawyer up—before she had a chance to ask him about Katie.

As Mary approached the house, Josh seemed oblivious to her presence. He gently swayed on the swing, his eyes closed as he listened to the MP3 player in his hand. He wore blue jeans and a red T-shirt, along with a pair of white tennis shoes—no black hoodie or green shoelaces today.

Mary climbed the porch stairs, and his green eyes opened, staring at her for a long moment. Then he tugged on the thin cord of his earbuds, pulling them loose from his ears. "Mom," he shouted toward the screen door. "Some lady is here to see you."

"Actually," Mary said, walking toward the swing, "I'm here to see you."

His dark eyebrows drew together as he stared at her. "Do I know you?"

"No...," she began and then turned when she heard the screen door open behind her.

Diana Foley, her ash-blonde hair pulled back in a ponytail, stepped onto the porch. Both her oversized, chambray shirt and her blue jeans were dotted with fresh white paint stains and Mary could see paint under her fingernails as well.

"Hello, Mary," Diana said with a smile.

Mary had wanted to talk to Josh alone, but maybe it was best if his mother was here.

"If you're looking for Roger," Diana continued, "he just left for Jimmy's Hardware to buy some more paint." Diana looked down at her clothes. "As you can see, we've got a project going, but knowing my husband, he won't be back for a while. He and Jimmy always have a lot to talk about."

Josh sat up on the swing. "The lady said she came here to see me."

"Mrs. Fisher," Diana corrected him.

Josh rolled his eyes. "*Mrs. Fisher* said she's here to talk to me."

"Oh?" Diana turned to Mary.

Mary took a deep breath. "This is rather difficult, but Anthony Cantuccio was mugged last week, and I think Josh might have some information about it."

"Why me?" Josh asked, his voice belligerent.

Mary turned and looked at him for a long moment. He slunk back onto the swing, not quite meeting her eyes.

"Josh?" Diana walked toward her son, her eyes full of concerned dismay. "What's going on?"

He shrugged his narrow shoulders. "I don't know."

"I think you do know," his mother said, her voice firmer now. "I thought you wanted to make a new start here. That once you stopped hanging around with those boys back at your old high school in Boston, you might be able to stay out of trouble."

Anger flashed in his green eyes. "Why do you always believe other people instead of me?" He waved one hand toward Mary. "You don't even know her, and you believe her."

Diana closed her eyes and sighed. Then she turned to Mary. "Is there proof my son did it?"

"Anthony described his mugger as wearing a black hoodie, black jeans, and tennis shoes with neon-green shoelaces. The shoelaces were special ordered for the cross-country team. Apparently, no store in Ivy Bay carries them."

"I know," Diana said, her voice strained as she looked over at her son. "We paid for the uniform and the shoelaces." Then her face cleared. "But he couldn't have done it. The cross-country team had a meet in Hyannis last Wednesday. Isn't that when Anthony was mugged?"

Mary's heart hurt for the woman next to her. It was bad enough that her son had probably committed this crime, but he'd lied to her about the meet too. "I talked to Coach Stover today." She heard Josh angrily mutter something under his breath but didn't let that stop her. Diana needed to know the truth—for her sake and for Josh most of all. "The coach said that Josh wasn't allowed to go to the meet because of academic problems in one of his classes."

Diana slowly turned to her son. "Josh? Is this true?"

A muscle flexed in his cheek, his gaze fixed on the porch floor. "Yes," he bit out.

A spasm of anguish crossed her face. "Why didn't you tell me?"

"I don't know," he mumbled. "You weren't going to make it to the meet because you had a bad cold, so I figured I could bring my grade up in Algebra and you wouldn't even have to know."

Diana's face hardened. "Did the school send a letter about it?" she asked, sounding as if she'd been down this road before.

"Yeah," he said quietly, still not looking at his mother. "I got it out of the mailbox before you could see it."

Diana covered her face with her hands and heaved a long sigh before looking at her son again. "And Anthony Cantuccio?"

Josh bit his lower lip. "It was an accident."

"Oh, Josh," Diana said, exasperated.

His head shot up. "No, really! I couldn't come home after school because you thought I was in Hyannis, so I decided to go for a long run. I figured that way I'd at least be in shape for my next meet. It was starting to get dark, and I was changing the song on my MP3 while I ran on the trail. The next thing I knew, I ran right into this older guy. He flew forward and hit the ground."

Josh raked one hand through his shaggy hair. "I don't know why I took his shopping bag. It was a mistake." He stared at his mother, his eyes imploring her to believe him. "I wanted to turn around and take the bag back to him, but I was scared. So I just stuffed it under my bed when I got home that night, and I haven't looked at it since."

Diana just shook her head. "Oh, Josh."

"It's true," he insisted, throwing his hands in the air. "I hate what happened. I lost my girlfriend because of it."

Diana blinked. "Paige knew?"

"No, and I figured if she ever found out, she'd probably dump me. Paige is...wonderful. And smart. I knew she'd never understand how I could do something so dumb, and I didn't want to lie to her. So I broke it off."

Diana sighed. "Do you realize you could lose a lot more than a girlfriend because of this? What you did was a *crime*."

Tears flooded his eyes. "I really did run into Mr. Cantuccio. I just wasn't paying attention." His hands clenched into fists. "I don't know why I did something so stupid. It was a mistake, Mom. I mean it."

Mary's heart hurt for both of them. Despite Josh's behavior, he seemed sincerely sorry. Or was it just an act? She thought about Katie. Mugging two people, if that's what happened, was more than a mistake.

She needed to tread carefully, though, since she had no proof that he even knew Katie. "Josh, can you tell me what you were doing last Tuesday?"

"Tuesday?" he echoed, looking perplexed by the question.

Diana turned to her. "We were at a funeral for my great-aunt in Boston last Tuesday. We actually left on Sunday night to help with the preparations. Why?"

Mary couldn't help but breathe a sigh of relief. Maybe Josh was being truthful about accidentally running into Anthony and then making a series of stupid decisions after that happened. "I'm just trying to put it all together."

Diana nodded, too distracted by her son's situation to process Mary's answer. She looked over at Josh. "Son, I think we need to go to the police."

Fear flashed in his eyes. "Mom, no!"

"Chief McArthur has been working on a case with me," Mary said gently, "and we thought Anthony's mugging might be connected to it. Now that I know it's not, I think you should talk to him, Josh. The chief is a fair man. And he'll be more impressed if you turn yourself in than if he has to chase you down."

"She's right," Diana said, walking over to her son and laying a hand on his shoulder. "I'll go with you."

He hung his head. "What will Roger think?"

Mary could tell by his tone that Roger's opinion was important to him. That was a good sign, Mary thought to herself. A man like Roger could be a good example for a boy.

"He'll think we're a family and we stand by one another, even during the tough times," his mother said gently. "Especially during the tough times."

Josh gave a slow nod. "Okay. I'll probably feel better no matter what happens to me." He met his mother's gaze. "Can I apologize to Mr. Cantuccio too?"

"I think that's a good idea," Diana replied. She looked over at Mary. "Thank you. I appreciate you coming here today."

"You're welcome," Mary said. "Josh is doing the right thing. I have a feeling everything will turn out all right."

Diana gave her a small smile. "I hope so."

Mary took her leave, praying for Josh and his family. The story he'd told about running into Anthony actually fit Anthony's story as well. Only Josh could know for sure if it was an accident or intentional, but she was confident that Chief McArthur would sort it all out.

She drove a few blocks away from the Foley house and then parked again to make a call to the police station. She was pleasantly surprised to find him there.

"McArthur," he barked into the phone after one of the officers transferred her call.

"It's Mary Fisher. I just wanted to update you about Anthony's mugging."

"Oh, hello, Mary. What did you find out?"

"Well, I did a little digging on my own," she explained, "and narrowed down the suspect list to Roger Foley's new stepson. He's about sixteen and his name is Josh Durant."

"Durant?" he echoed. "Is that the kid who's dating the Bailey girl?"

Mary smiled at the question. In a small town, even the police chief knew who the local teenagers were dating. "Yes, although he broke it off with her. I think the guilt was eating him up."

"Sounds like she might be better off," he said gruffly. "Hey, can you spell the kid's last name for me?"

Mary recalled the team roster that Coach Stover had given her. "It's d u r a n t."

"Got it," the chief said. "Good work, Mary. I'll send over a squad car to pick him up for questioning."

"Actually," Mary said, "that won't be necessary. When I talked to Josh, he said he was planning to come to the station and turn himself in."

"And you believe him?"

"Yes," she said without hesitation. "Especially because his mom, Diana, was there at the time and is none too happy with him. She'll make sure he gets there."

"Okay, good to know."

She heard the rustling of papers over the line. Then he cleared his throat.

"If the kid really is remorseful and makes restitution, then he'll most likely be placed on probation. I'll get in touch with Anthony and let him know. He's got some medical bills from the incident that will need to be paid too."

Mary felt bad that Roger and Diana had to weather this kind of storm so early in their marriage, but sometimes it brought a couple even closer together. But she also breathed a small sigh of relief for the boy, believing in second chances. She just hoped Josh took advantage of it.

A few minutes later, Mary walked into the shop to find Rebecca helping a customer and Katie straightening books on the shelves. She tucked her purse into a cubbyhole behind the front counter and quickly flipped through the mail and the notes near her computer. There was nothing urgent that needed her attention, so she walked over to Katie and started helping her straighten up the bookshelves.

Katie smiled. "You must have a busy schedule today. I've hardly seen you."

"It's been eventful," Mary said. "One thing I learned is that Anthony Cantuccio's mugger is planning to turn himself into the police."

Katie's eyes widened as she looked at Mary. "And?"

Mary shook her head. "And it turns out that he couldn't have caused your head injury. He has an airtight alibi for last Tuesday."

Mary was expecting Katie to be disappointed, but instead she just gave a small shrug. "Well, I guess I'll just have to keep waiting for the Dinsdales to return for the concert. At least I can be certain that I'll know who I am by next week."

Mary pulled out a book by Anne Perry that had been shelved with the J section and put it back in the P section. Katie might be resigned to waiting another week to discover her identity, but Mary wasn't ready to give up.

SEVENTEEN

❖◆❖

"I can't figure this one out." Ashley sat on a stool at the front counter, nibbling on the end of her pencil. School had let out early on this Thursday afternoon, and Ashley's dad had dropped her off at the bookshop.

Mary looked up from the invoices in front of her. The shop had been hopping, keeping Rebecca and Katie busy helping locate books while Mary worked the cash register. Things were much calmer now, but there was still a steady flow of customers in and out of the door.

"Figure what out?" Mary leaned over to look at Ashley's paper.

Until a few minutes ago, Ashley had been busy reading to Marnie Reid's children, keeping them occupied so Marnie could browse in the adult book section. The two toddlers had laughed at the voices Ashley had used for the characters, and they had chased Gus around the children's nook until Ashley had kindly but firmly told them to stop. Then she'd held Gus in her arms and taught the children how to pet him gently, without tugging on his ears or tail.

"Our teacher gave us a puzzle," Ashley said, sliding the paper closer to Mary. "We're supposed to move the letters around to form new words or something." Ashley scowled. "I don't understand."

The work sheet was entitled "Brain Food," which made Mary smile. "Well, these types of puzzles are called word scrambles. That's when letters in a word are all mixed up and you have to rearrange them to find the word. There are ten word scrambles on your work sheet, and the first one has the letters *k, c, a,* and *e.*" Mary slid the paper back in front of Ashley. "What word can you make if you rearrange the letters?"

Ashley frowned at the work sheet, deep in thought. Then she shook her head. "I don't know."

Mary reached for a piece of scrap paper. "Why don't you try writing it out? Just keep moving the letters around in different combinations until you discover the word."

Ashley copied down the letters from the first puzzle on the work sheet and then started rearranging them, putting the letters in different orders. The tip of her tongue peeked out one corner of her mouth as she worked. Soon her head popped up. "It's *cake!*"

"That's right," Mary said. "Good job. Now, can you figure out the next one?"

Ashley began playing with those letters, and it only took her a few seconds to figure it out. "*Cheese!*" she cried, a big smile on her face.

Mary laughed. "I think you've got it."

Now that Ashley was getting the hang of it, the words came fast and furious. *Carrot. Milk. Lemon. Ham.* "This is fun," Ashley said as she deciphered the next puzzle. "I wish there were more."

Mary liked word puzzles too. She liked to try her hand at crossword puzzles on occasion and even attempted acrostics once in a while. When they were preteens, Mary and Betty had tried to develop their own secret code so they could send messages to each other that no one else could understand. They'd given simple words new meanings, which often resulted in stilted messages that were difficult to understand. After a while, they'd given up on their secret code and moved on to other things.

She smiled at the memory. Then she thought of the note that Katie had found in her pocket. *Katie, Arrive at Mary's Bookshop at 1:12.*

She frowned as she thought about it. Why not write "Meet me at Mary's Bookshop at 1:12" or "Come to Mary's Bookshop at 1:12"? Either one of those would have sounded more natural. So why use the word *arrive*? And, she questioned once again, why the unusual time of 1:12?

Unless the note was trying to convey more than was obvious at first glance. Could it be some kind of secret code, with another message embedded in the letters?

A tingle of excitement shot through her. Is this what she'd been missing? A clue about Katie that had been there from the beginning?

Ashley continued to work on her puzzles, completely unaware that she'd just opened a new avenue into the mystery of Katie. Mary looked up to see Katie chatting with Simon Rafferty in front of the shelf of classic mysteries.

Her cranky neighbor could be gruff at times, but to Mary's surprise, Simon was actually smiling at Katie. She watched as Katie picked up a book by Rex Stout, featuring his famous fictional detective Nero Wolfe, and handed it to Simon. Then the two of them headed for the front counter.

"Did you find something?" Mary asked, moving to the cash register.

"I guess so." He frowned as he pulled his wallet out of his back pocket. "The price is pretty steep though."

"It's worth it," Katie told him. "I started reading the Nero Wolfe books last week, and I just can't get enough of him. I think you'll really like this one."

His gaze narrowed on Mary as she rang up the sale. "Can I return the book if I don't like it?"

Customers rarely asked her that question, although it didn't surprise her coming from Simon. He had a reputation as a miser around town, which made it even more impressive that Katie had convinced him to buy a brand-new book. "You can exchange it for a different book," she offered. "But I think you'll like it too."

He gave a little snort of disagreement but paid her cash for the purchase and headed for the door.

"Let me know what you think of the story," Katie called after him. Then she turned to Mary and grinned. "I think that's what you call a tough customer."

"Simon can be...difficult."

"The poor guy," Katie said, watching as he walked past the window. "He told me he lives alone. Maybe he's lonely."

Something in Katie's voice conveyed that she knew exactly how he felt. Even though Katie was surrounded by her new friends, Mary was certain that she longed to be around people who really knew her.

"Well, you did a good deed," Mary said. "Books can bring all kinds of new and interesting friends into our lives."

Katie grinned. "That reminds me. Now that things have quieted down here, I have a date with Hercule Poirot by the fireplace."

Mary laughed. "Well, before you go, I have a favor to ask."

"Name it."

"May I make a copy of the note you had in your pocket the day you came here?"

"Sure." Katie reached into her pocket and pulled out the note. She'd been keeping it with her constantly, so now it was so crumpled that Mary had to smooth it out on top of the counter before taking it over to the scanner.

Before Katie could ask Mary why she wanted it, Rebecca emerged from the back room where she'd been opening the new shipment of books that had just come in. "That took longer than I thought." She took a seat next to her daughter. "So what's going on out here?"

Ashley held up her work sheet with a triumphant smile. "I just finished my homework."

"Hooray," Rebecca said, reaching over to give her a hug.

"And I just managed to sell a wonderful book to Simon Rafferty," Katie announced, prompting applause from both Rebecca and Ashley. She gave a mock bow.

Rebecca turned toward the scanner. "How about you, Mary? Anything to celebrate?"

"Not yet," she said, pressing the Scan button on the machine. "But I'm working on it."

———

Later that evening, Mary sat on the sofa in her living room with Katie's note in one hand and a yellow legal pad in the other. Gus lay curled up beside her and slept. Every once in a while, one of his paws twitched, making her believe that he was dreaming of playing with a mouse. He had a stuffed mouse to play with at home and more toys at the shop, but something told her that he probably didn't feel that was as good as the real thing.

"How's it going?" Betty asked, walking into the room. She rubbed her hands together, massaging them, and then began to do individual finger stretches, slowly moving them back and forth.

"Slow," Mary said. She set down the legal pad and the pencil she'd been holding. "The more I work on this, the more I'm convinced it's some kind of code or riddle. I just haven't been able to figure it out yet."

"Well, keep trying." Betty headed toward the piano. "You'll get it eventually."

Mary hoped so. She was still trying to figure out the reason why the note would be a riddle or a code in the first place. Was it a game of some kind? A message for a secret rendezvous? Perhaps even something criminal?

She shook her head at that thought, realizing it might be a stretch. But the note still intrigued her. What did it mean? And what would it mean when she finally decoded it?

Betty sat down at the piano and began to play a series of scales.

"How's the song coming?" Mary asked her.

"A little better, I think," Betty said. "It helps to play an easier song first to warm up." She reached for a piece of sheet music and set it in front of her. Then she began to play.

The tune was instantly familiar to Mary and made her want to sing along. It was an oldie but a goodie called "A Wink and a Smile." Mary found herself smiling at the feel-good song and humming along with the music. Even Gus didn't seem to mind it as he cracked open his eyes and looked in the direction of the piano as if it were his archenemy.

"That's pretty good," Mary said as Betty ended the song. There had been a few errors and finger fumbles, but none that had made her wince. "Maybe you should play that one at the concert."

Betty shook her head as she shifted the sheet music in front of her. "Oh, I could never do that. It's too simple. People expect a lot more at a concert like this. Those tickets aren't cheap."

Then Betty dove into "Rondo alla Turca." Gus stiffened beside Mary, then bounded off the sofa and out of the living room. Mary was almost tempted to follow him, but she stayed put through the entire excruciating piece, wincing more than once at some of the wrong notes.

When Betty was finished, she turned to Mary. "Better, don't you think?"

Mary hesitated, not sure what to say. "It does sound better than before," she answered truthfully. "But are you sure you'll be ready to play it for the concert?"

"Only if I keep practicing," Betty said and started to play the song once more.

Mary picked up the legal pad, trying to turn her attention back to the puzzle in front of her.

After more than a dozen rounds of "Rondo alla Turca," she still couldn't figure it out. Her legal pad was full of letters and words from the note, all in different combinations, but nothing made sense.

Part of her dilemma was deciding whether to use the first word in the note, *Katie*, in deciphering the code or riddle. Perhaps that was simply a greeting and wasn't supposed to be part of the puzzle. She sighed, deciding to keep trying it both ways. Eventually, she'd figure it out, she told herself. "I think I can. I think I can," she said out loud.

"Did you say something?" Betty asked, stopping in midsong.

Mary scribbled out a series of words that was leading her nowhere. "I was just talking to myself. Go ahead and keep playing."

Betty closed the cover over the keyboard. "Actually, I think I'll stop for the night. I'm a little tired and sore. I don't want to overdo it."

Mary glanced at the clock, surprised to see that it was after ten. "Going to bed?"

Betty nodded. "I think I will. How about you?"

"Soon. I want to work on this a little while longer."

After Betty left the room, Mary stretched out on the sofa, her head propped against a pillow. A few minutes later, Gus padded into the room and resumed his spot on the sofa beside her, his tail flicking onto the legal pad.

Mary removed the word *Katie* from the mix and played with the letters in front of her, trying to make them come together into something meaningful. Gus's tail kept moving back and forth across the page in a way that was almost hypnotic. Her eyelids drifted shut and her head drooped. She caught herself nodding off and finally decided that it was time for bed.

She reached for the legal pad, Gus's tail now covering half of her scribbled combinations.

Then she saw it.

His tail had blocked out a few of the letters, leaving only the letters uncovered that formed the word *tomas*. She sat up on the sofa, unceremoniously dislodging Gus from his place beside her. He hopped off the sofa and moved underneath the coffee table, as if he needed to protect himself from any more sudden movements.

Mary grabbed her pencil and copied down the words from the note again. Only this time, she had an idea in mind. She began to circle different letters to test out her theory and grew even more excited when they fit the words she was trying to spell. Tomas was the first name of a new mystery author who was receiving raves from all the reviewers. His last name was Hooks and his debut novel was called *A River Apart*.

So the *A* from the word *Arrive* was the first word of the title. The remaining five letters comprised the word *River*. The letter *a* from *at* could be used to start the word *Apart*. Then she added the letter *p* from *Bookshop*, the letters *a* and *r* from *Mary*, and the letter *t* from the second *at*. The rest of the letters fell into place to form the message: "A River Apart by Tomas Hooks 1:12."

Mary tapped her pencil against the legal pad. Since *A River Apart* was a novel, then *1:12* must refer to something in the book. Was it a sentence on the first page, twelfth line? Or the first chapter, the twelfth page? Or even page 112?

She rose to her feet, so tempted to hop in her car and drive to the shop to check it out. But it was late, and she was tired. She'd already nodded off once tonight. Despite the short distance to the shop, Mary didn't want to risk falling asleep at the wheel.

"Let's go to bed, Gus," she said, picking up the legal pad and the note, and heading for her room. "We'll find the answer in the morning."

The next day, Mary couldn't wait to tell Katie what she'd discovered. She'd even resisted looking in the Hooks's novel until Katie arrived at the shop, wanting to share the moment with her. It was a real test of her willpower, and when Katie walked through the door, Mary didn't waste a second telling her the unscrambled message.

Katie stared at her. "I don't get it."

Mary hadn't told her about the note possibly comprising a riddle or puzzle. She'd been vague yesterday when Katie had questioned why she'd wanted a copy, just replying that she wanted to compile all the information about her into one place. Mary wasn't trying to keep secrets from her; she just didn't want to get the girl's hopes up only to see them dashed again.

Mary brought out her copy of the note. "When I saw Ashley trying to solve one of her word puzzles yesterday, it made me think about your note, especially the odd wording and the specific time. So I wondered if it might be some kind of riddle or puzzle itself. I made a copy to take home with me and spent all night trying to figure it out, but I think I finally did."

Katie dug the original note out of her pocket. "You mean this is some kind of clue?"

"It could be. Here, let me show you." Mary reached for a piece of paper, then wrote down the words on the note, leaving out the handwritten word *Katie*. Then she began to circle the letters like she had done the night before, to show Katie how they formed the message, along with telling her about the possible meanings of the 1:12.

"That's amazing," Katie said, breathlessly. "I think I've seen that book on the shelf."

"You have." Mary walked over to the counter and pulled it from a cubbyhole. "I took it off the shelf this morning when I arrived, but I've been waiting for you before looking inside." She handed the book to Katie. "It's all yours."

Katie stared at it for a long moment, then looked up at Mary. "Where should we start?"

"Wherever you want."

Katie shrugged. "Okay, let's start with what's easy—page 112." Then she opened the book and thumbed through pages until she reached page 112. Tucked deep in the crease of the book was a small piece of folded yellow paper.

"Something tells me that may be our next clue," Mary said as Katie pulled it free.

Katie opened the paper and read the words written on it. "Meet Alfonso Denali at the gallery."

"Is there a time?" Mary asked, leaning over her shoulder to look at the note.

"No." Katie wrinkled her brow. "Is the gallery that art place across the street from Cape Cod Togs?"

"Yes." Mary checked her watch as Rebecca walked into the bookshop. "And it opened five minutes ago."

———

Five minutes later, Mary and Katie were walking through the door of the gallery, setting off a tiny melodic chime. The gallery displayed several high-quality art pieces and was housed in an old restored Victorian. The venue added to the charm of the place, and Mary enjoyed going there to view the portraits and sculptures, even though most of them were way out of her price range.

Mary looked around the large, open space, wondering if coming here was a fool's errand. Whoever had left that note in the Hooks's novel must have expected Katie to find it on that Tuesday, not ten days later. Her intention not to let Katie get her hopes up only to have them crushed could fail if this turned out to be another dead end.

Mason Willoughby appeared at the top of the curved staircase, leaning over the railing just far enough to see them at the front entrance. He began to descend, wearing a light blue artist's smock and a pair of black denim jeans. He was usually more formally attired, but Mary thought he must be working on a project.

Mason was a painter in his own right and loved to talk about the craft and the many paintings that filled his gallery.

He had a small studio upstairs and had shown Mary some of his work in the past.

"Hello there, Mary," he said, the smile on his face revealing a perfect row of unnaturally white teeth. "You're here bright and early this morning." Then his gaze moved to Katie. "And I see you brought a friend." He cocked his head to one side, his gaze moving over Katie's face. "You have lovely features. Would you be interested in modeling for me?"

"I . . . don't know," she said, glancing at Mary.

"This is Katie," Mary told him. "We're actually here on somewhat of an urgent mission."

He arched a brow. "Well, that certainly sounds intriguing. What kind of mission?"

"We were wondering if you know someone by the name of Alfonso Denali."

He smiled. "I know him very well."

EIGHTEEN

❖◆❖

I n fact," Mason continued, "I believe that Denali is a hidden treasure as an artist."

"So he's an artist?" Katie said, looking a little perplexed. "Does he live in Ivy Bay?"

"Oh no," Mason told her. "I'm afraid he's not living anywhere. He passed away about sixty years ago in Paris at the age of ninety-four. What's so fascinating about his life is that his later years were his most productive. He dabbled in art as a young man, but after he married and had six children, he worked long hours as a farm laborer to support his family."

As Mason spoke about the artist, Mary thought about the clue. At first, she was disappointed to hear that Denali wasn't in Ivy Bay, but now she realized this was even better. Katie wasn't supposed to meet a person at the gallery. She was supposed to meet an artist—or more specifically—one of his paintings. That's probably where they'd find the next clue.

"Some in the art world say that Denali's experience as a common laborer is reflected in the stark realism of his work," Mason continued. "The scenes almost jump off the canvas."

Mary hurried to interject, aware that Mason could talk about art and artists for a very long time if a person let him. "May we see some of his paintings?"

"Of course," Mason said, turning to his left. "I know you'll fall in love with them. Just follow me."

Katie moved closer to Mary as he led them through the gallery. "Do you think the next clue is on one of his paintings?" she asked in a hushed voice.

Mary nodded, glad to see they were on the same page. "It has to be, doesn't it? Why else would the clue lead us here?"

Mason slowed his steps as they reached a display of oil paintings near the back of the gallery. "Here are the Denalis." He pointed to a painting of a farmer tending his grapevines. "As you can see, it's the detail in his work that makes it so enthralling. The perspiration on the laborer's brow. The callused hands. The way he crinkles his eyes against the glare of the sun."

Mary studied the painting, impressed with the work. Mason was right—the image did practically jump off the canvas. "Is this set in France?"

"Yes." Mason folded his arms loosely across his chest. "Denali spent most of his life in the Normandy region, and this painting depicts one of the local vineyards there."

Mary moved closer to it, her gaze moving over the canvas and the frame. She wasn't sure where the clue would be. Better to see all the Denali works and then let Mason know the reason they were there.

"As you can see, Denali did a series of three vineyard paintings." Mason motioned to the two other framed paintings. Then he moved a few steps away in front of another large painting. "Here is one of my favorite pieces in the entire gallery." He smiled at Mary. "I'm sure you can see why."

She looked at the painting. A man stood next to a large buhrstone with an open bag of corn in his arms. His shoulders were bent from the weight of the bag, and several of the kernels had fallen on the floor in front of him. There was something familiar about this painting.

She looked at Mason. "Is that the Hopkins-Emerson Gristmill?"

"Good eye," he said. "This one depicts a scene from the early twentieth century."

"So Denali was in Ivy Bay at one time?" Mary asked, still staring at the painting. The way the artist used shadow and light gave the painting a dark, brooding quality.

"He did spend some time here," Mason affirmed. "He'd achieved some success with his art at the turn of the century and had the money to travel. According to what I've read about him, Cape Cod was one of his favorite destinations."

Katie stepped closer to the painting, her gaze moving slowly over it. "Do you mind if we look at the back?"

Mason blinked. "What?"

Mary smiled, understanding his confusion. "I know it sounds like a strange request, but we have a good reason for it. You see Katie has amnesia—"

"Oh," Mason interjected, nodding his head. "So you're the one I've been hearing about. I've never met anyone with amnesia." He lowered his voice a notch. "Can you tell me what it's like? I know that may sound rather rude, but it must be fascinating in a way—not to remember anything about your life."

Katie hesitated for a long moment before she replied. "I'm not sure *fascinating* is the word I would use. Most of the time, I just feel confused. I don't really understand amnesia either." She gave a slight shrug. "I mean, once my memory returns, will I feel like the same person as I do now?"

Now Mason looked even more intrigued. "Does the painting have something to do with your amnesia?"

"We think it might be connected to figuring out her identity," Mary explained. She told him about the note and the clue in the mystery novel at her store.

"So that's why you asked if I knew Denali," Mason said, putting it all together. "You didn't know he was an artist. You thought he might have been waiting here for Katie."

Mary nodded. "That's right. And now we think the third clue might be attached to one of his paintings."

He turned to the painting of the gristmill and placed his hands on the frame. "Well, let's take a look." Mason lifted the painting off the wall, then slowly turned so that Mary and Katie could view the back of it.

"There's nothing there," Katie said with a frown. She looked over at Mary. "The clue must be attached to one of the other paintings."

"We can look at those too," Mason said, putting the painting back on the wall.

As Mary watched him remove the series of vineyard paintings for inspection, she began to believe the clue might not be another note. She looked at the painting of the Hopkins-Emerson Gristmill again. Denali had obviously been inside it sometime during his travels to Cape Cod. The depiction was too accurate to have come from a photograph.

Although it was no longer a working mill, it was now open on weekends as a tourist attraction. It would be easy for someone to plant a clue there.

Mason put the last of the vineyard paintings back on the wall. "It looks like whoever sent you here didn't manage to leave another clue."

"I think he did," Mary said, looking over at Katie. Then she pointed to the painting. "And I think it's at the mill."

As they drove to the Hopkins-Emerson Gristmill on Saturday, Mary gave Katie a brief history about it. "It's been in existence since the mid-seventeenth century. My sister was married to Edward Emerson, and it's been in his family for generations. It was called the Emerson Gristmill until recently. But the family learned that there was some dispute about its ownership, going back centuries. It's been resolved to the satisfaction of both parties and is now called the Hopkins-Emerson Gristmill. It's been restored recently, too, and turned into a tourist attraction."

"I wonder if I've been there before," Katie mused. "I don't have any memory of it, of course, but it seems a strange place to leave a clue."

"Stranger than inside a book or at an art gallery?" Mary asked as the road crossed through the marsh.

Katie smiled. "Good point. Especially since I don't know who sent me on this scavenger hunt or why. I'm curious to see what's at the end of it."

Mary was curious too. She still didn't understand why no one had come in search for Katie when they realized the clues weren't picked up. Perhaps whoever had planned the scavenger hunt didn't know that Katie hadn't embarked on it until now. It was even possible that the Dinsdales planned it, although she found that a little hard to imagine. Then again, she didn't really know Matthew Dinsdale. He might love to plan and execute this kind of game.

A small flock of salt-marsh sparrows soared over the front of the car as Mary rounded a curve. Then the Hopkins-Emerson Gristmill came into view. "There it is," Mary said, looking straight ahead at the historic site. "Seem familiar?"

She glanced over at Katie, who peered through the windshield as they approached the mill. The foundation was made of sturdy gray rocks, and the old-fashioned wheel, which used to tilt at an odd angle, now stood true and straight on its axis. The restoration had been costly, but worth it in Mary's estimation. The gristmill was a valuable piece of Ivy Bay history that needed to be cherished.

"No, it doesn't look familiar," Katie said, her voice hushed. "But it truly is lovely, isn't it? I can see why Alfonso Denali decided to set one of his paintings here."

Water ran from a large pond, down a raceway and past the mill to turn the waterwheel. The way the waterwheel slowly turned under the clear blue sky was so quaint and peaceful. Sometimes it took Mary's breath away to imagine that this bucolic scene had been here for over three hundred years.

Mary parked her car in the small gravel lot that had been cleared on the other side of the road from the mill. "Shall we go inside?"

"Lead the way," Katie said, a note of eagerness in her voice. They crossed the road to the music of birds singing in the trees and the sound of falling water from the working waterwheel.

Once inside, they were greeted by Stephanie, a college intern from Suffolk University, who had been hired to give tours on Saturdays. "This place is so cool," Stephanie said, straightening the name tag on her gray jacket. "I've learned more about gristmills than I ever thought possible."

Mary liked the girl's bubbly enthusiasm. "We'd love to take a tour. I want to see every nook and cranny."

Stephanie grinned. "Then you've come to the right place, because there are plenty of nooks and crannies!" Then the young intern began to tell them all about the mill, taking them around both the outside of the mill and the inside.

Stephanie pointed out the keystone block that had been etched with the date of the gristmill's founding, 1667. She then went on to explain the way the waterwheel worked and how the mill operated to grind corn into cornmeal.

As they walked around the mill, both Mary and Katie searched for any sign of a potential clue. After their experience at the gallery, Mary knew that the clue might not be on a piece of paper.

When they reached the millstone, Mary went into high alert. This was the scene from the painting, which made it likely that the clue was somewhere nearby.

"The buhrstone, or millstone as it's more commonly called, is used for grinding the grain," Stephanie explained, "and we can find a reference to a millstone all the way back to the Bible. In fact, putting a millstone around someone's neck used to be a method of execution in biblical times. It was tied around the condemned prisoner's neck, and he was thrown into a lake or river."

Mary looked around the stone for any type of clue as Stephanie continued the history lesson.

"Millstones actually come in pairs. The top stone does the grinding, while the bottom stone is slightly convex so that the ground grain moves to the outer part of the stones where it can be collected by the workers."

Mary saw Katie looking high and low also, both of them only half listening to the intrepid intern. As Stephanie started to move on, Mary called out to her. "Do you mind if we just look around this part of the mill for a while? It's really captivated our attention."

Stephanie nodded. "Of course. Take all the time you'd like." She waved one hand in front of her face. "It's getting warm in here, isn't it? I'll run back to the office and get us some bottled water while you look around."

"Thanks," Mary told her, watching as Stephanie disappeared down the narrow hallway. Then she turned to Katie. "Why don't you take that side of the stone and I'll take this side? The clue has to be here somewhere."

"Good idea," Katie said, rounding the stone to examine the other side of the grinding room.

Mary took a step back, taking in the heavy wood beams spanning the ceiling as well as the original beams that were spaced about four feet apart on the refurbished walls. On closer inspection, she noticed that one of the beams had a deep knothole in it about the size of a half dollar coin. "Katie, come and look at this."

Katie hurried over to her. "What is it?"

Mary squeezed two fingers into the hole and touched what felt like a round paper tube. She pinched the edges between the tips of her fingers and pulled it out. "I think it might be just what we were looking for."

Then she handed it to Katie, letting her do the honors. Katie unrolled the paper and stared at it for several seconds. "It's a claim ticket to Strings & Things."

"What?" Mary took a look at it. Katie was right. The paper had the Strings & Things logo printed on the top, along with CLAIM TICKET. And the number 235 was written in bold black ink below.

"Now we know the next clue," Mary said, eager to be on her way to Strings & Things.

Stephanie returned to the grinding room carrying three water bottles. "Here you go," she said, handing them out.

"Thank you so much," Mary told her, appreciating the intern's kindness. "And thank you for giving us a great tour. I think we're going to take these water bottles to go, if you don't mind. We found what we came to see."

"Closed?" Katie cried, staring at the sign in the window of Strings & Things. "We've come this far and the music store is closed?"

The sign read Closed for Repairs and indicated that it would be open again on Monday morning. Mary's car sat in front of the shop, located in a century-old stone cottage. It was located on Water Street, just south of the Tanaka Florist and Garden Center. When she was little, the cottage had been the home to the mayor of Ivy Bay and still had the same white picket fence surrounding it that she remembered.

Katie pivoted in the passenger seat to look at her. "If my real life is this frustrating, I'm not sure I want to remember it." Then she chuckled. "This is almost getting comical. It's like I'm not supposed to find out who I am. At least not yet."

Mary had started to wonder the same thing. Was God's hand at work here? Leading Katie on her life journey with His own perfect timing?

Before she could reply, the front door of the shop opened and Roger Foley stepped out, a tool belt strapped around his waist. "We may get in there yet," Mary said, unbuckling her seat belt and stepping out of the car. Katie did the same, following Mary as she made her way toward Roger. He stood with his back to them as he locked the front door of the music store.

"Don't put your key away yet," Mary said, her tone light. She knew the chances were low that they could gain entrance to the building. Even if they did, she'd need to figure out their ticket system to find the item that was tagged as number 235. Still, she was willing to give it a shot.

Roger turned around and smiled when he saw her. He wore a royal-blue baseball cap with a Jimmy's Hardware logo on it, the brim frayed and worn. "Hello, Mary. What are you doing here?"

"Hoping you can let us inside," she said bluntly. "I'd tell you the whole story, Roger, but it's a long one and a little odd as well." Then she held up the claim ticket they'd found at the Hopkins-Emerson Gristmill. "We really just need to pick up something inside."

He shook his head. "I'm sorry, Mary. I'd love to help you, but they had a water leak here during that last rain, and they wanted me to check the electrical system. The ceiling isn't stable, so I can't let you in for your own safety and for insurance reasons."

She understood, even if she was disappointed.

"How much damage was there?" Katie asked, a hint of concern in her voice. No doubt she was thinking about the item waiting for them and how easily it would be for ink to run if a piece of paper got wet.

Mary closed her eyes, stifling a groan at the thought. They'd already come this far. *Please, Lord,* she prayed, *let us make it to the end. Even if we have to wait until Monday.*

"Looks like most of the damage was isolated to the ceiling tiles and the carpet," Roger said. "Darius was able to get all the instruments and other valuables into the back room, where there was no leak."

Mary saw a flash of relief on Katie's face. She hoped that whatever was attached to their claim ticket had made it into that storage room.

Roger turned to her. "By the way, Mary, I want to thank you. Diana told me about your visit to the house and your talk with Josh." He heaved a long sigh. "I think he's a good kid at heart, but he's developed some bad habits and lost his way a bit."

"I just met him," Mary said, "but that's the feeling I got about him too."

Roger nodded. "He turned himself into the police and made a full confession. It looks like he'll have to do a bunch of community-service hours, which will probably be the best thing for him." He hitched up his sagging tool belt. "Anthony Cantuccio was really good about the situation. When Josh gave him his apology, he forgave him and said he'd made some dumb mistakes as a teenage boy too."

Mary was happy to hear the saga of the neon-green shoelaces had a good ending. She just hoped that Josh used this opportunity to turn his life around. Judging by Roger's expression, he'd make sure that the boy did just that. "I'm so glad it turned out that way."

"Me too," he said, and then turned toward his truck. "Well, I'd better get back to work."

After they parted, Mary and Katie returned to the car. Mary sat in the driver's seat and watched Roger climb into his truck and drive off.

"It's not even noon yet," Mary said, looking at the clock on her dashboard. "Where do you want to go now? Back to your cabin or to the bookshop?"

"Let's go to the bookshop," Katie said without hesitation. "That place always makes me feel good. There's just something special about it." She breathed a wistful sigh. "You must love working there."

"I do," Mary said with a smile. "Especially when I get to meet people like you."

NINETEEN

◆━◆◆◆━◆

A fter church on Sunday, Mary and Katie took Henry up
on his offer to go for a ride on his fishing boat, the *Misty
Horizon*. The day was glorious, with the temperature in the
midseventies and a clear blue sky, and there was just a whisper
of a warm breeze. Henry made a point to sail past some of
the landmarks around Cape Cod, hoping something Katie
saw might jog her memory, but she didn't recognize anything.
After about an hour, Henry anchored the boat in the open
water and announced it was time to eat.

Mary had packed a picnic basket for lunch, and all
three of them now dined on cold fried chicken, coleslaw,
and the cherry pie that Betty had pulled out of the oven
just before they'd left for church that morning.

"I wish Betty had come with us," Katie said, licking
the last of the homemade cherry pie filling off her plastic
fork.

"Why didn't she?" Henry asked. "The more the merrier."

Mary dabbed at her mouth with a paper napkin. "We
almost had her talked into it, but she decided to stay home
and practice for the concert. It's coming up this Tuesday, you
know."

"I can't wait," Henry said. "We're still planning to go together, right?"

Mary nodded. "Yes, but let's just plan to meet at the community center. I told Betty I would drive her to the concert, and she needs to arrive two hours early for hair and makeup."

"Wow." Katie placed her empty plate and fork into the trash bag that Mary had brought. "Just thinking about it makes *me* nervous. I can imagine how Betty must feel."

The *Misty Horizon* bobbed gently in the water as a gray-and-white herring gull soared overhead. Katie leaned back in the captain's chair and stared up at the sky. "This is the life. I hope I'm a fisherman in my real life—or should I say fisherwoman?"

Henry chuckled. "Either way is fine by me, but a fisherman's life isn't too relaxing."

Katie sat up, her blue eyes curious. "Tell me what you do. What kind of fish do you catch?"

"Well," Henry began, "I sell mostly to local restaurants and merchants, so I usually cater to their needs. Now that fall is here, I've been fishing for striped bass and bluefin tuna. There's been a high demand for both."

Katie stretched her legs out in front of her, then kicked off her Top-Siders and wiggled her bare toes. "I think it sounds great."

"Better than working in the bookstore?" Mary teased before taking the last bite of her pie.

Katie smiled. "Now that would be a dilemma if I had to choose between the two. Maybe I'd decide to have the best of both worlds and have a floating bookshop."

Henry laughed, his sea-green eyes filled with amusement. Mary found herself staring at him a little too long. She looked away, her cheeks warm.

"Well, that would be something to see," Henry told Katie. "The problem might be getting your customers *off* the boat. Especially if it's as cozy as Mary's shop."

Mary was happy that Katie felt comfortable with them, but she knew that the girl wasn't where she was supposed to be. Somewhere, people were waiting for her. There could even be children waiting for her, although that thought made Mary's heart ache. Yet Katie hadn't been wearing a wedding ring when she'd appeared in Mary's bookshop. Not that such a thing meant a lot these days, but the fact that no one had reported Katie missing was a sign that she was probably single.

They spent the rest of the afternoon on the boat, getting plenty of sun and sharing plenty of laughter. Henry took photos of Mary and Katie with his cell phone, promising to e-mail them to Mary soon.

When they finally docked at the marina, Katie and Mary stepped onto the dock while Henry finished mooring the boat.

"I can't remember when I've had so much fun," Katie said with an impish smile. "Of course, I can't remember anything past twelve days ago, so there aren't a lot of memories to choose from."

Mary chuckled. "I had fun too. And *two* pieces of Betty's pie, believe it or not." She sighed. "I just couldn't resist."

"Henry's a cutie," Katie said, glancing over Henry. "So are you two an item?"

"No," Mary said, feeling a blush creep up her cheeks again. "We're just good friends."

Henry stepped off the boat and joined them on the dock. "I'll walk you to your car, ladies. Then I need to hightail it to church if I want to make it in time for the men's Bible study meeting."

"When did you start going?" Mary asked, since it was the first she'd heard of it.

"A week ago," he replied with a small shrug. "I don't have time to attend regularly, but I enjoyed it, so I plan to go whenever I get the chance."

Mary was about to reply when a yellow Labrador retriever pranced up to them. He wasn't full size and, judging by the way he was bouncing around the dock, he still had plenty of puppy left in him.

Katie leaned down to pet him. "Well, aren't you a doll?" she said, rubbing him behind his ears and collar.

Albert Curran approached them, a leash in his hand and a sheepish smile on his face. "Finn might be a doll, but he's a rambunctious one. I barely got my boat docked before he jumped off. At least he hit the dock instead of the water."

Mary had always liked Albert. He was married to Frances Curran, a member of Betty's book club.

"Well, he'd probably be all right even if he did hit the water," Katie said, rubbing the dog's ears. "Labs are excellent swimmers." Then her hands stilled on the dog's head and her brow crinkled. She gently pulled one of his ears back so she could see the skin inside. "Looks like Finn has ear mites."

"He does?" Albert moved closer, leaning down to inspect the dog's ears. "You mean those white spots on the skin?"

"Yes." Katie carefully inspected Finn's other ear. "They're in both ears. That might be why he's so wired. They can cause intense itching."

Albert reached up and scratched his ear. "Are they contagious?"

Katie laughed. "No, don't worry. They're only contagious among dogs and cats, not people."

Mary stared at her, aware that Katie didn't even realize how she sounded. *Like a doctor*, Mary thought to herself. Just like she'd suspected before. Her only mistake was not realizing that Katie was probably an animal doctor—or had some kind of veterinary training.

"You'll want to clean his ears, both inside and out. Dirty ear canals can shelter mites and make it difficult for the medication to work." Katie stood up, her hands still resting lightly on Finn's head. The dog didn't move, obviously in love.

"Your vet can prescribe a miticide ear cream," Katie continued. "That will help the itching and should get rid of the mites."

Albert looked impressed. "Thank you." He leaned down to hook the leash to Finn's collar. "I'll call my vet first thing in the morning."

As the two of them continued to chat, Henry walked over to Mary and leaned in. "Did you just hear what I heard?"

Mary nodded. "I think Katie's memory may be starting to come back—and she doesn't even realize it."

"Are you sure you want me to stay for supper?" Katie asked Mary as they pulled up to the house. "I don't want to be a bother."

"You're no bother," Mary replied. "Besides, Betty is planning on you. She'll be disappointed if you don't join us."

Katie smiled. "And I do want to tell her about what happened at the dock. I still can't believe it."

Mary had pointed out to Katie that she'd basically diagnosed and advised treatment for Albert Curran's dog, exhibiting a knowledge about animals that most laypeople didn't have.

Katie had been both surprised and pleased, as well as hopeful that her memory truly was starting to return, even though it seemed to be coming back in bits and pieces.

They walked into the house, both of them excited to tell Betty the news. But one look at her sister's tear-stained face pushed everything else out of Mary's mind.

"Bets?" Mary cried. "What's wrong?"

Betty sat in the middle of the sofa, a small tape recorder on the coffee table in front of her. "Everything," Betty replied. She wasn't crying now, but fresh tears gleamed in her eyes. "I made the mistake of tape-recording myself playing 'Rondo alla Turca.'" Her shoulders sagged. "And it was bad. Oh, Mar, why didn't you tell me how bad it is?"

Mary's heart sank. She walked over to the sofa and sat down next to her sister. "It's not that bad. I'm sure you're just rusty and need practice."

Betty shook her head, then took a deep cleansing breath. "You may be right, but it's more than that." She held up her hands. "My rheumatoid arthritis means I can't play the piano like I used to. I may never play like I used to. I've tried, Mar; I really have."

Katie walked over and sat on the other side of Betty, not offering words of advice, just a comforting hand on her shoulder.

"Nobody does anything the same way they did forty years ago," Mary said gently. "I think you're expecting too much of yourself, Bets. You bought the piano less than two weeks ago, and you're already trying to play a recital-level piece."

"I know," Betty admitted. "That's why I called Eleanor this afternoon and asked her if she could find a replacement for me. But she said it was too late. The programs have been printed, and she made sure I got the prime spot." Betty winced. "I go on stage right before Adam Sullivan. I can just imagine what he'll think when he hears me play."

Mary hated to see her sister so upset, but blamed much of it on exhaustion and pain. Betty had been practicing such long hours and pushing herself to the limit, despite the pain in her fingers and hands. "Does the program indicate what music you're playing?" she asked.

Betty shook her head. "No, just our names and instruments."

"Then play 'A Wink and a Smile,'" Mary said. "It's a great song, and the crowd will enjoy it. You've almost got it down already."

Betty hesitated, her eyes clearing. "I don't know. There are still a couple of rough spots."

Katie stood up. "Will you play it for me? I don't know if I've ever heard it before and, even if I did, I probably won't remember it so you can't go wrong."

That brought a smile to Betty's face. "Don't be so sure." But she got up from the sofa and walked over to the piano. She plucked the sheet music for "Rondo alla Turca" from the music stand and placed it inside the piano bench. Then she sat down and reached for the sheet music for "A Wink and a Smile."

Katie walked over to stand beside the piano while Mary stayed on the sofa. As Betty began to play, she saw Gus pad into the room. He looked at the piano and then continued into the living room instead of running out, like he'd done so many times before. Mary took that as a positive sign.

The rhythm of the song was light and fun, and Mary found herself tapping her foot to the beat. Then Betty fumbled a few notes and stopped playing.

"That's where I always mess up," Betty said, exasperated with herself. "I just have so much trouble with the left hand fingering in those three bars."

Katie moved beside her and sat down on the bench. "Why don't you play chords there instead?" she suggested, then demonstrated what she meant, playing three perfect chords with her left hand while she played the melody with her right hand.

Betty stared at her. "You know how to play the piano." She turned to Mary, who had risen to her feet and begun moving toward them. "Katie knows how to play the piano."

Mary smiled. "I know. I just heard her."

Katie's mouth gaped. "Wow. I guess I do. I'm learning a lot about myself today." They told Betty about Katie's animal expertise at the dock, which indicated that she'd had some kind of veterinary medicine training.

"No wonder Gus likes you so much," Betty said, chuckling. "You're his very own house doctor."

Mary gave her sister's shoulder a gentle squeeze. "And he likes that song, and so do I. You should definitely play it for the concert."

Betty hesitated and then looked over at Katie. "Will you help me prepare? You seem to know what you're doing."

Katie grinned. "I'd love to. I can finally give something back after all you've done for me."

"Just teach me how to play those chords again," Betty told her, cheerful once more, "and we'll be even."

On Monday, Mary left Rebecca in charge of the shop so she and Katie could make a return trip to Strings & Things. This time, the store was open, and they both breathed a sigh of relief.

"Do you have the claim ticket?" Mary asked her as they made their way to the door.

"It's right here," Katie said, holding the ticket in her right hand. "I just can't wait to see what it's for."

Mary couldn't wait either. She'd tossed and turned last night, anticipating what the morning might bring. She'd even turned on the lamp next to her bed at three o'clock in the morning to read her Bible until she was ready to fall asleep again.

Katie had returned to the cabin last night after helping Betty adapt her piano fingering so she could play "A Wink and a Smile." Katie even showed her a few riffs to add some pizzazz to the music. The memory made Mary smile as they headed into the music store.

It specialized in guitars but had something for every music lover. There were different kinds of musical instruments as well as instructional books and even training videos.

Darius Kerner stood behind the counter, playing with one of the many windup musical toys displayed in the shop. With his teen years just behind him, Darius now sang in a band at local venues and was trying his hand at songwriting. He looked up as they entered. "Good morning."

"Hi, Darius," Mary said, walking with Katie to the counter. "We have a claim ticket we'd like to turn in."

He arched a brow. "I didn't realize you had something here, Mrs. Fisher."

Katie held up the ticket. "Actually, it's for me."

"Okay," he said, taking the ticket from her. Then he looked between the two of them. "If you ladies want to hear some good music, my band is playing at Sam's Seafood restaurant next Saturday night. Invite all your friends."

"Thanks," Mary said with a smile. "We'll keep it in mind."

Darius glanced at the ticket. "Number 235. That one is still in the back room," he said, then turned and walked through a door behind him.

"Invite all my friends?" Katie said wryly. "I don't even *know* my friends." She sighed as she turned to Mary. "Some of my memories seem to be returning, but so far, the only person in my life that I remember is Nana. I love her dearly, but aren't there others?"

"I'm sure there are," Mary said softly. "And we'll find them." *Please, Lord,* she prayed silently. *Help us find them. Help make Katie's life whole again.*

After a few minutes, Darius emerged from the back room with an old, battered saxophone case in his hands. "Sorry it took so long, but I had trouble finding it." He set it on the counter between them. "Here you go."

Katie stared at it, then lifted her gaze to Darius. "Do I owe you something?"

"Nope," Darius said with a smile. "It's already paid for."

"Do you know who paid for it?" Mary asked him. "Or if they paid by check or credit card?"

"I can't remember offhand," Darius said, turning to the computer in front of him. "Let me look it up."

Darius tapped a few numbers on the keyboard in front of him. "It looks like claim number 235 was paid with cash, but there's no name listed with it."

That was what Mary had suspected. Nothing about this scavenger hunt was easy.

Katie grabbed the handle of the saxophone case and picked it up. Then she and Mary headed out the door.

"Thanks for stopping," Darius called after them.

When they reached Mary's car, Katie set the saxophone case on the hood of the Impala, then glanced at Mary. "Ready?"

"Are you?"

Katie nodded, then flipped open the clasps to release the lid. She opened the case and emitted a tiny gasp.

Inside was something wrapped loosely in tissue paper. Katie carefully pulled the tissue paper away. "It's a dress. A *very nice* dress."

Mary watched her pull out the black-and-white cocktail dress. The cap sleeves, full skirt, and vintage-style neckline reminded her of the type of dress Grace Kelly used to wear in the movies. And it was the kind of dress carried by Cape Cod Togs. The material was expensive, and a quick look at the tag hanging from the sleeve revealed it was a designer label.

"It's gorgeous." Katie held it up to her. "And looks like it's my size. But why was it in this old saxophone case?" She wrinkled her nose. "This just doesn't make sense."

"It's probably the dress you tried on in Cape Cod Togs," Mary told her. "But the saxophone case confuses me too."

She sensed there was some secret meaning behind some of these clues that they hadn't figured out yet. She looked at the open case, then noticed a folded sheet of white paper nestled at the bottom of the tissue paper. "What's this?"

Katie moved closer to her. "Another clue?"

Mary unfolded the paper and saw two typewritten lines in extra-large font, centered in the middle of the page. "You're just too good to be true. Can't take my eyes off of you."

"Is it a poem?" Katie asked, bemused. "A *very short* poem?"

Mary cleared her throat. "It's actually the first two lines of a song that was recorded by a singer named Frankie Valli in the late sixties."

"Well, that's strange," Katie said, turning her attention back to the dress. "I wonder what it means."

So did Mary. She read the second line again. *Can't take my eyes off of you.* An image of a man wearing sunglasses flashed in her mind. The same man Katie had thought was waving to her when the marching band passed by on the street.

A shiver passed through Mary. What if Katie's head injury had been caused by someone she knew, not by an accident or even a mugger? That could explain why the person who created this unusual scavenger hunt hadn't come looking for her or filed a missing person's report. He already knew what had happened to her.

"What is it?"

Mary looked up to see Katie staring at her. "Nothing," she said, not wanting to scare the girl over a speculation. "I'm just trying to figure this all out."

Katie smiled. "Well, I know where we can go to do that." She held up a business card for the Harbor View restaurant. "I just found this tucked inside one of the sleeves."

TWENTY

◆◇◆

Mary and Katie walked into the Harbor View restaurant when the doors opened at eleven o'clock. The lunch crowd at the fancy seafood restaurant would be arriving soon, and Mary wanted to avoid trying to question harried wait-staff when that happened.

"Table for two?" asked the headwaiter, approaching them with two menus in his hand. He wore a tailored black suit and tie. His name tag read Tito.

"Actually, we're not here to eat," Mary told him. "We just have a couple of questions that we need answered."

Tito peered at them through a pair of thick black-framed glasses. "About the food?" he asked, turning toward the reception counter. "We have an allergen information sheet for all our dishes, as well as our gluten-free options, if you'd like a copy."

"No, thank you," Mary said, realizing she'd need to be more specific. But she wasn't sure if the restaurant was the site of another clue or the end of the scavenger hunt. She took a moment to think of how to phrase her question and then motioned toward Katie. "My friend was supposed to come here on Tuesday night, the week before last, but she was ... detained."

Tito arched a skeptical brow. "Almost two weeks ago?" He was a short man, only a few inches taller than Mary's five feet one, and had a feather-like brown mustache that matched his short, thinning brown hair. He appeared to be about fifty, but Mary sensed that he was probably closer to forty. The thinning hair and the glasses aged him.

She also sensed that he didn't have a lot of patience for nonpaying guests. For a moment, she considered taking a table and ordering a beverage but decided to give him a chance to cooperate.

"Yes," she replied. "I know this is a rather strange request, but could you look to see if she had a reservation on that day, if you still have that information available?"

"We do." He hesitated a moment, then moved toward the reception counter where a thick black binder lay open. "Name, please?"

Katie stepped forward and cleared her throat. "Katie."

Tito looked up from the book. "Your last name, please?"

"I don't know my last name," Katie said candidly. "That's the reason we're here." She glanced at Mary and then continued. "You see, I've had amnesia for about the last two weeks and I've been searching for my identity during that time. Mary's been helping, and our search has brought us to your restaurant."

He looked around him, then began hastily smoothing down his hair. "Is this a television show? One of those where you play a prank on someone and see how long it takes them to get it?"

Mary could understand why he might think so, given the oddity of Katie's story. "No, we don't have any hidden television cameras," she told him. "Katie really does have amnesia. You may call Dr. Teagarden to verify. I'm sure Katie would give him permission to talk to you."

Katie nodded. "I will."

He stared at her. "I know Dr. Teagarden. He and his lovely wife come here often."

"Then you can be assured that we're telling you the truth," Mary said.

Tito began paging through the binder. "Okay, two weeks ago Tuesday. He scanned the list of names on the register. "I'm sorry, but I don't see anyone by the name of Katie who made a reservation."

"Could you tell us if anything unusual happened that night?" Katie asked him. "I know it's been almost two weeks, but is there anything that sticks out in your mind? Any strange notes found or messages? Or even the lines to a song."

Tito slowly shook his head. "No, nothing like that."

Mary paused, not ready to give up yet. "We've found a series of clues that led us to this restaurant, but we're not sure why Katie was supposed to be here."

Tito shrugged his shoulders. "I'm not sure what to tell you."

Mary leaned toward him to get a glimpse of the book. "How about initials? Are there any reservations that start with a *K*?" Then she saw a name with the letters *S* and *U* following it.

"What does SU stand for?" she asked Tito.

He gave her a sheepish smile. "Stood up. It doesn't happen often, but once in a while, we have someone waiting for a date who never shows up." Then his eyes widened behind his glasses as he looked to Katie. "Could you have been his date?"

"Maybe," Katie said. "Who was it?"

Tito glanced down at his book and scowled. "A guy by the name of Kosmatka. I don't recognize the name, and that's one I would remember. He must have been a first-timer here."

"What can you tell me about him?" Katie asked, her fingers gripping the edge of the counter.

Tito shook his head. "We have so many people come and go through here that I really don't remember, but let me ask Bryan. He's listed as the waiter for that table, and he's working today."

Mary and Katie waited while Tito went in search of Bryan. "Do you think I was supposed to meet that Kosmatka guy?" Katie asked her.

"I don't know," Mary said honestly. "We don't even know if you would have wanted to meet him. Maybe when you saw the first clue in the scavenger hunt, you were running away from the person who left that envelope on your table rather than running to him."

Katie gave a slow nod. "I've thought the same thing. I guess I just don't want it to be true."

"And as far as we know, it's not," Mary told her. "My mother always used to tell us not to borrow trouble. That's what we're doing now, and we don't even have all the facts yet."

Tito approached them with a young man in tow, who looked as if he'd be more comfortable in shorts and sandals than the suit he was wearing. "This is Bryan," Tito said. "I've told him your... situation."

Bryan nodded toward them. "What do you want to know?"

"The man who was here two weeks ago, this Kosmatka," Mary began, pointing to the name in the reservation book. "What can you tell us about him?"

Bryan shrugged, then reached up to tuck a strand of sunbleached hair behind his ear. "He was just an average guy."

"What color was his hair?" Katie asked. "His eyes?"

Bryan's mouth puckered as he thought about the question. "Dark hair, and I'm not sure about the eyes." He shook his head as he looked at Katie. "I'm sorry. I just don't notice that kind of stuff."

Katie nodded, forcing a smile. "It's okay."

"I can tell you that he waited here for two hours," Bryan said, "and then left without ordering anything. He still left me a nice tip though."

Although it might seem insignificant, that little detail about the tip made Mary feel better. She believed you could tell a lot about a person's character by the way he or she treated waitstaff.

Tito looked at him. "Anything else you remember, Bry?"

Bryan shook his head. "Not really. I overheard him on his cell phone right before he left. It sounded like he was leaving Ivy Bay and never coming back."

After they thanked him and left the restaurant, Katie reached out and gave Mary a hug. "I just want to thank you again for everything. You've stuck by me since the moment you found me in your shop."

"You're welcome," Mary said, hugging her back. "I wish we would have won the scavenger hunt by finding out your identity, or at least who wrote all those clues. But we'll know tomorrow night when the Dinsdales come back to town for the concert."

"I'm going to wear my saxophone dress," Katie said, and then laughed. "I know that's a strange name for it, but that's how I think of it."

"A strange name for a strange two weeks," Mary said, chuckling. "I think it sounds perfect."

———

The night of the Wildlife Rescue Foundation concert, Mary sat in her chair near the middle of the auditorium, her stomach in knots. She didn't even realize she was clenching the arm of her chair until Lizzie grasped her hand and gave it a warm squeeze.

"Relax, Mom," Lizzie whispered. "Aunt Betty will be great."

Mary nodded and took a deep, calming breath, so happy to have her daughter here beside her. Henry sat on the other side of Mary with Katie beside him in her saxophone dress. It looked gorgeous on her.

She tried to tell herself that Lizzie was right, but Betty had been so nervous backstage, pacing back and forth in the small waiting room. Both Mary and Betty's son Evan had tried to calm her, but she couldn't hide the way her hands were shaking when she took a sip of water.

When Adam had walked in, looking so handsome in his tuxedo, he'd taken one glance at Betty and known she was suffering from stage fright. It had never afflicted her before, as far as Mary knew, but tonight was different. Adam had taken some time to offer Betty some reassuring words, telling her everything would be fine. Mary prayed that he was right.

Katie leaned forward in her chair to talk to Mary. "Have you seen them yet?"

Mary glanced around the large auditorium, in search of the Dinsdales. Evan and his wife, Mindy, were seated near the front row with their girls. She'd seen Lori Stone here earlier but hadn't gotten a chance to speak with her. Diana and Roger Foley were seated a few rows behind her, and she saw Tess Bailey and her husband as well, along with Bea Winslow, Simon Rafferty, Millie Russell, and so many other people she knew. There was such a crowd here now that there was no way to tell if the Dinsdales had arrived.

Mary turned back to Katie. "I don't see them yet."

Katie nodded and sat back in her chair as Henry leaned toward Mary. "Poor kid has been waiting to get her life back for the last two weeks and still has to wait. I don't know if I could do it."

Mary could see the anticipation was fraying Katie's nerves this evening. She kept rubbing her temples and looked a little pale. Hopefully, Katie could relax enough to enjoy the performance. Then Mary and Henry would help Katie track down Matthew and Madeline at the reception later.

Chad was seated on the other side of Lizzie, looking quite dapper in his navy-blue suit and striped tie. He opened his program and checked his watch. "Time to get this party started."

As if on cue, the lights dimmed in the auditorium and a spotlight lit the stage. A moment later, Eleanor walked out, looking very regal in a long silver gown and matching heels.

"Good evening," Eleanor said into the microphone, smiling broadly at everyone in the sold-out auditorium. "I am Eleanor Emerson Blakely, and I want to welcome all of you to the annual Cape Cod Wildlife Rescue Foundation fund-raiser. One hundred percent of this evening's proceeds will be used for the rescue and treatment of wounded and displaced wildlife around Cape Cod."

Her words were met with an enthusiastic round of applause.

Eleanor waited until the applause died down and then continued. "Our very special guest this evening is Adam Sullivan of the Boston Grand Opera Company. He's volunteered his time and considerable talents to make this evening a success."

More applause followed and, in the interim, Mary wondered how Betty was holding up backstage. She wished Eleanor had placed her sister at the beginning of the program instead of the end. That just gave Betty more time to fret about her performance.

"We have some of Ivy Bay's finest local talent here tonight," Eleanor said. "Our first performer is Cynthia Jones, playing a violin solo."

Mary applauded with the rest of the crowd as Chief McArthur's sister took the stage. The spotlight centered on her as Eleanor moved behind the curtain. Cynthia stood with her violin tucked under her chin and her bow poised above it. She stayed that way for several long seconds, building the anticipation. Then her bow flew into action as she played a classical piece.

Cynthia was followed by her husband, Nick, who sang "Climb Every Mountain." Then Jeremy and Kaley Court played a duet with their clarinets. Tricia Miles followed with

238 SECRETS of MARY'S BOOKSHOP

a hauntingly beautiful song on her flute and received a long ovation from the crowd. As more performers took the stage, Mary kept checking their names on the program, waiting for Betty's turn.

At last, her sister took the stage.

Lizzie leaned over and whispered, "She looks great!"

Mary agreed. Betty had chosen a blue silk jacket and skirt that matched the color of her eyes. Her honey-blonde hair was swept up in a neat chignon, not one strand out of place. She sat down at the piano and positioned her music on the stand.

Mary held her breath, praying that Betty would get all the way through the song without any major problems. Thanks to her long hours of practice and Katie's assistance and helpful tips, she'd done it at home. But onstage, in front of this large crowd, was much different than playing in their living room.

A hush fell over the audience as Betty placed her hands on the keyboard and took a deep breath. Then she began to play. The first few notes were clear and true. Then a man's voice began singing the lyrics to the song. "I remember the days, of just keeping time." Adam appeared on the stage to the delighted gasps of the audience. "Of hanging around in sleepy towns forever. Back roads empty for miles. . . ."

To Mary's surprise and delight, Betty didn't miss a note as she continued playing the song on the piano. Adam's strong voice carried throughout the room, blending well with the music and hiding a few of the small imperfections in Betty's music.

Lizzie squeezed her arm. "Oh, wow! This is so awesome."

Mary smiled as she looked at Henry, who smiled right back at her. Katie leaned forward in her chair, her face tense, as if willing Betty to get through the song.

Adam continued to sing as he strolled over to the piano. Then he was singing directly to Betty as she played. Betty smiled up at him, and Mary could see her sister visibly relax. She even added a few of the impressive piano flourishes that Katie had taught her toward the end of the song.

The moment the song was over, the audience burst into thunderous applause. Adam held out his hand to Betty. She took it, and they walked to the front of the stage and together took a bow. Many in the audience rose to their feet, with Evan and his family leading the way.

Tears of joy stung Mary's eyes. The expression on Betty's face at this moment warmed her heart.

"Mom, she was perfect!" Lizzie exclaimed, clapping loudly beside her.

Mary agreed, but that perfection came in the fact that Betty hadn't given up in the face of adversity, even if she may have wavered once or twice. That made her perfect in Mary's eyes.

When the applause finally faded, Betty left the stage with a bounce in her step. Then Adam performed several songs, receiving another standing ovation when he was finished.

When the show was over, everyone in the audience began to stand up and mingle. Mary spoke with Amy Stebble and Lynn Teagarden, as well as Sherry Walinski, Jayne and Rich Tucker, and Jill Sanderson. The general consensus was that the concert had been a huge success and that Betty's song with Adam had been one of the highlights of the evening.

As she moved through the crowd with Henry and Katie beside her, Mary kept her eyes and ears open for any sign of the Dinsdales. "There's Lori," she said, pointing out the Realtor a few feet away.

The three of them made their way over to her. Lori turned to greet them. "Hello! Wasn't that a wonderful performance? You must be so proud of Betty."

"We are," Mary said. "We've been looking for the Dinsdales. Have you seen them?"

Lori winced, then looked at Katie. "Oh dear. Aren't they here yet?"

"No," Katie said, her voice sounding a little strained. "Not yet."

"I'm sorry," Lori said. "Maybe they were detained."

Dorothy Johnson grabbed Lori's arm and started talking to her, leaving Mary out of the circle of their conversation. She saw Lizzie and Chad laughing with Evan and Mindy and was thrilled that her daughter and son-in-law were staying at the house tonight, but her heart ached for Katie.

She looked over at the girl, who had gone even paler since talking with Lori. "Are you all right?"

Katie rubbed her head. "I'm not feeling too well. I may be coming down with something. I think I might walk back to the cabin and lay down."

"You're not walking," Henry said with a gentle firmness. "I'll be happy to drive you there. Do you want to go now?"

Katie glanced toward the stage, where Betty and the other performers were surrounded by well-wishers. "I wanted to talk to Betty, but it looks like she may be busy for a while. I'll come over to the house tomorrow and congratulate her."

"Do you want to stay with us tonight?" Mary asked, concerned about Katie being at the cabin alone when she wasn't feeling well. "Lizzie and Chad are staying with us, but we still have an extra room."

"No, I'll be fine," Katie said with a wan smile.

Mary watched Henry escort Katie out the door, almost certain that the Dinsdales' delayed arrival had contributed to Katie's discomfort.

She felt a tap on her shoulder and turned around to see Bob Hiller standing behind her. It was strange to see the town mailman out of his uniform, but he wore a nice dark suit and tie tonight.

"That was quite a performance," he commented. "Tell Betty she did a fine job. That's one of my favorite songs."

"I will," she promised.

"And what a treat for her to play for a big star like Adam Sullivan." Bob whistled low. "He's got some voice. I heard he's a nice guy too. It's hard to believe he's related to old Simon Rafferty."

Mary blinked. "Simon and Adam are related?"

"Sure," Bob said. "Simon is his uncle. Simon's sister studied in Europe and ended up marrying a guy in Poland named Klomska or something like that."

Or something like that.

Bob looked past his shoulder, his eyes lighting up. "Looks like the dessert table is open. Would you like to join me?"

"Thanks," she said, barely aware of his question, "but I think I'll wait a bit."

Mary stood alone after Bob headed for the dessert table, still trying to process what she'd just learned. Adam had a family tie to Ivy Bay, and his father was Polish. Sullivan certainly didn't sound like a Polish name to her. She had a hunch, but she didn't want to tell anyone about it until she knew for sure.

She stood on the toes of her shoes and searched the crowd for Simon Rafferty. When she spotted him by the south wall, standing alone and holding a plate of mini cream puffs, she hurried over to him.

"Simon," she said. "I'm happy to see you here tonight."

"I'm not much for going out at night," he grumbled. "But at least they're serving food." He popped a cream puff in his mouth.

Mary took a step closer to him. "I hear that you're Adam Sullivan's uncle. He's quite talented."

"He gets that from the Rafferty side of the family." Simon licked a dollop of sweet cream off his finger.

"Not the Kosmatka side?" she asked, wanting to confirm her hunch.

"Nope," he said. "My sister's husband is tone deaf."

Her heart skipped a beat. "So Sullivan is Adam's stage name?"

"Yep." Simon picked up another cream puff. "I don't know why he didn't pick Rafferty. That's a good, upstanding name." He shrugged. "No skin off my nose. Keeps all his crazy fans away from my door."

Mary wanted to hug him, but she resisted the urge. "Thank you, Simon! Thank you so much."

She could feel him staring after her as she went in search of her sister. Henry walked back inside the auditorium and intercepted her. "Hey, what's your hurry?"

Mary smiled up at him. "I just won the scavenger hunt."

TWENTY-ONE

──◆◆◆──

It took some finesse, but after about twenty minutes, Mary, Henry, and her family were able to separate Adam from his crowd of admirers and corral him into the waiting room backstage. Lizzie and Chad were there, along with Betty, Evan, and Mindy. Evan's two girls were at the refreshment table, having fun with the chocolate fountain.

Adam looked at Mary. "What's going on? Why did you want to talk to me in private?"

Mary looked at Henry beside her and then took a deep breath. "Because we have something to talk about that can't wait." She'd been thinking of a way to broach the subject of Katie to Adam, not sure what his reaction would be. But first, Mary had to be sure that she had the right man. "Did a woman stand you up at the Harbor View restaurant two weeks ago tonight?"

Adam blinked. "How did you know that?"

Betty's mouth gaped. Then she pointed at Adam. "That's him?"

"Yes," Mary said, her voice shaking a little. After all this time, they'd finally found someone connected to Katie. And he wasn't a crazed stalker but a kind, handsome, talented man.

He was also a very confused man, judging by the expression on his face. "You still haven't told me how you know about what happened at the Harbor View."

Mary met his gaze. "I know the reason why the woman you were supposed to meet didn't show up."

Now Evan looked confused. "I feel like I just walked into the middle of a play. What's going on?"

Lizzie grabbed Evan's arm and motioned to Mindy to follow her out the door. "I'll fill you two in," she said. "Come on, Chad, why don't you join us?"

The four of them left, leaving Adam alone with Mary, Betty, and Henry. The young tenor looked like he didn't know whether to stay or make a run for it.

"Maybe you should start from the beginning," Henry suggested. "The day you found Katie."

"Found Katie?" Adam blanched. "What does that even mean?"

"It means," Mary began, "that I found her in my bookshop two weeks ago and she didn't know her name or anything about her life."

"She had amnesia," Betty told him. "She was completely lost."

"Amnesia?" All the color drained from Adam's face, and his knees wobbled. "I can't believe it. How?"

Henry reached out and grabbed a chair. "Take a seat, Adam. There's still more to the story."

Adam half sat, half collapsed, into the chair, looking as if he might pass out.

Betty approached him, her face creased with worry. "Are you all right?"

"Yes," he rasped, his gaze on Mary. "Just tell me everything."

"The only clue to her identity," Mary continued, "was a note she found in her pocket that had the name Katie on it. A note that told her to arrive at Mary's Bookshop at 1:12."

Adam stared at her. "My note?"

Mary nodded. "We didn't realize that note was an actual clue in your scavenger hunt until several days later."

"Days that Katie kept showing up at the bookshop," Betty said softly. "Waiting for the person who wrote that note to meet her there."

Adam groaned, raking one hand through his thick dark hair. "I didn't know. Katie is my girlfriend—*was* my girlfriend," he said, correcting himself. "We had a big fight a few weeks ago and broke up. That scavenger hunt was my way of trying to get us back together. When she didn't show up at the Harbor View that night, I figured that was her way of telling me that it was over for good between us."

"So you left Ivy Bay and went back to Boston?" Mary said.

Adam nodded. "With no intention of ever coming back. But I'd already committed to performing at the fund-raiser, and once I'd licked my wounds, I realized I couldn't back out. I just kept myself as busy as possible and tried to forget Katie."

"The irony is Katie forgot you," Henry said. "And everyone else in her life."

"What I don't understand," Betty said slowly, "is why no one seemed to notice that she was missing. Doesn't she have family or friends who were looking for her?"

"Yes, she does have family and friends," Adam said. "But she works so hard that they were probably leaving her in peace on her vacation. That's what they've always done in the past." Then his brow creased as he turned to Mary. "Are you sure we're talking about the same woman? My Katie would have figured out the anagram in that note right away. She's a genius with word puzzles."

"I have something to show you." Henry pulled his cell phone out of his pocket and brought up the photograph of Katie and Mary that he'd taken on Sunday during their boat ride. "Does she look familiar?"

Adam stared at the view screen, and he swallowed hard. "That's her," he said, his words almost a whisper. He sucked in a deep breath, his fingers shaking as he reached out to touch her face on the screen. "That's my Katie."

"She's an amazing woman," Betty told him. "Even through the frustration and fear of not knowing her own identity, she kept a good attitude and went out of her way to help other people."

"That's what I love about her," Adam said. "We met at a fund-raiser for canine companions in Boston. She almost always has a smile on her face, no matter what obstacles are in her path." He shook his head. "I should have never let her go."

A twinkle lit Henry's sea-green eyes. "So what are you going to do about it now?"

Adam met his gaze. "I'm going to win her back. Only this time, I'm not running off if she doesn't fall into my arms. I'm going to stay by her side, even if it's just as a friend. I've discovered my life just isn't as full without her in it."

Henry moved toward the door. "Are you ready to tell her that yourself?"

Adam stood up, still a little wobbly. Then he squared his shoulders. "Yes, I am."

Henry smiled. "Then let's go."

Betty stayed behind at the community center so she could explain why the star of the show had suddenly taken off. Henry offered to drive his car to the cabin and, along the way, Adam explained how Katie had come to Ivy Bay.

"Before we broke up," Adam began, "I talked to Matthew Dinsdale about a rescue organization Katie wanted to start at her vet clinic. Matthew is a great patron of the opera, and I knew from our many conversations that he loved animals, especially the wildlife around his beach house."

"So Katie *is* a veterinarian?" Henry said, driving carefully through the packed parking lot of the community center.

"She's a great veterinarian," Adam replied. "And as soon as Matthew saw her business plan for a nonprofit rescue organization, he agreed to pay all the start-up costs."

"So he wrote out a check for $8,300," Mary said as it all started to make sense.

"That's right," Adam affirmed. "He wanted her to cash it and make the donation anonymously. He and Madeline had gotten so much press at that diabetes fund-raiser that they decided to keep a lower profile in their charitable giving. The one condition Matthew made when he gave her that check was that she couldn't tell anyone where the money came from."

"Oh my," Mary said with an amused smile. "He sure didn't have to worry about that. We didn't even know where

Katie came from." Then Mary remembered that she hadn't called Katie yet to tell her that they were on their way. She dug her phone out of her handbag and dialed the number for Katie's prepaid cell phone.

Something started ringing in the front passenger seat. Mary shifted slightly and reached behind her, pulling out Katie's phone. "Looks like Katie left her phone in your car," she told Henry. "I guess our arrival will be a surprise."

"I just hope it's a good one," Adam said in a low voice. "I can't even imagine how she must feel right now, not able to remember anything. And to know that I wasn't there for her when it happened just eats me up inside."

"But you were the guy who bought the dress for her at Cape Cod Togs, right?" Mary asked him. "The guy wearing the sunglasses and ball cap."

He smiled. "Yes, that was me. I'm not too skilled at going incognito, but if someone recognized me around town, then I thought it might put a damper on the romantic reunion I had planned for us. I wasn't even planning to buy her a dress until I walked by the store window and saw Katie standing in front of the three-way mirror in that beautiful dress. When she left the store without buying it, I stayed in the shadows until she was out of sight, then walked in and bought it for her."

"And you paid cash for the dress to stay incognito," Mary continued, putting it together in her mind. "And used your real surname, Kosmatka, at the restaurant."

Adam nodded. "My waiter wasn't an opera fan, so he didn't recognize me. When I thought I'd been stood up, I was very happy that no one knew me there. I tucked my tail between my legs and just headed back to Boston."

"Don't be too hard on yourself," Henry said as he turned the car onto Main Street and headed east. "You thought she'd rejected you."

"I did." His mouth curved into a sardonic smile. "I have to admit it was humbling. I've been used to women chasing after me, not pushing me away."

Mary was still trying to put the story together and had a few more questions. "How did Katie get to Ivy Bay? There was no car found by her cabin or anywhere else."

"Matthew and Madeline brought her," he explained. "When they heard she was planning to vacation in Ivy Bay, they offered her the use of their private cabin and told her she could hitch a ride with them after their meeting with the lawyer in Boston to get the ball rolling on her animal-rescue organization."

"Well, it's not like you really need a car to get around Ivy Bay," Henry said.

"That's right. Although I'm not sure how she was planning to get back to Boston," Adam replied. "We weren't talking much by that point, so I assumed she'd rent a car or take a bus or something."

"And the clues you left for her?" Mary asked. "They were...unusual. Did they have any special significance?"

"Of course," Adam said, chuckling. "The first thing I did was convince Madeline to let me in the cabin while Katie wasn't there. I left the envelope on the table for her and took off so I could make all the preparations."

"Like leaving a clue in the Hooks's novel in my shop," Mary said.

"Exactly," he replied. "Katie had given me that novel for my birthday six months ago. And Alfonso Denali was her favorite artist, so I was thrilled when I found some of his paintings at the Ivy Bay Gallery. I knew I had to plant a clue with one of them."

"How did you pick the Hopkins-Emerson Gristmill?" Henry asked.

"Well, believe it or not," Adam said sheepishly, "Hopkins is the name of Katie's pet rabbit. So when I saw the painting and that Mason guy told me it portrayed the Hopkins-Emerson Gristmill, then I knew I had to use it."

"So that leaves the saxophone case and two lines from the Frankie Valli song." She didn't mention that the song lyrics had seemed creepy when she thought they might have been from a stalker wearing sunglasses. Now that she knew they were from a man in love with Katie, it seemed like a sweet gesture.

"Katie used to play the saxophone in high school," Adam said. "And the song is from our first date. We sang it together at a karaoke party."

Mary gazed out the window, wondering once more how Katie would react when she saw Adam. Would she even remember him or the sweet, romantic gestures that were behind the scavenger hunt that he'd created for her? He'd based it on the memories of their romance, never realizing that she'd lost all her memories before the hunt even began.

Henry turned onto the gravel road leading to the Dinsdale cabins. As the car's headlights illuminated the path in front of them, she hoped Katie was still awake.

Henry parked the car in front of the cabin and cut the lights and engine. Then they made their way to the front door. Mary raised her hand to knock when she felt Adam's hand on her shoulder. She turned to look at him.

"Please, Mary," he said. "Let me."

She nodded, touched by the emotion she heard in his voice. Then she and Henry stepped back as Adam moved in front of the door and knocked. Mary watched the rapid rise and fall of Adam's shoulders as they waited for the door to open. She couldn't even imagine what he was thinking and feeling at this moment.

After what seemed like a lifetime, the door cracked open. "Who is it?" Katie's voice called out.

"It's me, Katie."

Mary found herself holding her breath as the door slowly swung open. Katie stood on the other side. She'd changed out of her fancy saxophone dress and now wore a gray T-shirt and Bugs Bunny pajama pants.

"Adam?" Katie said, her voice tremulous.

He stared at her. "You remember me?"

"Yes," Katie said, stepping out of the cabin and into his arms. "I remember you."

Mary put her palm over her mouth as emotions welled up inside of her. Henry placed a comforting hand on her back as they watched the reunited couple embrace.

At last, Katie stepped out of Adam's arms. "Please come in. You too, Mary and Henry." Tears of joy streamed down her face as they all walked inside.

"I can't believe this is happening," Katie cried. She sat down on the sofa, and Adam sat beside her. Henry and Mary each took a seat in the two remaining chairs.

"When did you start to remember?" Mary asked her. "When Adam was at the door?"

"No!" Katie exclaimed. "It was before—at the concert. I started getting a headache almost right away. I think I saw his name in the program. Then when he started singing while Betty played the piano, something just came over me." She smiled. "I felt hot and cold at the same time. Then I felt dizzy. I thought I was coming down with the flu!"

Adam reached for her hand. "I'm so sorry that you had to go through all of that. I'm sorry I wasn't there for you."

"Oh, Adam," she said. "I think I missed you even when I didn't remember you. It just felt like there was this . . . emptiness inside of me, you know?"

"I know," he said softly. "That's why I followed you to Ivy Bay and left those scavenger-hunt clues for you. I couldn't live without you anymore."

Katie's eyes sparkled. "I remember finding the envelope. I was so happy. I knew you'd written it, and I couldn't wait to see you." She closed her eyes, taking a few moments before she continued. "I remember walking back outside and locking the cabin door behind me. Then I saw a seabird, a tern, I think, dragging itself under the porch. I knew it was hurt, so I followed after it."

"I'm not surprised," Adam said with a wistful smile.

"I scraped my knees on some concrete blocks half-buried in the sand as I was crawling under the porch. I must have made too much noise because the bird got spooked and flew at me," Katie continued. "I reared back and hit my head on a beam so hard that I saw stars." She sighed. "And the next thing I knew, I was on the beach with no name and no memory."

Henry got up from his chair. "Excuse me," he said, heading for the front door. "I'll be right back."

Mary stared after him, sensing where he might be going. She just hoped he'd find what he was looking for.

"Standing on that beach," Katie continued, "with no idea who I was or how I got there, was the worst feeling in the world."

"Oh, Katie," Adam said, anguish etched on his face.

"But then I found your note," Katie continued, "and that feeling changed to one of hope. I didn't know it was an anagram and the first clue in a scavenger hunt. I just knew that it was a piece of my past—of my life—something that I could hold in my hands, like a lifeline, until I found my way home."

The front door opened, and Mary watched Henry walk back inside. He carried a small flashlight in one hand and a woman's purse in the other. Katie's purse had been under the cabin porch all along.

But Adam and Katie were too intent on each other to even notice his return.

Katie reached her hand into the front pocket of her pajama pants and pulled out the wrinkled note. "I've been keeping it with me all the time. I guess it was my way of keeping you close even when I didn't remember you."

"I did the same thing," Adam admitted. He reached into the front pocket of his suit pants and pulled out an engagement ring with an exquisite solitaire diamond.

Katie gasped when she saw it.

"This is what I had waiting for you at the end of the scavenger hunt. I thought the Harbor View restaurant, with its formal dining room, fancy meals, and the windows overlooking the bay, was the perfect spot to ask you to marry me.

"But now," Adam continued, "I think this cabin, with you in your Bugs Bunny pajamas, is the most romantic place in the world." He knelt down on the floor and then tenderly took her left hand in his own. "Katie Ann Barnes, will you marry me?"

"I will," she said tenderly, then watched as he slid the ring onto her finger. "It's a perfect fit."

"Yes," he said, smiling up at her. "We are."

Mary was still smiling when she walked into the house later that night. She and Henry had toasted Adam and Katie's engagement with hot chocolate. Then they'd taken their leave so the couple could have some privacy.

"There you are," Betty said, walking into the living room. "How did it go with Adam and Katie?"

Mary's smile widened. "Well, they're engaged, if that tells you anything."

Betty clapped her hands together. "Wonderful! Does that mean Katie's memory is back?"

"Most of it. But she definitely remembers Adam and her deep love for him. I made them promise to stop by for lunch tomorrow so you can see her ring and hear all about it."

"Perfect," Betty replied. "And now you need to come with me." She turned and headed toward the kitchen. Mary followed her, hoping that Lizzie was still awake. She'd hardly had a chance to visit with her daughter since she'd arrived today.

But when Mary walked into the dining room, she not only saw Lizzie seated at the table, but Chad, Evan, Mindy, and their daughters, ten-year-old Betsy and eight-year-old Allison. They were eating chocolate cake and strawberry ice cream.

"What's all this?" Mary asked, overjoyed at seeing so many of her family members together.

"We're having an after-party," Chad told her. "It's something all the celebrities do after a big show."

"And Grandma is a celebrity now," Betsy announced, before scooping up a big spoonful of ice cream. "She even gave me her autograph."

Mary laughed. "Did she now?"

Betty smiled. "Well, I did accompany Adam Sullivan on the piano. He's a celebrity, so I guess that makes me one by proxy." She laughed. "It was my farewell performance."

"Farewell?" Mary asked, confused. "What does that mean?"

"It means I'm giving the piano away," Betty told her. "It doesn't match the decor in the living room, and more important, it's simply too painful for me to play."

"I noticed," Mary said softly.

Betty's eyes twinkled. "The best part is that the piano is going to a good cause. I met a couple this evening who run a music center for underprivileged children in Boston. When I asked if they'd be interested in the piano, they were thrilled and offered to pay all the transportation costs."

"What a wonderful gift," Mary said, sharing the joy she saw on her sister's face. "We have so many things to celebrate tonight."

"Including this delicious cake," Chad said, digging into the piece in front of him.

Everyone laughed, and the dining room was filled with the sounds of love and kinship. Lizzie patted the empty chair beside her. "Mom, come and sit down by me. We have so much to talk about."

Mary made her way to the table, taking a moment to send up a silent prayer of thanks and praise for Katie's recovery and for all the blessings she had in her life.

There were so many precious memories from her past— and so many wonderful new memories to make for the future.

And now was the perfect time to start.

ABOUT THE AUTHOR

Kristin Eckhardt is the author of more than forty books, including eighteen books for Guideposts. She's won two national awards for her writing, and her first book was made into a TV movie. Kristin and her husband have three children and live in central Nebraska. Kristin enjoys quilting, traveling, and spending time with family.

CRANBERRY APPLE PIE

◆◆◆

1 nine-inch deep-dish pie crust
6 apples—peeled, cored, and chopped
1 twelve-ounce package fresh cranberries, roughly chopped
1½ cups white sugar
⅓ cup quick-cooking tapioca
1½ cups all-purpose flour
¾ cup packed brown sugar
1 teaspoon ground cinnamon
½ teaspoon salt
⅔ cup unsalted butter
1 egg lightly beaten

Preheat oven to 325 degrees. Invert pie shell over another pie pan of equal size. This will keep the crust from shrinking down in the pan. Bake in this position for ten minutes, until partially baked. Turn right side up and remove the extra pie pan from inside the crust.

In a large bowl, combine apples, cranberries, and white sugar. Cover and set aside for about twenty minutes. Mix in tapioca and set aside for fifteen to twenty minutes, until tapioca has absorbed fruit juice. Spread mixture into the partially baked pie shell.

In a medium bowl, combine flour, brown sugar, cinnamon, salt, and butter. Work mixture with fingertips until crumbly. Spread mixture over the apple-cranberry filling. Brush exposed pie shell with lightly beaten egg.

Place the pie on a cookie sheet to catch drips. Bake forty-five to sixty minutes on the bottom rack of the oven or until apples are tender when tested with a wooden toothpick.

FROM THE GUIDEPOSTS
ARCHIVE

————◆◆◆————

Thou crownest the year with thy bounty; the tracks of thy chariot drip with fatness. —Psalm 65:11 (RSV)

Even with one hundred years in which to practice, my Aunt Betty will be the first to say she's not perfect. When she recounts her past, I detect certain "memory grooves"— perceptions about people and events in her life that are deeply entrenched in her mind and continually resurface.

There is her irritation: As a minister's daughter whose family was moved every year, she always showed up each October as the "new" kid in school. And she still resents her father for not having kissed her mother good-bye when he boarded the train for chaplain service in World War I.

She's absolutely convinced that her husband's mother wanted her son to marry another Elizabeth, who was a family friend and heiress to an oil fortune. She's never gotten over feeling she was the "wrong" Elizabeth.

On the plus side, Aunt Betty remembers her college roommate Ginny, a wool merchant's daughter, who hid her expensive dresses in the back of the closet so she wouldn't outclass her friends. She tells us how her husband Bill never said a word against anybody. She recalls with pleasure how he, a bass baritone, and she at the piano gave concerts all over

China in their missionary years. "I've had a wonderful life," she keeps repeating.

Where will my "memory grooves" be when I am old? What themes will I attach to myself and others? Will resentment or alienation or disappointment kick up like stinging gravel? Or will my life's momentum crest the hill and catch the glow of the setting sun? The time to choose is now.

Dear God, today's perceptions become tomorrow's memory grooves. Help me to set mine deep in You. —Carol Knapp

A NOTE FROM THE EDITORS

Sign up for the

Guideposts Fiction Newsletter

and stay up-to-date on the Guideposts fiction you love!

You'll get sneak peeks of new releases, hear from authors of your favorite books, and even receive special offers just for you.

And it's free!

Just go to

Guideposts.org/newsletters

today to sign up.